MW01026664

BLOODBATH

A small cluster of soldiers were racing toward the fountain, determined to reach their commander.

Hickok saw there was no way Bertha could hold them off, that some of them might even reach the fountain. He dropped his Henry and drew his Pythons, running at full speed now, firing as he ran, going for the head as he invariably did, his shots spaced so closely together it was almost impossible to tell them apart. He reached Bertha's side, the two of them shoulder to shoulder.

Blade suddenly wrenched free of Bertha and rose, the Commando chattering, swinging the machine gun in an arc. Four charging troopers jerked and danced as the heavy slugs stitched a crimson patchwork across their chests.

THE ENDWORLD SERIES

Also by David Robbins

THE WERELING

DAVID ROBBINS

ENDWORLD

ARMAGEDDON
RUN

LEISURE BOOKS 🕸 NEW YORK CITY

Dedicated to.......
Judy & Joshua
Michael & the DM
and
Yul Brynner, Steve McQueen,
Charles Bronson, Robert Vaughn,
James Coburn, Horst Buchholz,
Brad Dexter, Elmer Bernstein,
John Sturges,
and
the greatest Western ever made.

A LEISURE BOOK

Published by

Dorchester Publishing Co., Inc.
6 East 39th Street
New York, NY 10016

Printed in the United States of America

1

It was time to kill again.

The big man cautiously raised his head, his penetrating gray eyes scanning the scene directly ahead, counting the soldiers once more. He had to be sure. Too many lives depended on his judgment. Cautiously, insuring his dark, curly hair wouldn't be visible above the lip of the ditch he was lying in, he verified his earlier count: 12 guards and 48 prisoners.

So far, so good.

The soldiers obviously weren't expecting trouble. They ringed the prisoners at regular intervals, idly watching the captives work at repairing the road. Three of the troopers, an officer and two others, stood near a pair of parked troop transports and a jeep, engaged in conversation. Every soldier carried an M-16 and had an automatic pistol strapped to his waist.

It wasn't going to be easy.

The man in the ditch flexed his huge muscles, alleviating a sharp cramp in his left arm. His bulging biceps and triceps, as well as his black leather vest and green fatigue pants, were caked with dirt from his prolonged crawling along the ditch. A pair of Bowie knives dangled from a brown belt, one on each hip. In his right arm he cradled a Commando Arms Carbine, a 45-caliber machine gun. Suspended under each arm in a shoulder holster was a Vega 45 automatic pistol.

Just a few more feet!

The soldiers and their prisoners were south of his position, coming toward him at a slow pace as the captives, each one of them shackled at the ankles, labored at repairing this stretch of U.S. Highway 85. The prisoners were filling in the potholes, using ready-mixed asphalt taken from a stack of sacks piled on the eastern side of the road.

Startled, the man with the Bowies suddenly noted an interesting fact about the 48 prisoners: they all seemed to be Indians.

Could it be?

A slight movement to his left arrested his attention. He caught sight of a lean, blond man dressed in buckskins crawling up behind the stack of asphalt sacks. Hickok. The gunman's pearl-handled Colt Python revolvers were strapped around his narrow waist. He clutched a Navy Arms Henry Carbine in his hands.

The big man glanced to his right, searching for another of his companions, but there was no sign of the stocky Geronimo. If figured. With his green shirt and pants, both constructed from the remains of an old canvas tent, Geronimo would blend into the scenery.

"Move your butts!" one of the soldiers abruptly barked, goading on the workers.

The afternoon sun was high in the sky, the early November weather mild with the temperature hovering in the 60s, typical of northeastern Wyoming for this time of the year.

The man with the muscles tensed, hoping the others in his party were set in their assigned spots. Except for Hickok, Geronimo, and Bertha, the rest of his group were strangers, and he felt uncomfortable about working with the newcomers. Still, orders were orders. If it was necessary to join forces

with Lynx, Rudabaugh, and Orson, so be it. He had
heard about Lynx, about how deadly the genetic
deviate could be, but Rudabaugh and Orson were
unknown quantities, and he disliked relying on them
in matters of life and death.

The nearest soldier was now only ten feet away.

The big man looked at the officer and the other
two troopers standing near the vehicles at the far
end of the work detail. It would be up to the
diminutive Lynx to insure none of the soldiers
escaped in those vehicles. Lynx had better be as
good as his reputation, or all of their plans would be
for naught.

Six feet separated him from the closest trooper.
The soldier was facing in the other direction,
watching the laborers.

The man in the ditch placed his right index
finger on the trigger of the Commando.

Four feet. The soldier, backing toward him, took
another step.

Now!

"Get down!" the big man shouted as he rose to
his knees, not bothering to wait and see if any of the
prisoners complied with his command. He angled
the Commando upward and pulled the trigger, the
stock bucking against his shoulder as a burst ripped
into the nearest soldier, the heavy slugs catching
the man at the neck and nearly decapitating him,
showering blood and flesh everywhere.

The trooper never knew what hit him.

"Get down!" the man with the Bowies repeated,
rising, sweeping the Commando to the right.

Another soldier was attempting to bring his
M-16 into play.

The big man let him have it in the chest, the
impact flinging the trooper to the ground, his chest

exploding in a crimson spray.

Bedlam ensued.

The prisoners dropped to the asphalt, removing themselves from the line of fire as quickly as possible.

Hickok popped up from behind the pile of asphalt sacks, the Henry leveling as he sighted on a nearby guard. The 44-40 boomed, and the soldier was propelled backward, collapsing in a disjointed heap. Hickok swiveled and fired again, downing a second foe.

The man in the black vest started toward the prisoners, spotting Geronimo as the black-haired Warrior rose from concealment in a cluster of sagebrush and let loose with an FNC Auto Rifle, ripping one of the hapless soldiers from his crotch to his forehead. Geronimo was also armed with an Arminius .357 Magnum in a shoulder holster under his right arm and a genuine tomahawk tucked under the front of his leather belt.

Beyond the stack of asphalt bags, a tall man with a bristly black beard and bushy eyebrows, dressed in tattered, patched jeans and a faded brown-flannel shirt, jumped up from the ditch and pulled the trigger on a Winchester 1300 XTR Pump Shotgun. A soldier in front of him was struck in the stomach and almost cut in two by the buckshot. The bearded man, the one called Orson, pivoted and blasted a youthful trooper vainly turning to flee.

The man in the vest saw two soldiers at the far end of the work detail running in the direction of the vehicles.

Where the hell was Rudabaugh?

Even as he mentally asked the question, Rudabaugh came into view near a small bush, his black Western-style clothes a sharp contrast to the

surrounding vegetation, his hawkish features grim
and determined, a Heckler and Koch Double Action
Automatic held in each hand. The 45s cracked, and
the pair of fleeing troopers dropped in their tracks.

The big man glanced toward the vehicles in time
to see a furry figure pounce from the top of one of
the troop transports. The figure landed on the
officer, knocking him to the ground. There was a
flash of lightning claws, punctuated by a hideous
shriek, and in an instant the officer and his two
companions were dead, their throats torn open,
gaping at the blue sky with lifeless eyes.

And that made it 12.

Geronimo approached the man in the black vest.
"Any orders, Blade?"

The big man nodded. "Check the bodies," he
instructed. "If any are still alive, then put them out
of their misery."

"Will do." Geronimo ran off to comply.

Hickok strolled over to Blade, a grin on his
handsome face, his long blond mustache drooping
over the corners of his mouth, his blue eyes
twinkling. "I knew these wimps wouldn't be a
problem," he stated. "It was a piece of cake."

"It's just the beginning," Blade reminded him.
He stared at the Indians. All 48 were prone on the
highway. Miraculously, none of them had been hit.

Orson, Rudabaugh, and Lynx walked up to the
muscular giant.

"Orson," Blade directed, "see if you can find the
keys to these shackles on one of the soldiers. Your
best bet would be the officer."

Orson's pudgy features twisted in a frown.
"Why should I do it? I'm not your errand boy. Have
somebody else do it."

Hickok took a step toward Orson, his right hand

lowering near the pearl handle of his right Python.
"You keep flappin' your gums like that, pard, and
I'm just liable to put a hole between those beady
eyes of yours."

Orson glared at the gunman. "You don't scare
me, Hickok! Oh, sure, I've heard all about you. How
you're supposed to be the fastest man alive with
those Colts. But you don't scare me! Personally, I
think you're a lot of hot air!"

Before Hickok could respond, or Blade could
intervene, a quiet, high-pitched voice interrupted
them. "What about me, chuckles? Do you think I'm
a lot of hot air too?"

Orson glanced at the speaker, and the faintest
flicker of fear was visible in his face. "No, Lynx. I
never included you in the same catagory as
Hickok."

Lynx chuckled, delighted at the unnerving
effect he had on the towering Orson. Where Orson
stood well over six feet in height, Lynx was only
about four feet tall. While Orson weighed over 220
pounds, Lynx weighed in the vicinity of 60. Lynx
wore a leather loin cloth. The rest of his wiry body
was coated with thick, grayish-brown fur. His ears
were pointed, his eyes vivid green orbs. Smiling, he
raised his right hand and stroked his pointed chin,
displaying the bloody nails on the tips of his thin
fingers. "That's real decent of you, bub," Lynx said.
"So I know you'll believe me when I tell you to stop
griping every time Blade tells you what to do, or I'm
going to gut you and eat your entrails for a snack."

Orson swallowed hard.

Blade stepped up to Orson and placed the barrel
of the Commando against Orson's abdomen. He
tapped the handle of his left Bowie. "And if Lynx
doesn't gut you, I will. When I give an order, I

expect it to be obeyed. Do you understand?''

Orson's brown eyes narrowed in resentment, but he nodded.

"I don't get you, Orson," Rudabaugh interjected, his hands on the pistols resting in the holsters attached to the black belt around his slim waist. "You volunteered for this mission, just like the rest of us. You agreed, before we left, that Blade would be our leader. Yet you've been bucking him at every turn, and usually over the most chicken-shit things imaginable. What gives?"

"Maybe I don't want to be here," Orson replied bitterly.

"Then why'd you volunteer?" Blade asked him.

"I didn't," Orson revealed.

"What?" Blade demanded in surprise. "Everyone here, each of us involved in this plan, was to be a volunteer."

"Not me," Orson said, frowning. "Wolfe told me to come or else. There's no way I could say no to Wolfe. You know that."

"I know," Blade admitted, his brow furrowed. What was going on here? Why hadn't Orson told the truth earlier? What was Wolfe up to? "Go look for those keys now and we'll talk about this later." Blade watched as Orson walked off.

"What the blazes is this, pard?" Hickok inquired.

"I wish I knew," Blade admitted. He glanced at Lynx and Rudabaugh. "Thanks for backing me up. I appreciate it."

"No problem, big guy," Lynx said.

"We've got to stick together," Rudabaugh commented. "If we don't, the Doktor will make mincemeat out of us."

"Not if I get to the Doktor first," Lynx vowed.

Blade stared at the genetic deviate, impressed by the sheer hatred in Lynx's tone. "Lynx," he commanded, "you and Rudabaugh gather up the weapons from the dead soldiers. We'll add them to our arsenal."

Lynx and Rudabaugh left as Geronimo approached.

"All of them are dead," Geronimo confirmed.

"Good." Blade glanced over his shoulder at a curve in the road 500 yards distant. "Hickok, I want you to run back and get Bertha and the SEAL."

"On my way." Hickok jogged off.

"What's the matter?" Geronimo asked Blade. "You look troubled."

"I'll tell you about it later," Blade promised.

"Uhhhh, excuse me," someone said to their left.

Blade turned.

One of the Indians, a lean man with shoulder-length black hair and angular features, was slowly rising. Like all of the captives, he wore dingy gray pants and a matching shirt. "Who are you?" he inquired. "Where did you come from?"

"What's your name?" Blade requested.

"I am called Red Cloud."

"Are you a Flathead Indian?" Blade asked.

Red Cloud's mouth fell open. "How did you know?"

Blade ignored the question. "How far are we from Catlow?" he inquired.

Red Cloud pointed to the south along U.S. Highway 85. "Catlow is about ten miles from here," he replied.

Blade smiled in satisfaction. "Perfect. We're right where we want to be."

"Everything is going according to schedule," Geronimo commented.

Red Cloud looked at Geronimo. "What is your name?"

"Geronimo."

Red Cloud studied Geronimo from head to toe. "And what tribe are you from?"

"The Family," Geronimo divulged.

Many of the other Flatheads, about a third of them women, were cautiously standing, wary of their liberators.

"What is the Family?" Red Cloud asked, perplexed. "Where are you from?"

"All you need to know about the Family," Blade answered, "is that we have the same enemies you do, namely the military forces of the Civilized Zone and their leaders, the Doktor and Samuel the Second."

Red Cloud stared at one of the dead soldiers. "I noticed you are not especially fond of them."

"If you feel about them the same way we do," Blade said, "then maybe you will join us in our cause."

"What is your cause?" Red Cloud asked.

"We have declared war on the Civilized Zone," Blade disclosed.

Red Cloud's astonishment showed. "Do you know how powerful they are? They defeated my people!"

"We know," Blade stated. "We were in Kalispell, Montana, a couple of months ago." He slung the Commando over his right shoulder.

Red Cloud's features saddened. "That is where they vanquished us." He sighed. "We were holding our own against the regular troops. They had us surrounded, but we had plenty of food and ample water. We believed we could hold out indefinitely. Some of us were even able to sneak through the enemy lines.

Our chief had his wife and daughter escorted to
safety." Red Cloud stopped.

"And then what happened?" Geronimo
prompted him.

Red Cloud seemed to withdraw within himself
as he spoke, his facial lines hardening. "Then they
unleased the Doktor's demons on us." He twisted
and glanced at Lynx, engaged in gathering up the
firearms of the slain soldiers. "Creatures much like
that one, only different."

"Don't worry about him," Blade said. "He's on
our side."

"We fought them off once," Red Cloud
continued his narration. "That was when they used
the clouds."

"The clouds?" Blade repeated.

"Yes. Giant green clouds. These clouds would
drift over our lines, and the people swallowed by the
clouds would never be seen again. The clouds ate
them."

Blade took a step toward the Flathead. "You're
certain about this? They actually caused the clouds
to drift over your positions?"

Red Cloud nodded. "I am positive."

"What happened after that?" Geronimo asked.

"They sent in the demons again, backed by the
regular troops. Our numbers were too depleted, and
there were too many gaps in our defensive
formations. They overran us." He paused and
shuddered. "It was horrible! They killed men,
women, and children without mercy. The demons
were the worst! It was like they went crazy for our
blood! There was no way we could stop them! If the
demons hadn't been called off, they would have
annihilated us. As it was, they took all of our
youngest children, all of our babies, to the Cheyenne

Citadel. The rest of us were scattered in groups and
sent throughout the Civilized Zone as slave labor.
They told us we weren't even good enough to be sent
through one of their Reabsorption Centers."

"Would you like to get back at them?" Blade
asked him.

Red Cloud's eyes brightened. "Of course."

"Do all of your people feel the same way?"

Red Cloud gestured at the nearest Flatheads.
"Let them answer for themselves. How do you
feel?" he asked them. "Do you want to take revenge
on those who conquered us?"

There was a chorus of vehement affirmatives.

Blade nodded. "I was hoping you would say
that." He raised his voice so every Flathead could
hear him. "Listen to me! I have an offer for you! We
will free you from your shackles if you will agree to
aid us in our fight against the Doktor and Samuel
the Second. Are you willing to fight?"

All of the Flatheads began shouting in unison,
"Yes! Yes! Yes!"

Blade waited until they quieted, then held his
arms aloft to attract their attention. "We will
supply you with the arms you will need. If you will
stand by us, after it is all over we will reunite you
with the daughter of your chief."

Red Cloud gripped Blade's right arm. "Star?
You know where Star is?"

"Yes," Blade confirmed. "She is staying with
my Family in our Home."

"How can this be?" Red Cloud inquired in
amazement.

"It's a long story," Blade responded, "and we
don't have the time to tell it right now."

"What about Rainbow, Star's mother?"

Blade glanced at Geronimo. Would it be wise to

divulge the whole story? How Rainbow had led them to Kalispell under the pretext of locating desperately needed medical supplies, when all she really wanted to do was steal the SEAL? How she had shot Geronimo, and herself been shot by soldiers from the Civilized Zone? No. It was unnecessary to elaborate now. He could always tell them the full truth later, after the upcoming battle was over. "Rainbow passed on to the higher mansions," Blade replied.

"But Star is all right?" Red Cloud queried.

"Star has been adopted by our Leader and his wife," Blade explained. "Plato and Nadine are taking excellent care of her."

"Plato? What an odd name," Red Cloud remarked.

"He took it from a book," Blade stated.

"A book? I don't understand."

"We call it our Naming," Blade elaborated. "It's a special ceremony every Family member goes through when they turn sixteen. We are encouraged to go through the books in our vast library and select whatever name we want for our own. The Founder of our Home started the practice. He wanted us to always be aware of our history, so we wouldn't find ourselves committing the same stupid blunders our ancestors did, the mistakes which led to World War Three. Most of us pick names from our history or literature books. Some of us take a name of our own choosing."

"I have never heard of such a thing," Red Cloud stated.

Lynx suddenly appeared at Red Cloud's left elbow, and the Flathead inadvertently recoiled in shock.

"What's the matter, chuckles?" Lynx chattered.

"Don't you like kitty cats?"

Red Cloud and the rest of the Flatheads were gazing at Lynx in wide-eyed stupefaction. "What are you?" Red Cloud blurted out.

"Don't you know?" Lynx retorted.

"My people call you, and the other creatures like you, demons," Red Cloud answered. "We have heard fantastic tales about the Doktor, about how he creates you out of the thin air to do his evil bidding."

Lynx shook his head. "Someone's been feedin' you a line, dimples. The Doktor creates us, sure, but he does it from test-tubes. Ever heard of genetic engineering?"

"No," Red Cloud admitted. "My parents taught me to read, and I did own a dozen or so books, but I never heard of genetic engineering. What is it?"

At that moment, Orson ran up, holding a key chain in his left hand. "Look at what I found," he announced.

Blade took the keys and knelt in front of Red Cloud. There were seven keys on the chain; with the third key, the shackles came unlocked.

Red Cloud reached down and placed his right hand on Blade's left shoulder. "Thank you. For this act of kindness, you have my undying friendship."

Blade stood, smiling. "I would be honored to consider you a friend." He handed the keys to Red Cloud. "Would you like to finish freeing the rest of them?"

Red Cloud beamed from ear to ear. "I would!" He turned and walked to the nearest prisoner.

"So what's next?" Geronimo inquired.

Blade thoughtfully stroked his chin. "We'll give them some of the weapons we've confiscated, and let them take the two troop transports and the jeep—"

"Why don't we keep the jeep for ourselves?" Orson asked, interrupting. "It's too crowded in that SEAL of yours with all seven of us inside. Why not let a couple of us ride in the jeep?"

"Could you drive it?" Blade demanded, his jaw muscles tightening.

"No," Orson confessed. "But I know Hickok could, 'cause he drove the SEAL part of the way here. Let him do it."

"We all stay in the SEAL," Blade declared.

"When we have a jeep we could use?" Orson countered. He snorted derisively. "Sounds like a dumb idea, if you ask—"

Orson never completed his sentence.

In a blur of motion, Blade stepped up to Orson and gripped the malcontent by the front of his flannel shirt. Blade's powerful muscles rippled as he heaved, lifting Orson an inch off the ground. Orson dropped his shotgun and frantically attempted to break Blade's iron hold, to no avail.

Lynx laughed.

Blade's lips were a compressed line as he stared into Orson's eyes. "Listen to me, Orson, and listen good," he said, his voice harsh and grating. "I won't tolerate any more back talk out of you. The fact that you were forced to come along on this assignment doesn't give you the right to be impudent. From now on, when I say we're going to do something a certain way, then that's the way we'll do it. And I don't want any sass out of you."

Orson's bearded face was a bright red.

"Now if you have any objections," Blade stated with a hint of menace in his tone, "speak right up. We're going to settle this here and now. The lives of all of us will depend on how well each of us follows orders when we reach Catlow. If I can't rely on you,

I don't want you with us."

Blade released Orson and shoved. Orson stumbled backward for several steps before he regained his balance. He rubbed his neck, glowering at Blade.

"Wipe that scowl off your face," Blade threatened, "or I'll do it for you!"

Orson gulped and managed a feeble grin. "I didn't mean anything by what I said!"

"What's it going to be?" Blade angrily demanded. "Are you with us or not? If you want out, just say the word. I'll send you with the Flatheads."

"I've got to stay," Orson whined. "Wolfe will have me killed if I leave."

"If you stay," Blade warned him, "you'll do what I tell you, when I tell you, with no lip. Is that understood?"

Orson nodded.

"I can't hear you," Blade said.

"I understand," Orson shouted.

Blade picked up the shotgun and tossed it to Orson. "I want you to walk south a couple of hundred yards. Keep your eyes peeled. If you see anything coming our way, report back on the double. Move!"

Orson whirled and hurried away.

Lynx was beaming. "I like your style, big guy! You should have punched his lights out, though."

"If we didn't need Orson in Catlow," Geronimo interjected, "you can bet Blade would have."

Rudabaugh walked up. "Was Orson being a bad boy again?"

Blade simply nodded.

"So what's next?" Geronimo asked one more time.

"Like I was saying," Blade said, "we'll give the Flatheads the jeep and the two troop transports, as well as some of the weapons. I'll give them explicit directions so they can join up with our main column." He paused and glanced at Red Cloud, who was still busy releasing his fellow Flatheads. "Hey, Red Cloud!"

Red Cloud looked at Blade. "Yes?"

"Can any of your people drive a vehicle?"

Red Cloud nodded. "Some of us were assigned to the garbage detail in the Citadel about a month ago. They forced us to drive their garbage trucks to the dump. Under guard, of course. Why?"

"I'll explain after a bit," Blade said.

"After they leave, what then?" Geronimo inquired.

"We proceed as originally planned," Blade responded. "We'll drive to Catlow, subdue the garrison there, and send our message to the Doktor."

"Message? What kind of message?" Rudabaugh asked.

Blade grinned. "We're going to send the good Doktor an invitation to tea."

2

He couldn't get the images out of his mind.

No matter how hard he tried.

All he kept seeing, repeating over and over again, were vivid scenes of death and destruction. A tremendous battle, the ultimate conflict between good and evil. Thousands upon thousands died on both sides, the innocent as well as the guilty.

And it was all his fault.

He had formulated the initial plan, and set the wheels of combat in motion. Whatever happened next, the outcome would be on his shoulders.

Maybe he should have waited for the Doktor to make the next move. Maybe he should have upgraded the fortifications protecting the Home and waited for the Doktor to show up.

"Plato, it's getting late."

Plato sighed and shook his head, clearing the cobwebs, his reverie shattered. "What did you say?" he absently asked.

The speaker was standing on the bank of the moat in the northwestern corner of the 30-acre plot known as the Home. The moat was a stream, diverted under the northwestern corner of the 20-foot-high brick walls surrounding the Home. The stream was channeled along the base of the inside of the walls, providing a secondary line of defense as well as the essential water for the inhabitants of the Home, the descendants of followers of a wealthy survivalist named Kurt Carpenter. They called themselves the Family, and at the moment, their

aged Leader, Plato, was supervising a special
project. The stream entered the Home through an
aqueduct in the northwestern corner, with half of
the water flowing to the south and the remaining
volume flowing to the east. Eight-foot-deep trenches
carried the water along the four walls until they
merged in the southeastern corner and exited the
Home via another aqueduct. In addition to the walls
and the moat, strands of barbed wire were strung all
across the top of the wall to impede potential
attackers. Of the six huge concrete blocks Kurt
Carpenter had had constructed on the property, one
of them was a well-stocked armory. Carpenter had
known civilization would revert to bestial levels
after World War III, and he had wanted his beloved
Family to be prepared to repel any assault on the
Home. He had tried to project probabilities and
cover every contingency.

But he had left one weak spot.

Actually, two.

Plato stared at the stream while seated on a
small boulder, watching the water rush past,
wondering why Carpenter hadn't thought to install
a screen or grid over the aqueducts to prevent
anyone or anything from gaining entry to the Home
by swimming through them.

Live and learn.

Twice the Family had been attacked *inside* the
compound, and it wasn't until after the second
attack that Blade had deduced the faulty link in the
Family's armor. First, some time back, a mutated
frog had leaped from the moat and savagely assailed
some nearby Family members. Then, only recently,
two of the nefarious Doktor's deadly genetic
assassins had invaded the Home. One of them had
let it slip that they had gotten into the Home by

swimming. It didn't require a genius to ascertain their method.

Plato glanced at the four men in the moat near the aqueduct. They were putting the finishing touches on the large screen they had attached to the interior aqueduct opening.

"It's getting late," the speaker on the bank reiterated. "It will be dark soon. Should we wait until morning to put the other screen on the southeastern aqueduct?"

Plato looked at the speaker, a tall man with blue eyes and short blond hair. He wore a brown shirt and buckskin pants, as well as the traditional Family footwear: moccasins. Strapped to his waist was a long broadsword, just one of the many unusual and exotic weapons Kurt Carpenter had stocked in the Family armory. Plato grinned. "The aqueducts haven't had a screen on them in the one hundred years since World War Three," he said. "One more night won't hurt. Yes, we'll wait until daylight to complete our task, Spartacus."

Spartacus nodded. "Wrap it up!" he shouted to the four men in the moat. "We'll be doing the second one tomorrow." He faced Plato, noting the Leader's haggard appearance and the stringy condition of Plato's long gray hair and beard. Plato's clothes, kept in spotless condition by his wife, Nadine, consisted of faded tan trousers and a buckskin shirt. "What were you thinking about just now?" he inquired.

"Nothing much," Plato said evasively.

"Come on," Spartacus rejoined. "I've seen that look before. You're worried about Blade and the others, right?"

Plato sighed and frowned. "Of course."

"Try not to think about it," Spartacus advised.

"If only it were so easy," Plato said wearily.

"You did what you had to do," Spartacus
pointed out.

"That's what I keep telling myself," Plato said.
"But it doesn't seem to help much."

"Blade is a Warrior," Spartacus noted. "He
knew what he was getting into. He knows the risks
involved. It's all part of being a Warrior."

Plato absently nodded. A Warrior.

The Founder of the Home, Kurt Carpenter, had
been a firm believer in social equality. To that end,
he had instituted a practice whereby each and every
Family member would receive an official title.
Whether it was Tiller, Empath, Warrior, or one of
the others, every Family member would be assured
equal social footing. Of the over 6 dozen Family
members now alive, 15 had been selected as
Warriors, the defenders of the Home and the pro-
tectors of the Family. The 15 were divided into 5
Triads of 3 Warriors apiece. These 5 Triads were
known as Alpha, Beta, Gamma, Omega, and Zulu.
Each Triad had a head or leader, but the head of
Alpha Triad, Blade, was the chief Warrior, responsible for the Home's security. Blade, Hickok, and
Geronimo comprised Alpha Triad, and since they
and Beta Triad were currently away from the Home,
Spartacus, as the head of Gamma Triad, had become
the chief Warrior in their absence.

Spartacus walked over to Plato and gently
placed his right hand on Plato's narrow shoulder.
He had never seen the Family's Leader look so sad.
"Cheer up!" he stated as happily as he could.
"Everything will work out."

"I hope so," Plato said softly.

"Hey! What's the matter? Aren't you the one
who is always telling us to have faith?"

Plato gazed up at Spartacus. "If it's spiritual

enthusiasm you want, I suggest you see Joshua."

"I haven't seen Joshua around lately," Spartacus noted.

"Neither have I, come to think of it," Plato said thoughtfully.

"So what's got you so down in the dumps?" Spartacus said, pressing the issue. "The senility?" he queried tactlessly.

"It has been affecting me greatly of late," Plato divulged. "If only we could find a cure . . ."

A mysterious form of premature senility had befallen the Family. The Family records indicated that each previous generation had had a shorter life expectancy than the one before it. Some of the Family Elders were now showing unmistakable symptoms of the senility, and Plato was one of them. Although not quite 50 years of age, Plato looked the way a 70-year-old man would have looked in the days before World War III.

"You'll find a cure," Spartacus predicted. "With all that medical and scientific equipment Blade and Geronimo brought back from Kalispell, and the help you're getting from Gremlin, you should find a cure real soon."

"Those four hardbound notebooks Yama found at the Citadel are proving to be of more help than the scientific instruments," Plato noted. He had sent Yama, one of the Warriors from Beta Triad, on a spying mission to the Cheyenne Citadel. While there, Yama had managed to steal four notebooks belonging to the Doktor. He'd also rescued one of the Doktor's genetically engineered creations, Lynx, from certain death. Before they had fled the Citadel, Yama and Lynx had destroyed the Doktor's headquarters.

"What did you find in those notebooks?" Spartacus asked.

"Much of it is over our heads," Plato replied, "but we are still in the process of examining them. They're written in the Doktor's own longhand, and he doesn't have the most legible writing in the world. A lot of the contents concern highly technical medical and scientific experiments and data."

"Are the rumors I hear true?" Spartacus inquired. "About the Doktor being so old?"

Plato's brow furrowed and he scratched his neck. "If the dates in the notebooks are correct," he said slowly, "then the Doktor is one hundred and twenty-seven years old."

"Is it possible? How could he be that old? He would have been alive before World War Three started."

"The Elders have researched the matter thoroughly," Plato detailed. "We've consulted pertinent books in the library." One of the concrete blocks was devoted entirely to housing the library Kurt Carpenter had amassed for his followers, hundreds of thousands of books on every conceivable subject. "We discovered references to a number of individuals who lived beyond the century mark before World War Three. True, they were the exception rather than the rule. But the records conclusively prove that living to a hundred, or beyond, is possible. The Doktor seems to have devoted considerable energy and his brilliant mind to discovering a viable way of achieving that goal. Apparently, before the war, some scientists had discovered biochemical causes for aging. They had identified two substances in particular, oxyradicals and peroxide, as crucial to the aging process. These substances are formed from oxygen. They're emitted by the red blood cells in the body as the cells carry oxygen through our system. Nature requires us to use oxygen for energy, but it turns against us in our later years. When we're young and healthy, like you, the body is able to resist the onslaught of the oxyradicals and the peroxide. But when we're older, the oxyradicals and peroxide gain the upper hand by causing the destruction of our red blood cells. Are you following me on this?"

"Uhhhh, not really," Spartacus confessed.

"Well, suffice it to say the Doktor hit upon a technique to inhibit the development of the oxyradicals and the peroxide, thereby drastically reducing the rate of which he aged."

"What kind of technique?" Spartacus asked, his curiosity aroused.

"Transfusions," Plato answered, "in conjunction with a unique chemical he synthesized."

"Transfusions?" Spartacus repeated. "Isn't that where you take the blood from one person and give it to another?"

"Precisely. And in the Doktor's case, he uses the blood of infants."

Spartacus grimaced in revulsion. "Babies? You mean he uses blood from babies?"

"That's exactly what I mean," Plato confirmed. "His notebooks indicate he has used the blood of thousands of babies over the decades."

"Dear Spirit! Why?"

"By having regular transfusions, and using only the blood from healthy, compatible infants, the Doktor is able to prevent the oxyradicals and peroxide from increasing in his own system and triggering the aging process. The longer he lives, the more frequently he must have the transfusions. The notebooks reveal he starts to age if he neglects the transfusions, although the process is partially reversible if caught in time." Plato paused. "So, to answer your earlier questions, yes, I do believe it is possible for the Doktor to be one hundred and twenty-seven years old."

Spartacus patted the hilt of his broadsword. "I wish I was with Blade and the others!" he declared. "I'd like to find this Doktor on the business end of my sword."

"The use of the infants is not the only horror we've discovered," Plato commented.

"There's more?"

"We're working on one notebook in particular, striving to decipher the writing," Plato said. "But if the information we've found so far holds up, there is a definite link between the Doktor and the mutates. Probably the green clouds as well."

The mutates were pus-covered, perpetually ravenous mammals, reptiles, and amphibians. They infested the countryside, stalking and slaying any living thing they encountered. No one knew what caused their condition, nor did anyone know the origin of the green chemical clouds. The clouds appeared out of nowhere, drifting over the landscape, and any person unfortunate enough to be covered by a cloud, to be caught by its eerie, opaque fog, was never seen again.

"Is there anything the Doktor isn't involved with?" Spartacus asked.

"We'll know more after we have finished analyzing the four notebooks," Plato said. "We've gleaned considerable knowledge concerning the Doktor's research and work with genetics. In the realm of genetic engineering, he's phenomenal. Before World War Three, scientists were able to produce babies from a test-tube. They even designated them test-tube babies, and would implant them in a female's womb—"

"Really?" Spartacus marveled.

"Really. The Doktor has refined their technique.

He is capable of tampering with a human embryo in a test-tube, of somehow altering the genetic code and creating mutants like Lynx and Gremlin, and the monstrosities in the Doktor's own Genetic Research Division." Plato shook his head. "If the Doktor weren't so unspeakably wicked, I could readily admire the man and his sensational accomplishments."

"No one should be allowed to fiddle with nature," Spartacus opined. "The Spirit designed us a certain way, and we should leave well enough alone."

"We in the Family may believe that," Plato stated, "but the Doktor obviously doesn't, nor did many in the scientific community before the war. Some of them would perform any type of research for money. Money talked."

"Talked?" Spartacus appeared puzzled. "I thought their money was made from paper and metal?"

"Just a quaint colloquialism from prewar times," Plato explained. "A figure of speech, they called it."

"Women have figures," Spartacus retorted playfully. "Speech has style."

"Why, Spartacus!" Plato said, genuinely impressed. "Such eloquence! I'd hardly expect it from you."

"I guess some of my schoolteachers must have rubbed off on me." Spartacus grinned. "At least, one of my teachers."

Seven of the Family Elders shared in the responsibility of training the young children, each Elder instructing in areas in which he or she enjoyed expertise. Plato was one of those teachers.

"I wonder what it was like," Spartacus

continued thoughtfully.

"What *what* was like?" Plato asked.

"Living in a world where they used money. From what I've read, money was responsible for a lot of greed and sorrow and even war."

"The root of all evil, they called it." Plato turned and watched several of the children playing tag 30 yards away. "Men and women committed all manner of immoral and wicked acts to acquire monetary wealth."

"It's a good thing the Family doesn't use money," Spartacus stated.

"We're fortunate. With only slightly over six dozen members, the Family is small enough so that we don't need it. Each of us performs our work to the best of our ability, and we all share in the fruits of the Tillers' efforts," Plato said.

"Wasn't our system called Communism before the Big Blast?" Spartacus asked, referring to World War III by the slang expression the majority of the Family used.

"Our system is called sharing," Plato expounded. "Any resemblance to Communism, the tyrannical scourge of the planet, is purely superficial. If the Family were larger, we would require an efficient economic system. Capitalism was the best, but even Capitalism is only as good as the Capitalists practicing it."

"What was wrong with Communism?" Spartacus queried.

"Think back to your history studies," Plato directed. "Remember how it was before the war erupted. Global Communism was on the verge of collapse. Communism stifles individual initiative, and contains a major, fatal flaw. No economic system can survive when it forces the worker to become a slave to the idler. Also, the Soviet Communists, and the other Communist Governments, were determined atheists. No social system that denies the reality of the Spirit can long survive. I firmly believe that the Communists realized their system was close to falling apart, that it was disintegrating under their very noses, and they pressed the nuclear button as much in desperation as for any other reason. They probably believed the propaganda disseminated by both sides, that a nuclear conflict was survivable. The ignorant, destructive idiots!''

"I've got another question," Spartacus declared.

"What is it?" Plato was pleasantly surprised by this behavior of Spartacus. He had erroneously assumed Spartacus was a lot like Hickok: living for the moment with nary a thought about profound matters.

"You mentioned that the Communists denied the Spirit, and that reminded me of something I've wanted to ask for some time, but kept forgetting to bring up. We, the Family, call the Creative Force the Spirit. In many of the books in the library, I've noticed that before the Big Blast they called the Spirit by another name. They usually used the term God. So how come we use the Spirit instead of God?"

"You amaze me!" Plato was sincerely surprised by this unexpected philosophical interest of Spartacus. "Your question is easily answered. You're right in that the prewar society did use the designation God, or Lord, for the First Source. Unfortunately, the terms lacked any special significance to the average user. They were commonly taken in vain. The term God was

routinely prostituted by incorporation into a
standard curse word, 'goddamn.' Some people could
use the word six times in a seven-word sentence. Our
Founder was a religious man, and this verbal
violation of the special relationship existing
between Man and Maker revolted him. He urged the
Family to avoid using the crude slang, and to adopt
instead the term Spirit. To this day, the Family
usually employs the word Spirit when referring to
the Divine Presence.''

"So that explains it,'' Spartacus said.

Plato stood and stretched. "I'd best be getting
along. Nadine will have my supper waiting, and she
can become quite cross if I'm detained.''

"I'll see you in the morning,'' Spartacus stated.
"Don't worry about the guard schedules. I have
everything worked out, which Triad is supposed to
be on duty and when.''

"You're doing a superb job. Blade will be proud
of you.'' Plato smiled. "And thank you for the
stimulating conversation. It has perked me right
up!''

"My pleasure,'' Spartacus said, satisfied with
himself. He had wanted to rouse Plato from his
depression, and he knew there were few pursuits
Plato relished more than an invigorating chat. He
watched the Family's adored Leader shuffle off
toward his cabin. The current situation had to be
rough on the old man. Plato loved Blade as though
he were his own son, and now Blade was hundreds of
miles from the Home in northwestern Minnesota,
preparing to fight the Doktor to the death.

Spartacus gazed up at the darkening sky,
noting the first visible stars. What was Blade doing
at this very moment? he wondered.

3

Catlow, Wyoming. Located on U.S. Highway 85 between the junctions of Highways 18 and 16. Present population: approximately 400. Catlow was one of the many communities which had sprung up after World War III, after the Government had evacuated thousands of people into the area later known as the Civilized Zone. The Constitutional Republic of the United States had deteriorated into a dictatorship controlling most of Wyoming, Colorado, eastern Arizona, New Mexico, Oklahoma, the northern half of a state once called Texas, and most of Montana, as well as the former states of Kansas and Nebraska. Catlow was one of the northernmost settlements in Wyoming, and a garrison of 40 Government troops were stationed there.

All of these facts flitted through Blade's mind as he viewed the town using binoculars. He was lying on a small rise 200 yards north of the outskirts of Catlow. The town had quieted considerably since darkness had fallen. Lights had come on all over the place, indicating the town had electricity.

How long would it be, he speculated, before the garrison commander became concerned about the 12 missing troopers?

How soon before a patrol was sent out to ascertain why the work detail was overdue?

Blade glanced over his shoulder at the SEAL, parked on the highway below.

The SEAL. Kurt Carpenter's most important

legacy to the Family, a gift costing Carpenter
millions. He had wisely foreseen the need for an
exceptional vehicle after World War III, knowing
conventional cars and trucks would only last as long
as fuel was obtainable and parts could be replaced.
Consequently, Carpenter had personally financed the
research on and construction of the SEAL. The
Solar-Energized Amphibious or Land Recreational
Vehicle, more commonly referred to by the acronym
SEAL. The SEAL was van-like in its contours, its
body composed of a heat-resistant and shatterproof
plastic, tinted green to enable those within to see
out but preventing anyone outside from looking in.
The SEAL's source of power was the sun; sunlight
was collected by two revolutionary solar panels
affixed to the roof. The energy was then converted
and stored in a bank of six singular batteries, stored
in a lead-lined case under the transport. Four huge
tires completed the exterior picture.

Almost.

Because, after the automakers had completed
this prototype, Carpenter had spent even more
money, hiring skilled mercenaries, weapons experts,
who had modified the vehicle, installing various
armaments.

Blade saw a buckskin-clad figure emerge from
the SEAL and climb toward his position. He
glanced through the binoculars one more time, then
turned to face his friend. "Why didn't you stay in
the SEAL?" he inquired.

"I got tired of hearin' Orson bellyache, pard,"
Hickok said as he knelt alongside Blade. "I
reckoned I'd best skedaddle before I was tempted to
call him out."

Blade stared at the vehicle, frowning. "Bringing
him along was a mistake," he stated.

"It wasn't our idea," Hickok reminded him. "Plato was the one who said each outfit should send at least one fighter."

"At least Orson can fight," Blade commented. "He proved that when we ambushed those twelve earlier."

"Doesn't mean a thing," Hickok disagreed. "We took them by surprise. The real crunch will come when we're on the receiving end. Personally, I don't think Orson will hold up."

Blade gazed at the starry sky. "We'll wait a while longer before we make our move."

"Should we break out the jerky and water?" Hickok asked.

"Sounds like a good idea," Blade said.

Hickok started to go.

"Wait," Blade said.

"What is it, pard?"

"I never got around to asking you," Blade noted. "How did Sherry take to this campaign?" Sherry was Hickok's wife.

The gunman laughed. "She didn't want me to come. She said she thought Plato's plan is too risky, and I had to agree it is a mite on the cockamamie side. She was worried I might get hurt, which is only natural seeing she worships the ground I walk on."

Blade chuckled. "I'll bet what she loves the most about you is your humility."

"How did Jenny take it?" Hickok queried, referring to Blade's spouse.

"The same as Sherry. Geronimo's wife probably reacted the same way," Blade commented.

"Not quite, pard," Hickok said.

"What do you mean?"

"I was talking to Geronimo a while ago," Hickok explained. "He claimed Cynthia told him to kick ass and bring back some white scalps."

"He was pulling your leg."

"I figured as much," Hickok said. "That mangy Injun wouldn't tell me the truth if his life depended on it."

Blade smiled. "You do the same to him. That's what you get for having him as one of your best friends."

"Yeah." Hickok smiled also. "We know we can count on him when the going gets rough."

"And Bertha has proven herself in combat," Blade remarked. "How do you rate Rudabaugh and Lynx?"

"I like Rudabaugh," Hickok declared. "He's right handy with those pistols of his, but the poor boy suffers from delusions."

"Delusions?"

"Yep. He told me he'd like to have a shooting contest. The dummy thinks he might be able to beat me."

"One of these days," Blade told him, "you may meet your match."

Hickok snorted. "Thanks for the vote of confidence! The only way anybody is going to beat me is if they tie my hands behind my back."

"What do you think of Lynx?" Blade inquired.

"That hombre is downright loco," Hickok responded.

"Nathan," Blade said, using the gunfighter's given name, the name his parents had bestowed, the one he had used for the first sixteen years of his life before he had selected Hickok at his Naming. "Are you sure you're talking like the real James Butler Hickok would have talked when you try to sound like him?"

"What?"

"Never mind." Blade sighed. "So do you like

Lynx or not?"

"There's no doubt the furry runt can kill," Hickok said. "He just takes some getting used to, is all. I mean, when you saved Gremlin from the Doktor in Kalispell and brought him back to the Home, he took some getting used to also. But I like him fine. I do know I could count on Lynx to back my play in a pinch, which is more than I can say for that wimp Orson." He paused. "I wonder how the Doktor does it?" he asked thoughtfully. "How does the madman make critters like Lynx and Gremlin and all the others?"

"Beats me," Blade confessed. "I think Plato and the Elders are close to understanding the process."

A twig abruptly snapped behind them, and Hickok reacted instantly, his hands flashing to his Pythons, the revolvers clearing leather faster than the eye could follow. His thumbs were cocking the hammers when he recognized his intended target.

"Damn it, you idiot!" Hickok exclaimed. "I could of blown you away!" His body was half-twisted in the direction of the newcomer.

"Not the pitiful way you shoot," a husky feminine voice taunted him.

"Bertha! What are you doing up here?" Blade demanded. "Did somebody call a meeting and forget to tell me about it?"

"Be cool, baby," Bertha advised him, kneeling next to Hickok. She was a lovely, statuesque woman, with dusky skin and curly black hair; one of her parents had been black, the other white. Her clothing, fatigues confiscated from a deceased soldier, blended nicely with the night. Alpha Triad had rescued her months before from an Army contingent in Thief River Falls, Minnesota. Originally from the Twin Cities of Minneapolis and St. Paul,

where she had served as a "soldier" in a faction
called the Nomads, she had later become instru-
mental in assisting the Family in relocating the
inhabitants of the Twin Cities to a deserted town
known as Halma, situated very close to the Home.
The Home itself was located on the outskirts of the
former Lake Bronson State Park. "I wanted some
fresh air," Bertha stated. "Besides, you got no call
to get on my case. But I want you to know I'm still
ticked at you for what you did today."

"Me?" Blade touched his chest. "What did I
do?"

"You left me behind to babysit the buggy while
you *boys*"—she emphasized that word—"went off
to get your jollies. I didn't like it but I didn't want
to say anything in front of the others and show them
you don't know what you're doing."

"I don't know what I'm doing?" Blade retorted.

Bertha playfully slapped Hickok's shoulder.
"Do you hear this bozo? He has a short memory.
Who was it who almost got us killed when we made
that run to the Twin Cities? Who was it who almost
lost his gonads to the Wacks?" She stopped and
pointed at Hickok's Pythons. "You gonna put them
away or shoot me, White Meat?"

Hickok, absorbed in her tirade against Blade,
had forgotten to replace his Colts. He promptly
twirled them into their respective holsters. "Keep
goin', Black Beauty," he urged her. "I'm enjoying
this."

"I'll bet you are," Blade cracked.

Bertha faced Blade. "You ain't off the hook yet,
sucker! Why'd you do it? I can hold my own, and
you know it. Why didn't you let one of them other
jerks guard the SEAL today?"

"You've got it all backwards," Blade informed
her.

"Oh, yeah?" Bertha responded skeptically. "Then set me straight."

Blade put his brawny right hand on her shoulder. "Bertha, I'd never treat you differently because you're a woman. Remember, I'm the one who picked two women to be Warriors in the Family. I happen to think women can handle combat as competently as men, provided it's the right woman—"

"What do you mean by that?" Bertha curtly cut him off.

"Just what I said. Certain women are natural fighters, others aren't. It's the same with men. Some make excellent fighters, while others don't. You've met Joshua. He's a case in point. He's too spiritual to become an effective fighter. Why do you think my Family has such an arduous selection process for the status of Warrior? Why is our screening of potential candidates so rigorous?"

"You still haven't told me why you left me behind today," Bertha noted.

"You were the logical choice."

"How so?"

Blade pointed at the SEAL. "You know how important our transport is. It's essential to the Family's welfare. So put yourself in my shoes. There I was, about to leave the SEAL unprotected in enemy territory. I had to leave a guard. But who could I pick? Lynx or Rudabaugh or Orson? Not likely. I don't know any of them well enough to trust them alone with something as valuable as the SEAL. Hickok or Geronimo? They're my Triad partners. We trained together, and we've fought side by side for years. I needed them with me to maximize our capability. There was only one person I trusted enough to leave with the SEAL, only one person whose ability and reliability I could count on."

Bertha beamed. "Me?"

"You," Blade affirmed.

Bertha leaned down and kissed Blade on the left cheek. "You adorable hunk, you!"

"Uh-oh," Hickok said.

"Don't worry," Bertha said to Hickok. "I ain't about to fall for him. Not like I did for you, before you went and got yourself married to someone else."

"I wasn't talking about you," Hickok corrected her. He pointed toward Catlow. "Look."

A pair of headlights was just leaving the outskirts of the town, bearing north on U.S. Highway 85.

"Damn!" Blade cursed his carelessness. "*Move it!*"

The three of them raced down the rise to the SEAL. The rise and a slight curve temporarily blocked their view of the town and the approaching vehicle.

Blade grabbed Bertha's right elbow and pushed her to the center of the road. "Lay down," he ordered.

"What?"

"Lay down!" he directed.

Bertha dropped to the tarmacadam, lying on her stomach, with her arms outspread.

"Hickok!" Blade said, pointing at a cluster of boulders and rocks at the side of the highway only ten feet away.

Hickok ran to the boulders and disappeared from sight.

Blade quickly clambered into the SEAL, into the driver's seat.

"What's going on?" Geronimo asked.

The interior of the SEAL was spacious. There were two bucket seats in the front, one for the driver and the other for a passenger, with a console between them. A comfortable long seat ran the width of the transport right behind the bucket seats. The rear section of the SEAL was utilized as a storage space for their provisions. Two spare tires and tools were stocked in a recessed compartment under the rear storage area.

"Company," Blade said. Geronimo was in the other bucket seat. Rudabaugh and Orson sat in the wide seat behind them, and Lynx was reclining on top of the pile of supplies.

"What kind of company?" Orson questioned.

Blade hastily placed the key in the ignition and gunned the motor. He kept the lights off and carefully backed the vehicle from the highway, into the cover of the rise. He stopped the SEAL 20 yards from the road and switched off the engine.

"What kind of company?" Orson impatiently repeated.

"Don't know yet." Blade glanced at Geronimo. "Stay put and watch the SEAL."

Geronimo nodded his understanding.

Blade climbed from the transport and sped to the boulders Hickok was hiding behind.

The gunfighter spun at his approach.

"I want them taken out quietly," Blade said as he crouched near Hickok.

"You got it. Mind if I borrow one of your knives?"

Blade raised his right pants leg. A stiletto was strapped to his calf below the knee. Another stiletto was secured to his left leg. He gripped the hilt and handed the weapon to Hickok.

"Thanks, pard," Hickok whispered. "I hope you won't fuss if I get it bloody."

"Be my guest."

Further conversation was terminated by the

appearance of headlights coming around the curve.

Blade recognized the vehicle as a jeep, alleviating his concern it might be civilians. Traffic in this area was sparse, almost all of it comprised of military conveyances. Jeeps were exclusively used by the Army of the Civilized Zone. The garrison commander had undoubtedly sent a patrol to check on the missing work detail.

The jeep was traveling at a sedate speed, not more than 30 miles an hour, when the lights illuminated Bertha's prone form. The driver promptly slowed to a crawl.

Bertha didn't move a muscle.

The jeep drew to a stop about eight feet from Bertha. A door on the passenger side slowly opened and a soldier cautiously stepped out, his M-16 at the ready. He carefully walked to Bertha and nudged her with his right foot.

Bertha lay still.

Two more soldiers emerged from the jeep, one of them the driver. They also carried M-16s.

The first trooper, a sergeant, put the barrel of his M-16 on Bertha's head. With his right hand on the trigger, he used his left to reach down and touch her cheek.

"Is she dead?" one of the others asked.

The sergeant straightened. "I don't think so."

Blade hesitated in making his move, hoping the troopers would spread out a bit more or turn their bodies in another direction. As it was, the three were practically facing the boulders.

"I think she's faking it," the sergeant was saying. "Look at the uniform she's wearing."

Damn!

Blade mentally lambasted his stupidity. Bertha was wearing a trooper's uniform! Why hadn't he thought of it before he had her lie down? Did they have female troopers in the Army?

Damn!

"If you don't open your eyes right this instant," the sergeant stated harshly, "I'm going to add another hole to your head."

Bertha opened her eyes and rolled over. She grinned at the sergeant. "Hi, there! Thanks for waking me from my nap."

"Cut the crap, bitch," the sergeant rejoined. "I happen to know for a fact that women aren't stationed at outposts like Catlow. So where did you come from? And how did you get out here in the middle of nowhere? Where'd you get that uniform?"

"My, ain't you a bundle of questions," Bertha said.

The sergeant jammed the barrel of the M-16 against her right breast. "I want answers, and I want them now."

Blade detected a motion out of his left eye.

Hickok was moving to the right, crouched over, heading for the highway.

What did he think he was doing?

"I'm going to count to ten," the sergeant told Bertha. "If you haven't told me what I want to know by then, I'm going to ram this thing up your snatch and let you have it."

Bertha, incredibly, smiled. "Ohhh, how kinky! I love it!"

"One," the sergeant began.

"You sure are friendly to strangers in these parts," Bertha quipped.

"Two."

Blade had lost sight of Hickok. What the hell was the gunman up to now?

"Three."

Bertha went to rise, but the sergeant shoved her down.

"Four," he said.

"Ain't I gonna get a last request?" Bertha demanded.

"Five."

"Anyone ever tell you that you've got a one-track mind?" Bertha asked.

"Six."

Bertha glanced at the other soldiers. "Are you just gonna stand there and let him blow me away? Didn't your momma ever tell you it ain't polite to waste a lady?"

"Seven."

"Seven always has been my lucky number," interposed a new voice.

The three soldiers looked up, elevating their weapons, covering the interloper.

Hickok was nonchalantly standing in the very middle of the highway, not 15 feet from the troopers, his thumbs carelessly hooked in his gunbelt. He began walking casually to his left, to the far side of the road, forcing the soldiers to pivot and follow his movement, compelling them to turn their backs to the near side of the road and the boulders. "Howdy, neighbors," he said politely. "I think the lady might have a point. You guys sure don't know how to impress a woman, do you?"

"Who the hell are you?" the sergeant demanded, flabbergasted at his audacity.

"Would you believe Little Bo Peep?" Hickok responded, still moving.

"Hold it!" the sergeant growled. "Another step and you're history!"

Hickok stopped, his hands dropping to his sides.

"Are you with her?" the sergeant snapped.

"I got better taste than that," Bertha interjected.

"Shut up!" the sergeant shouted at her. "You!" he bellowed at the gunman. "Unbuckle that belt!"

"What? My pants will fall down. Do you want me to expose my knobby knees to the world?" Hickok asked.

"I'm not fooling!" the sergeant warned. "Do it right now or else!"

Hickok's left hand drifted to his belt buckle. "I don't reckon I could prevail upon you to surrender peaceably?"

"What? Are you nuts?"

"Nope. I'm alive," Hickok stated, "which is more than I can say for you."

The sergeant never saw the massive arm encircling his neck, nor did he feel more than a twinge of pain as the razor point of a Bowie knife ripped up and into his neck, piercing his jugular, driving past his jawbone, and imbedding itself in the base of his skull. He gurgled once, blood erupting from the wound and cascading down his chest.

The remaining pair of soldiers, intent on keeping an eye on the man in the buckskins, glanced at their sergeant, astonished to see a steely giant looming behind him. One of them tried to bring his M-16 to bear, but the woman on the ground suddenly swung her legs in an arc, clipping him behind the knees and sending him sprawling to the highway.

Frantic, the third trooper swung toward the giant in the black vest. Before he could fire, the gunman was there.

Hickok charged in a rush, grabbing the stiletto from behind his back and lunging, the narrow blade penetrating the third trooper's left eye.

The trooper screamed and fell to his knees, futilely striving to extract the stiletto from his eye.

He quivered for a moment, then toppled over, dead.

Bertha was on top of her foe, pinning him to the road with the M-16 pressed against his neck. He was gaping at her in sheer horror.

"Please don't kill me!" he wailed.

Blade and Hickok joined her.

"What should I do with him?" Bertha asked.

"Watch him for a moment," Blade instructed her. He turned and strode into the darkness.

Bertha stood, the M-16 in her hands. "Don't move!" she told her prisoner. "And keep quiet!"

The young soldier froze, his eyes wide.

Bertha looked at Hickok. "Thanks for the assist, White Meat."

"Any time."

"Too bad you had to go and marry Sherry," Bertha stated. "We would of made a great combo."

Hickok nodded at the captive. "Now's not the time nor the place. Besides, I thought we had this all settled."

"I never made any promises," Bertha mentioned.

Hickok, desperate to change the subject, leaned over the soldier. "Did I just see your eyelid twitch?"

"No, sir!" the trooper timorously replied.

"You sure?"

"Yes, sir!"

"Well, don't let it happen again!"

"Yes, sir!"

"Leave the poor boy alone," Bertha said. "He might pee his pants if you keep it up."

They clearly heard the sound of the SEAL starting, and a few seconds later Blade drove the transport onto the roadway. He braked, turned it off, and jumped outside to the ground. Geronimo and the others followed his example.

"What do we have here?" Orson demanded. He

walked up to the soldier and, without warning or explanation, kicked him in the side.

"What the hell do you think you're doin', big belly?" Bertha angrily inquired. "There was no need for that!"

"Just giving him some of his own medicine," Orson answered, surprised by her attitude. "What's the big deal."

"Leave him alone," Blade commanded, stepping up to Orson.

The bearded grumbler started to say something, decided it wouldn't be wise, shrugged instead, and walked away.

"What are we going to do with him?" Geronimo asked.

"First things first," Blade said. He looked at Rudabaugh. "Take the binoculars up that rise and keep your eyes peeled. If you see anything heading our way, come running."

Rudabaugh nodded and left.

Blade squatted next to the soldier. "I'm going to ask you some questions. I want honest answers." He drew his right Bowie, the one he'd used to kill the sergeant. "If I suspect you're lying, you know what I'll do."

"Yes, sir."

"Fine. How many soldiers are left in Catlow?" Blade inquired as a test question.

"Let me think," the trooper said hastily, calculating. "About twenty-five," he concluded.

Blade nodded. The number fit. He'd already known there were originally 40 in Catlow. They had wiped out the 12 guarding the Flatheads. The 3 here made it 15. Subtract 15 from 40, and the result was 25. The trooper was telling the truth.

"Where is the garrison located?" Blade wanted to know.

"There's a large square in the center of town," the soldier said. "Our headquarters is a concrete building to the south of the square."

"Were you sent to check on the road crew, on the Flatheads?"

"How did you know?" The trooper asked, gawking.

"Who's in charge in Catlow?"

"Captain Reno."

"When will he expect you back?" Blade queried.

"Not before morning," the soldier stated. "He told us he thinks they had mechanical trouble, and they wouldn't want to leave one of the transports with a load of Indians out overnight. He said they were probably camping out and would send the jeep back in the morning for a mechanic. It's happened before."

"Why wouldn't they just send someone back at night?" Blade inquired.

"We don't do a lot of driving at night, not unless it's really necessary."

"I don't get it. Why not?"

The soldier fearfully gazed skyward. "There are . . . things . . . out at night."

"But the captain sent you?"

"He felt it would be safe," the trooper responded. "The moon is not out tonight."

"What the blazes does the moon have to do with anything?" Hickok questioned.

"I don't rightly know. I'm kind of new here. I was assigned to Catlow only a month ago. I've heard a lot of stories—"

"Maybe we shouldn't be standin' out here," Bertha said, looking up.

"What do we do with him?" Geronimo mentioned again.

"We could tie him up and leave him at the side

of the road," Hickok suggested.

"Please! No!" the soldier pleaded. "They might get me!"

"Who might get you?" Blade asked.

"The . . . things."

"Why not give him to me?" Lynx requested. He had been quietly leaning against the SEAL, but now he moved forward and stood near Blade. "I could use a tasty snack."

At the sight of the genetic mutant, the young soldier recoiled in stark fear. "Keep him away from me!"

"He won't hurt you," Blade promised.

"Sure, sonny," Lynx said, grinning, his green eyes twinkling. "I was only foolin'."

"I know who you are," the trooper informed Lynx.

"Oh, you do?"

"Yeah. I saw you on the news. You're the one who tried to kill the Doktor! You're the one who nuked the Citadel!" The trooper's eyes were terrified saucers.

Bertha glanced at Lynx. "You *nuked* the Citadel?"

"What's the big deal?" Lynx demanded defensively. "It wasn't a *big* nuke! Just a little thermo, the portable missiles they used a lot during World War Three."

"You *nuked* the Citadel?" Bertha shook her head in disbelief. Her knowledge of nuclear weaponry was scanty, a result of her lack of schooling. But she had heard many tales during her gang years in the Twin Cities, and she knew from firsthand experience some of the horrifying results of the nuclear devastation caused by the Third World War.

"You're the one they call Lynx!" the soldier

exclaimed. "You're the reason they had to evac—"
He abruptly stopped, his head cocked to one side.

"SSSShhhhh," Hickok said.

"Does anybody hear anything?" Geronimo
asked.

They all listened intently. There was a faint
swishing sound in the air.

"What is that?" Hickok queried.

"Where's it comin' from?" Bertha questioned.

Blade stood. "It's an odd noise, isn't it?"

"It's coming from overhead," Geronimo
declared.

"It sounds like a colossal canary to me," Lynx
commented.

"It's one of the things!" the young soldier
screeched.

"It's what?" Blade inquired. "What are these
things you keep talking about?"

The swishing increased in volume, resembling
the rhythmic beating of monstrous wings.

"What the blazes is it?" Hickok demanded.

"I can barely make out . . . something,"
Geronimo mentioned.

"It's going to get us!" the trooper yelled. Before
any of them knew what he was doing, in a surprising
display of speed, he twisted, pushed himself erect,
and bolted into the night, into the field on the far
side of the highway.

Geronimo attempted to grab him, but missed.

"I'll get the dumb kid," Lynx volunteered, and
took off in pursuit.

The swishing had diminished in intensity.

"Should we give kitty a hand?" Hickok asked
Blade.

Blade shook his head. "Lynx can move faster
than any of us, and those eyes of his enable him to
see in the dark much better than we can. He'll catch

the soldier."

A piercing scream abruptly rent the enclosing blackness, a scream inexplicably terminated in midcry.

"It was the trooper!" Hickok stated.

"Great Spirit, preserve us!" Geronimo exclaimed.

Bertha started to run in the direction of the outcry.

"Stay put!" Blade ordered.

Bertha stopped. "But—"

"But, nothing! You can't help him now!"

They waited in the glare from the jeep head-lights, their hands on their respective weapons. Blade debated having the jeep headlights doused, but discarded the notion. Whatever was up there had fallen upon the soldier in the gloomy field, not in the bright headlights. Maybe the . . . thing . . . didn't like the glare.

Lynx startled them when he suddenly appeared at the edge of the highway. "I didn't get to him in time," he said, stating the obvious.

"What happened?" Blade demanded.

Lynx stared up at the stars. "Something, I don't know what, swooped down and grabbed the kid before I could reach him. The thing was so damn quick. . . ." He left the sentence unfinished.

"Did the thing kill him?" Bertha queried.

"I don't know," Lynx replied. "I saw this form diving from the sky, and I could make out a gigantic pair of wings. You heard the kid when the thing got hold of him? It never slowed, just grabbed the kid and up it went again. There was nothing I could do."

"Do you think there could be more of them?" Geronimo questioned.

Footsteps pounded nearby and Rudabaugh ran up to them. "I heard a scream," he said. "What happened?"

"Did you see anything?" Blade asked him.

"Nope. I was watching the town, like you said."

"Any sign of activity there?"

Rudabaugh shook his head, breathing deeply from his dash down the rise. "Not a peep."

"Okay." Blade noticed Orson standing near the SEAL, fear on his features. "Hickok, I want Geronimo and you to put the bodies in the jeep and drive it into the field. See if you can find a suitable hiding place, like a ravine or arroyo. Then get back here on the double. Watch out for colossal canaries!"

"You don't have to tell me twice," Hickok said.

"The rest of you," Blade addressed them, "inside the SEAL. We'll spend the night inside, just in case there are more of . . . whatever they are . . . around here."

Lynx climbed into the rear section, while Orson, Rudabaugh, and Bertha took the wide seat. Blade retrieved the arms from the dead soldiers and passed them to Lynx, then stood outside observing Hickok and Geronimo comply with his instructions. When Hickok drove the jeep into the far field, he clambered into the driver's seat.

A minute elapsed in strained silence.

"We just gonna stay here on the highway?" Orson asked. "What if some traffic comes along?"

"We'll wait here for Hickok and Geronimo," Blade replied.

"What's the matter?" Orson said sarcastically. "Don't tell me you're worried about them! I thought the vaunted Warriors were indestructible!"

Before Blade could reply, Bertha rammed the barrel of her M-16 into Orson's fleshy chin.

Orson straightened and made like a rock.

"You know, honky, I'm gettin' real tired of your

face," Bertha said in a hard tone. "First, you beat on that boy out there, a kid just doin' his job, when he couldn't fight back. And now, you badmouth the Warriors. You must be one stupid honky! I've seen these Warriors in action, and I'm here to tell you they can be mean mothers if you tick 'em off. But don't take my word for it. I've seen how you like to get on Blade's case all the time. Do me a favor. Do all of us a favor! Why don't you pick on Hickok, but do it when Blade ain't around, 'cause Blade is a nice guy and wouldn't let Hickok do a number on you. You see, lover," Bertha mentioned softly, leaning nearer to Orson, "you don't know Hickok like I know Hickok. That man is stone crazy when it comes to killin'. You might be able to cross him once and get away with it, if he had a reason to let you live. But dump on him twice . . ." Bertha paused and laughed. "Well, let me put it to you this way. I don't know of anyone who's crossed Hickok twice and is still alive to tell about it. Do you, Blade?"

Blade suppressed a grin. "No," he confirmed.

"This is real interesting, Bertha," Lynx chimed in. "You should have been with us earlier, when we jumped the work detail guards."

Bertha glanced at Lynx, reclining on the supplies in the back of the transport. "Oh? Why?"

"Because fatso here told Hickok he was full of hot air." Lynx frowned and snapped his fingers. "And dummy me! I had to go and butt in before Hickok made his play!"

Bertha looked at Orson, her brown eyes dancing with delight. "Did you really?" she inquired sweetly. "Orson, I'm here to tell you, I haven't met anyone in all my years with less brains than you have." She removed the barrel of the M-16 from his bearded chin.

Orson turned and glared at her. "You talk real

big when you have a gun in my face!"

"Are you . . ." Bertha began, then hesitated, her face creasing in a pleased smile.

The passenger side door was jerked open and Geronimo entered the SEAL, followed by Hickok. Geronimo sat on the console, the gunfighter in the remaining bucket seat.

"Any problems?" Blade inquired.

"No," Geronimo answered.

"It was a piece of cake," Hickok affirmed. "Not more than fifteen yards thataway"—he pointed to the southwest—"is a gully. Not very big, but the jeep fit in it real nice."

"Good," Blade declared. "We'll back up behind the rise and spend the night there."

Bertha eased forward on her seat. "Say, White Meat?" she said, using her pet expression for Hickok.

"What is it, Black Beauty," he responded.

"Would you do something for me?" Bertha innocently asked.

Hickok glanced over his shoulder. "Anything except marry you. I keep tellin' you I'm already hitched."

"Oh, it's nothin' like that," she assured him.

"Then what is it?"

"Would you kill Orson for me?"

A pin dropping would have been the equivalent of tumultuous thunder.

Hickok stared at Orson. "Have you been bothering her?"

"He sure has," Bertha verified. "Me, and Blade, and everybody else, for that matter."

Hickok's blue eyes narrowed. "I told you I'd put a hole between those beady eyes of yours if you kept it up." He reached for the door handle. "I'll wait for you outside."

Orson's mouth fell open. He shot a glance at Blade. "Are you just going to sit there and let him shoot me?"

Blade slowly stretched. "Orson, I'm tired. It's been a long day. I don't have the energy to waste trying to talk Hickok out of killing you."

"But you can't!" Orson protested.

Blade stifled a yawn. "Why not?"

"This is supposed to be a joint venture," Orson said. "We were sent here as a team! Your Family and my people have signed a treaty!"

"True," Blade admitted. "The Family and the Moles did agree to a pact."

"So, if you let Hickok kill me, it would violate the treaty!" Orson declared.

Blade stared at Orson and allowed himself the luxury of an innocent smile. "Who would know?"

"What?"

"How would your people find out? I'm not about to tell them," Blade asserted.

"I know I won't," Bertha said.

"My lips are sealed," Lynx interjected. "And besides, I really could use the snack!"

Orson gazed at Rudabaugh for support.

Rudabaugh chuckled. "Don't look at me! My people, the Cavalry, could care less about one slimy Mole."

Hickok opened his door. "There you have it. I won't wait long."

Orson paled.

"Oh, darn!" Geronimo said, then sighed. "I hate to be the party-pooper, but I don't think you should kill him."

Hickok exhaled through his nose. "You're always spoiling my fun!"

"I'm sorry," Geronimo apologized.

"Why don't you think I should do it?"

Geronimo looked at Orson. "Don't get me wrong. I want you to do it. I've been thinking about scalping him myself. But don't you recall what Plato said to us right before we departed the Home?"

"Refresh my memory."

"He told us he was counting on us," Geronimo said. "He said all his hopes and aspirations were riding with us. And he added it would be up to us to set an example for all the others. If all of us can't get along, how could anyone expect the Family, the Cavalry, and the Moles to exist in peace?"

"Ain't no skin off my nose, pard."

"Plato is counting on us," Geronimo stressed.

Hickok sighed and slammed his door. "All right." He glanced at Orson. "It's against my better judgment, but I'm gonna give you one more chance."

Orson gulped. "I appreciate it."

"But if I were you," Hickok added, "I'd take the advice of my grandmother. If you don't have anything nice to say about others, keep your damn trap shut!"

Blade grinned and started the SEAL, wondering if Hickok really would have shot Orson or if the gunman was merely applying some basic psychology. Because, as much as he hated to admit it, they would need Orson in the days ahead. Need him badly.

Bertha reached over and tickled Orson's chin. "No hard feelings, are there?"

"No hard feelings," Orson mumbled.

Lynx cackled. "This is just what I like."

"What is?" Rudabaugh asked.

"We're all one big, happy family!"

4

He was bedded down for the night, camped under an overhanging rock at the base of a steep ridge. His horse was tethered nearby, munching on the grass and other edibles he'd gathered before nightfall. He deliberately maintained a low fire to minimize the risk of detection. Absently chewing on a piece of jerky, he gazed out at the twinkling stars.

Why was he doing this? he asked himself for the umpteenth time. What was he trying to prove?

The going had been easier than he'd expected. Staying on course wasn't difficult; every Family member was taught to read the stars and navigate by the sun at an early age. Even hiding in one of the convoy trucks when they departed the Home had been simple, facilitated by the stacks and stacks of provisions affording ample hiding places. Once the column was on its way, the hard part had begun: keeping out of sight of Beta Triad and anyone else who might recognize him. Mingling with the Moles and the Cavalry had posed no problem, nor had stealing his mount to complete his journey.

So here he was, not half a day from his destination, if he read the map right.

Could he really go through with it?

Should he really go through with it?

Yes! he told himself.

He had to do it.

Even if he failed, even if they put him to death, at least he would know for certain before he died.

He had to know.

The question demanded an answer. It had been burning at his insides for weeks.

Longer.

Even since the trip to Thief River Falls.

Hickok couldn't be right! He couldn't be! There had to be more to life than kill or be killed!

He wearily rubbed his forehead.

It wasn't as if he hadn't tried to see it their way. Dear Spirit, he had even killed! Killed! Taken the lives of his spiritual brothers and sisters!

How could he have fallen so far so fast? How could he have permitted himself to be drawn down to their level? Was it a lack of faith? A lack of dedication? What?

Whatever it was, this trip was essential to his well-being. He would try it his way for a change. There was always the distinct possibility he would fail, but the prospect of defeat was secondary to knowing he had tried his best.

After all, perfection of purpose counted for something.

He closed his eyes and silently prayed. "O Divine Maker and Sustainer, please guide your servant Joshua in this enterprise. Lead me by the hand, and enable me to reveal the full glory of the knowledge of sonship with the First Source and Universe Center. We are all your children, and you have commanded us to love one another even as you love us. Help me, Father, to love others. Let my light so shine with the brilliance of your love that all others will recognize your presence in me and be led to worship your greatness. Steady me in the confrontation ahead. I pray I may be successful in my goal. I pray I may reveal your love to the Doktor."

5

Yet another sleepless night compelled Plato to arise early and tiptoe from the cabin without awakening his darling wife, Nadine. He stood near the door and sadly gazed at the first trace of light on the eastern horizon.

Was it the senility or something else? Why was he so uneasy?

Plato clasped his hands behind his stooped back and walked eastward, toward the fields and wooded sections preserved in the eastern part of the Home. The cabins for the married couples and families were aligned in the middle of the 30-acre plot, while the western portion contained the six concrete blocks and the open space used for Family social and religious activities.

If all was proceeding according to plan, Blade and the others would be assuming control of Catlow today. If the Doktor took the bait, the next phase would swing into operation. And if the column adhered to his explicit dictates, the Freedom Federation would score a major victory in its battle against the oppressive Civilized Zone.

There were so many ifs.

So many variables.

The Freedom Federation had been his idea. Actually, he had favored the designation Freedom Confederation, but when the final tally had been taken, after Zahner had expressed his preference for the "snappier" Freedom Federation, the leaders of the unifying factions had opted for Zahner's choice.

Quibbling over the title would have been inane. The primary achievement was effecting the union of such diverse groups.

The Cavalry people had been easy to convince. They had suffered repeatedly from raids by Civilized Zone forces. Based in eastern South Dakota, the Cavalry was the closest to the Civilized Zone. Originally formed as a protective association immediately after World War III, a vigilante group devoted to defending the residents from looters, scavengers, and Government troops, the Cavalry was now a precision military force with approximately 700 armed and mounted riders at its disposal. Its leader, a rugged man named Kilrane, had eagerly embraced the concept of the Freedom Federation and an assault on the Civilized Zone. Kilrane and over 500 of the Cavalry were now leading the attack column. Because 6 of the Family's 15 Warriors were also on the expedition, Kilrane had graciously left 20 of his men, under the command of a gunman called Boone, at the Home as support for Spartacus and the other remaining Warriors.

The refugees from the Twin Cities had also been happy to join the Federation. Alpha Triad had led about 550 people, the surviving members of three separate groups, to safety. The three groups, known as the Horns, the Porns, and the Nomads, had been fighting among themselves for years over their miserable turf. Now all three were working to build a new home in Halma, not far from the Home. The Family was industriously aiding the refugees in adapting to their new locale. After their arrival in Halma, the heads of the groups had held a conclave and decided to strive to bury their animosity and begin anew. They had selected a title for themselves, using the Family as an example, and called them-

selves the Clan. Elections had been held, and Zahner
had been chosen as their first collective leader. A
man named Bear and another known as Brother
Timothy had been appointed as Zahner's
lieutenants.

The final faction comprising the Freedom
Federation was the Moles. Initially discovered by
Hickok, they existed in a subterranean city over 50
miles east of the Home. They were led by a man
called Wolfe. Plato distrusted this Wolfe, but didn't
know why. There was simply some quality about the
man engendering unease, an air of deviousness, as it
were. Still, Wolfe had agreed to the Federation
concept and sent 150 men as his share of the
attacking force.

With the 500 or so Cavalry riders, and the 150
Moles, plus the 200 fighting men the Clan could
spare, the Freedom Federation was launching an
attack on the Civilized Zone with only 850
"soldiers." The number seemed considerable, until
one compared it to the amassed might of their foes.

The Civilized Zone was dominated by a dictator
named Samuel II, abetted by the Doktor. Both were
supported by the military. Apparently, during the
Third World War, a member of the deceased
President's cabinet, Samuel Hyde, had assumed
control of the reigns of Government and declared
martial law. That had been the end of the United
States of America's Constitutional freedoms. The
capital of the country had been moved to Denver, as
the military and political forces still operational
withdrew to the Midwest and Rocky Mountain
region. While in Kalispell, Montana, Blade had
learned of Samuel II's ambition to reconquer all the
former territory of the United States.

Plato watched the edge of the sun appear above
the horizon.

And now the Freedom Federation was poised to strike before the dictator could realize his vision of conquest. The first major blow had already been struck, when Yama and Lynx had destroyed the Doktor's headquarters at the Cheyenne Citadel. After Yama had returned from Wyoming and detailed his adventures, Plato had concocted the current plan. The beginning phase necessitated seven fighters entering the Civilized Zone. A conference had been held, and it had been agreed that each faction—the Family, the Clan, the Cavalry, and the Moles—should pick someone for the seven. Plato, Zahner, Kilrane, and Wolfe had agreed to use the SEAL for the operation, and the SEAL never went anywhere without Alpha Triad. With three of the seven automatically chosen, the Cavalry had nominated Rudabaugh as one of its best men, the Clan had opted for Bertha, and the Moles had volunteered Orson. Lynx had stepped forward on his own initiative. His intense hatred of the Doktor, combined with his thorough familiarity with the Civilized Zone, had made him an ideal candidate.

Seven against the Doktor.

Several sparrows darted from a nearby tree, chirping their greeting to the fresh day.

Plato somberly watched their flight, hoping he would have something to sing about too when this was over.

6

The morning sun was slightly above the eastern horizon when the garrison commander, a portly officer with a crew cut and a neatly trimmed black mustache, emerged from the front door of the concrete command post. He lazily stretched and idly gazed across the town square. How odd, he thought. Usually, even at this early hour, there would be people in the square, most enroute from one side of the town to the other. With vehicles at a premium, the majority of them having been confiscated by the military over the years, "pedal power," as the officer preferred to refer to it, was the normal means of locomotion. Civilians walked everywhere.

Why weren't there any in the town square?

There was a fountain in the center of the square, the geyser long since defunct. The white basin mainly served as a catch for rain water, and at the moment was two-thirds full.

The officer walked toward the fountain, hoping he could spot the young woman he had seen at the fountain the day before at about this same time. His fatigues had been pressed and starched, and his Government Model Series 80 Automatic Pistol hung on his left hip. He wanted to present a favorable impression when he ordered her to join him for supper, a candlelit repast for two.

Smiling smugly, the officer stopped near the fountain and scanned the area, disappointed that the young woman was nowhere in sight. He was about to return to the command post to arouse his men when he saw someone heading his way. At first, he mistakenly assumed it was one of his men. Several seconds elapsed before he realized it was a woman.

His initial reaction was to admire her beauty.

His second response was to wonder what she was doing in fatigues. All of the troopers under him were men.

His next move was to drop his hand to his pistol. He started to draw, then hesitated, perplexed by her friendly smile. She waved to him, as if she knew him. An M-16 was slung over her left shoulder, but otherwise there wasn't the faintest indication of hostility on her part.

Who the hell was she?

There was a commotion in the fountain behind him, and the sound of water splashing.

The officer glanced over his right shoulder and froze.

The barrel of a machine gun was an inch from his nose, being wielded by a huge man with bulging muscles. He wore a black vest, fatigue pants, and moccasins, all dripping wet.

"Captain Reno, I presume?" the giant asked.

Reno gingerly released his pistol and slowly raised his hands to shoulder height. "You have the advantage of me, sir," he stated.

"Do you keep up with the intelligence reports?" the stranger inquired.

Reno was confused by the unexpected query. "I beg your pardon?"

"I know the Army has been spying on us for years," the giant said. "Have you ever heard of the Home and the Family?"

Reno's eyes widened.

"Ahhh. I take it you have." The big man

grinned. "Then I can assume you have heard of the Warriors?"

"You're Blade!" Reno exclaimed.

"This varmint ain't as stupid as he looks," commented someone to Reno's right.

A blond man in buckskins stood at the east end of the fountain, a rifle in his hands, two pearl-handled revolvers on his hips.

"You're Hickok!" Reno stated.

"And where Hickok and Blade are," interjected another voice to the left, "can their faithful, smarter, and braver Indian companion be far behind?"

Reno glanced at the west end of the fountain.

The one known as Geronimo was there, an FNC Auto Rifle at the ready.

"What are you idiots doin', standing out in the open like this?" demanded the woman in the fatigues as she joined them.

"Shootin' the breeze with Captain Reno here," Hickok replied.

Reno recognized he had been set up. Blade must have been lying in wait in the fountain, with Hickok and Geronimo on either side. The woman had served as a distraction, allowing Blade to get the drop on him. "My compliments on your strategy," he said, addressing Blade. "How did you know I would be coming out here so early?"

"We didn't," Blade admitted. "I was expecting your men to come out first."

"And what is it you want?" Reno inquired. He struggled to maintain a calm demeanor, although he was extremely nervous. Every officer knew about the Warriors and had heard of their decidedly deadly reputation. He was astonished to discover these three so far from their usual stamping grounds. Who was the woman and how did she fit into the scheme of things? What was going on?

"What we want," Blade said, "and what we will get, is Catlow. You can make it easy for us, or hard on yourself. The choice is yours."

Reno looked at the command post. Where the hell were his men? He stalled, acting friendly. "Just the four of you against my garrison? You can't be serious!"

"There's more than four of us, bub!"

Reno casually turned, completely unprepared for the sight he beheld.

One of the Doktor's genetic creations, a short creature resembling a cross between a man and a feline, was strolling his way, coming around the eastern arc of the fountain, past Hickok.

Reno gaped, nonplussed.

The creature, smiling, stopped next to Reno and tweaked his chin. "What the matter, chuckles? Cat got your tongue?" He laughed.

"You!" Reno exploded. "You're Lynx!"

Lynx made a show of examining his own body. "Are you sure?"

"How is it everybody knows you?" the woman asked Lynx.

"You tell her," Lynx instructed Reno.

"Lynx, here, is famous," Reno explained. "He was in all the papers and on all the newscasts after he tried to kill the Doktor. He actually turned against the Doktor!" Reno said in a stunned disbelief.

"Too bad I wasn't able to rip him to shreds, like I wanted," Lynx stated regretfully.

"Did you know the Doktor has posted a reward for your capture?" Reno asked Lynx.

"Oh yeah? How much?"

"One million credits," Reno revealed.

Lynx whistled appreciatively.

"The Doktor wants you real bad," Reno elaborated. "I can imagine the reason. Everyone knows what you did to the Biological Center. All the newscasts reported how you used a thermo on the Doktor's headquarters."

"A million credits, dead or alive," Lynx said, marveling at his notoriety.

"No," Reno corrected him, "a million credits alive."

Lynx's brow furrowed in perplexity. "I don't get it. The Doc doesn't want me dead?"

Reno grinned. "The Doktor has made it clear he wants you alive. He has threatened to kill anyone who harms you."

"How would you like to impress the Doktor and win his good favor?" Blade asked Reno.

"I don't follow you," the officer admitted.

"It's simple. You drive to the Citadel and tell the Doktor Lynx is waiting for him here in Catlow," Blade explained. "Along with us, of course."

Reno looked from Blade to Lynx to Blade again. "You must be crazy! You want me to inform the Doktor you're here?"

"That's what I just said," Blade noted.

"Why would you want me to do something like that?" Reno asked.

"You let us worry about the reason," Blade said. "Just take your men, drive to the Citadel, and let the Doktor know we're here. It's easy enough, isn't it?"

"I find two problems with that scenario," Reno stated.

"What?" Blade responded.

"First, I'm not certain the Doktor is still in the

Citadel," Reno said.

"Who are you kidding, dimples?" Lynx
snapped. "The Doc has always used the Cheyenne
Citadel as his base of operations."

"That was before you obliterated his headquarters and all of his scientific equipment," Reno
retorted. "Don't you know how many thousands of
people you killed when you used that thermo? Do
you have any idea how much hardware you
destroyed? They had a panic on their hands! The
civilian populace went bananas! The Doktor and
Samuel the Second believe you've joined the rebels.
They're concerned you might have access to
additional thermo units. The last I heard, they were
in the process of evacuating Cheyenne."

"Evacuating the Citadel?" Lynx declared.

"Precisely. The Doktor salvaged what he could
from the rubble. You annihilated most of the
Genetic Research Division. The last I knew, there
were rumors the Doktor was relocating his
operations in Denver. So you see, I might not find
the Doktor in the Citadel to deliver your message."

"You said you had two problems with the idea,"
Blade commented. "What's the other?"

"I'm not stupid," Reno said harshly. "What
you're proposing is certain suicide for all of you. You
must have an ulterior motive."

"Like what?"

"Like setting a trap for the Doktor," Reno
asserted.

"Uh-oh," Hickok interrupted. "Look who
finally rolled out of the sack!"

Four troopers were congregated outside the
command post, observing the conversation near the
fountain. They were armed with the inevitable
M-16s, but they were reluctant to use their arms,

hesitant to initiate a conflict when their superior officer was obviously being covered and might be one of the first to fall.

"It's up to you," Blade told Reno. "Which way will it be? Easy or hard?"

Captain Reno was calculating his move. If the Warriors and Lynx were here, in Catlow, it did not bode well for his missing work detail. In addition, the patrol in the jeep he'd sent out the night before had not reported back as yet. And there was no sign of the guard he always posted on the roof of the command center each night. Which could mean only one thing: 16 of his men were more than likely dead, leaving him with 24. More than enough to polish off Blade and his companions! Blade was a fool if he expected a career military man to capitulate so readily! Reno's lips tightened in resolve. His friends did not call him "Bulldog" for nothing!

"Tell your men to drop their guns," Blade directed.

"And if I don't?" Reno inquired.

"I'll kill you," Blade vowed.

Reno slowly twisted, staring at his men. Eight of them were now outside, and the rest would join them any second. He smiled at his men, hoping to convince Blade he was going to comply. "Men!" he shouted. "Listen to me real good!"

Three more of his men exited the command post.

"Do exactly as I tell you!" Captain Reno yelled.

Hickok, tensely surveying the growing group of troopers outside of the command post, saw them begin to spread out. He glanced at Reno, noting the officer's calm countenance, positive the captain would obey. He was all the more amazed when the officer abruptly bellowed at the top of his lungs,

"Get them!" Reno then whirled, brushing the Commando barrel aside, and plowed into the much larger Blade.

The town square erupted into concentrated violence.

Blade and Reno tumbled into the fountain.

The soldiers started firing, advancing toward the middle of the square.

Hickok backed up, raising the Henry to his shoulder and pulling the trigger.

One of the troopers was struck in the chest and propelled to the ground.

Bertha and Geronimo opened up, both of them crouching to pose less of a target.

Lynx, unarmed, dove into the fountain.

More and more soldiers were bursting from the command post on the run, fanning out, deploying with an eye to encircling the fountain.

Hickok downed two more troopers.

Rudabaugh suddenly appeared on the roof of the command center, directly above the front door and the soldiers, a lit stick of dynamite in his right hand. He tossed the dynamite and dropped from sight.

The explosion was tremendous, spraying dirt and dust and chunks of flesh and blood in every direction.

Dumfounded by the blast, the soldiers still alive were looking for the source, unaware of the man on the roof above them. The concentration of gunfire directed at the fountain momentarily slacked off.

Rudabaugh jumped up again, another stick of dynamite clutched in his right fist. His arm swept down, then up, and he threw the explosive under-hand.

One of the troopers spotted the man in black on

the roof and tried to get off a hasty shot.

A second blast rocked the town square. Soldiers were screaming in pain and fear. Three of the troopers broke from the rest and ran toward the east side of the command post.

Orson leaped into view at the corner of the structure, his shotgun thundering.

The three troopers went down in a bloody heap.

Hickok held his fire, waiting for an enemy to show himself. The air was choked with dust and dirt, obscuring both sides in the clash. The area near the fountain was still relatively clear, and the gunman clearly saw Blade and Reno thrashing inside along the rim. What was taking Blade so long to finish off that wimp?

Lynx rose up next to the struggling pair, his lips contorted in a feral snarl. His right hand flicked out, and his claws closed on the back of Reno's squat neck. Lynx heaved, yanking Reno away from Blade and shoving the officer under the water. His pointed teeth exposed, Lynx piled on top of Reno.

Something was wrong with Blade. He was leaning on the rim of the fountain and gasping for air.

Hickok started toward his friend.

Bertha beat him there, reaching Blade and lifting his head in her left arm.

What the blazes was the matter with Blade? Hickok was less than ten yards from them when the dust and dirt dispersed enough for the soldiers to see their opponents. Without warning, the remaining troopers bore down on the fountain.

Geronimo was providing covering fire.

Rudabaugh entered the fray, using a Winchester from the roof of the command post.

Orson added to the carnage from the corner of

the building.

Caught in a withering cross fire, the soldiers were getting the worst of the battle, littering the ground with their dead and dying. A small cluster was racing toward the fountain, determined to reach their commander.

Hickok perceived there was no way Bertha could hold them off, that some of them might even reach the fountain. He dropped his Henry and drew his Pythons, running at full speed now, firing as he ran, going for the head as he invariably did, his shots spaced so closely together it was almost impossible to tell them apart. He reached Bertha's side, the two of them shoulder to shoulder.

Blade suddenly wrenched free of Bertha and rose, the Commando chattering, swinging the machine gun in an arc. Four charging troopers jerked and danced as the heavy slugs stitched a crimson patchwork across their chests.

The ensuing silence seemed unnatural.

Bodies filled the area between the fountain and the command post. Some of the injured were moaning. Pools of blood dotted the square.

Hickok took hold of Blade's right arm. "Are you all right? You look a mite pale."

"I'm fine," Blade replied, his voice ragged.

"What happened?" Hickok asked.

Blade ignored the question. He pointed at the fallen troopers. "Bertha! Geronimo! Check on them! See if any are faking. Be careful!"

Bertha and Geronimo began their circuit of the bodies.

"What happened?" Hickok repeated.

Blade doubled over, grimacing. "The bastard kneed me in the family jewels."

"You mean he got you in the nuts?" Hickok

said, snickering.

"It isn't funny," Blade stated. "Jenny and I may never have kids!"

"Yeah, I know how that can hurt, pard," Hickok agreed sympathetically. He glanced at the pool of water in the fountain. "What happened to . . ." He stopped, shocked.

Blade turned.

Lynx was standing near the center of the fountain. Floating next to his left leg was Captain Reno's body. Floating next to his right leg was Captain Reno's head, the neck a jagged ring of red flesh, the captain's eyes open and seemingly alive as the head bobbed in the murky water. Blood dribbled from Lynx's mouth and over his hairy chin. He walked to the rim of the fountain and stepped over it to firm ground. "That was my idea of a fun time," he quipped. "I can't wait for the Doc to show his ugly face so we can do it again."

Hickok scrutinized the genetic deviate. "You like doing what you just did?"

Lynx nodded. "It's in my blood."

Hickok gazed at the grisly corpse in the pool. "Lynx, I've been accused of being trigger-happy now and then. But you, pard, plumb take the cake."

"You gotta understand something, Hickok," Lynx said earnestly. "The Doktor created me from a test-tube. He did whatever he does to a human embryo and, presto, I'm the result. He created me, and all the others like me, for only one purpose: to kill. We're his personal assassin corps. Oh yeah, some of us in the Genetic Research Division perform other functions, but primarily we're bred to kill. It's what I do best. I only feel comfortable when I'm fightin' or killin'. You, more than any of the rest, should be able to appreciate that."

Hickok slowly nodded. "I reckon I do."

Blade strode several yards from the fountain, scanning the town square. The residents of Catlow were wisely staying in their homes. Earlier in the day, just before sunrise, when Blade and his strike force had surreptitiously entered the town, they had inadvertently bumped into several of the local citizens. Without exception, each one had gawked for a few seconds, then wheeled and fled.

Geronimo and Bertha were still verifying the status of the soldiers sprawled on the square.

Blade looked at Hickok. "Take Lynx with you. Bring the SEAL here."

Hickok nodded and ran off, Lynx in tow. They had left the vehicle parked behind a dilapidated shack four blocks to the north.

Rudabaugh and Orson jogged up to Blade.

"We made a quick sweep of the command post," Rudabaugh reported. "It's all ours."

"What's inside?" Blade inquired.

"Not much," Rudabaugh detailed. "Two big rooms with cots for sleeping, a smaller room with a bunch of tables and a stove, an office, and a room with a lot of electronic equipment."

"What type of electronic equipment?" Blade asked.

Rudabaugh shrugged. "Beats me. We don't have anything like it in the Cavalry. All the fancy stuff we had like that wore out years ago. I did see an old shortwave set once, and I think this stuff inside could be a radio of some kind."

"Stay here and keep alert," Blade ordered. "I'm going to have a look." He took two steps, then paused. "You both did a good job," he praised them.

"Even me?" Orson asked.

"Even you," Blade confirmed.

Orson grinned sheepishly.

Blade headed for the command post. He sincerely hoped there was a radio inside. Unless they could find a trooper relatively unscathed, capable of driving an extended distance, they would need to devise another method of contacting the Doktor. A radio might be just what the . . . doctor . . . ordered.

Grinning at his thoughts, he entered the concrete structure and found himself in a hallway. There was a door to his left, partially open, and he walked to it and shoved.

One wall of the room was filled with sophisticated electronic equipment. There was a wooden table aligned against the wall, and several pieces of equipment were on top of the table. In front of the table was a swivel chair, and in the chair, slumped forward so his forehead was resting on the edge of the table, was a trooper, a pair of headphones on his ears.

Blade crossed to the chair and touched the trooper's left shoulder.

The chair swiveled to one side, causing the trooper to begin to slide toward the cement floor. There was a neat hole in the back of the soldier's head, and a larger cavity where his right eye had once been.

Rudabaugh, Blade guessed. It looked like the type of wound a Winchester would make. Evidently, Rudabaugh had caught this trooper in the act of radioing for assistance.

The soldier slipped from the chair and landed in a disjointed pile on the floor.

Blade leaned down and stripped the headphones from the soldier. He placed them over his own ears.

"Charlie-Alfa-Tango-Lima-Oscar-Whiskey, come in, please!"

Blade sat down in the chair and studied the
equipment on the table.

"Charlie-Alfa-Tango-Lima-Oscar-Whiskey,
come in, please!" a faint voice requested.

Blade racked his memory. The Warriors had
confiscated some portable radio equipment during
their previous encounters with the Army, but the
items on the table were completely different in many
respects. He recalled his hours spent in the Family
library, and one book in particular.

Kurt Carpenter, the Founder of the Home, had
personally stocked the hundreds of thousands of
books included in the library. Books on every conceivable subject. History books, literature books,
humorous books, music books, books on math,
geography, astronomy, and all other branches of
science. Encyclopedias, dictionaries, and reference
books galore. How-to books proliferated. Carpenter
had foreseen the Family's future need for sources of
knowledge and instruction. Accordingly, he had
included books on the fundamentals of everything
from gardening and weaving to metalworking and
gunsmithing. As an added treat, Carpenter had
added scores upon scores of photographic books to
the library. These photographic books, filled as they
were with pictures of the prewar society and its
incredible accomplishments and lifestyle, were
especially cherished by the Family, affording a
glimpse of the wonders of the previous age. One of
the books, a book Blade remembered at this instant,
contained glossy photos and a fascinating narration
of the astonishing array of electronic means of
communication: television, radios, CBs, telephones,
and more.

Blade reached out and took hold of a metallic
stick on a stand. If his memory served, this thing

was called a microphone. There was a black switch on the base of the microphone. He depressed it and heard an audible click.

"This is Charlie-Alfa-Tango-Lima-Oscar-Whiskey," he said into the microphone, hoping his hunch was correct, and released the switch.

There were several seconds of static in the headphones.

Had he been wrong? Did he have to do something else to get this contraption to send a signal?

"Charlie-Alfa-Tango-Lima-Oscar-Whiskey, we receive you," the faint voice stated. "What happened to you? You were cut off in midsentence. You were saying something about an emergency. What emergency?"

Blade cleared his throat and pressed the switch. "The emergency is over," he informed the man at the other end. "But I do need to ask a favor."

"A favor? What are you talking about?" the man demanded.

"I need you to relay a message for me," Blade told him.

"Say, who is this?" the man asked. "Is it you, Darren?"

"No, this isn't Darren."

"Then who is it?" the man impatiently queried.

"My identity isn't important," Blade replied. "Will you relay my message or not?"

"I don't know who you are, buddy," the man snapped, "but you're in violation of standard operating procedure. Identity yourself!"

"Will you relay my message?" Blade reiterated.

"What message are you talking about? Why don't you send it yourself? Who the hell is this?"

"I need you to send a message to the Doktor," Blade stated.

"The Doktor? Are you crazy?" The man sounded fearful.

"Will you do it?" Blade prompted him.

"Are you serious? The Doktor? I could be taking my life in my hands!" The man paused. "What's this message, anyway?"

"You'll do it?"

"I didn't say that. First tell me what this message is that's so important."

Blade smiled. "I can assure you the Doktor will want to receive this message. You have nothing to worry about."

"So what the hell is it?"

"Tell the Doktor this: Lynx sends his love."

"Lynx! Lynx!" the man sputtered. "Is this some kind of sick joke?"

"It is no joke."

"Are you trying to tell me Lynx is there, in Catlow? Who is this, anyway? What the hell kind of game are you playing? If you don't—"

Blade removed the headphones and switched off the set. He had no doubt the message would get through to its destination. The radioman would consult with his superior, and they would endeavor to contact Catlow again. After failing several times, the radioman's superior would notify his superior, and so it would go on up the line until someone with the proper authority decided to report the situation to the Doktor. Hours might pass, but the Doktor would be apprised of the message.

Would the Doktor respond as Plato and Lynx had predicted? From what Captain Reno had said about the million-credit reward, the Doktor just might take the bait. Certainly, a man with the Doktor's intellect would deduce the setup was a trap of some kind. But the key to the success of this operation was the Doktor's monumental ego; would the Doktor march into the ambush anyway, confident in his ability to exterminate his adversaries? Another factor would be the Doktor's unquenchable thirst for revenge against Lynx. According to the diminutive mutant—and verified by the statements Captain Reno had made—the Doktor would want to get his hands on Lynx personally.

Which meant, if the assumptions were valid and events proceeded as projected, the tiny community of Catlow, Wyoming, was going to be visited by a prestigious psychopath and his murderous misfits.

Blade walked outside and spotted the SEAL parked next to the fountain.

Geronimo and Bertha walked up.

"There are eleven injured," Geronimo reported. "Seven or eight will die soon, and the rest might pull through with the proper medical help."

"We're not Healers," Blade stated. "There's nothing we can do for them."

Hickok, Lynx, Rudabaugh and Orson approached and joined them.

"We were lucky today," Blade declared. "We can thank the Spirit none of us was killed. Now we have to get ready for the Doktor—"

"How are we going to let him know we're here if none of the garrison can take the word to him?" Geronimo interjected.

"I've taken care of that," Blade disclosed. He jerked his right thumb toward the command post. "There's a radio inside. I've just sent a message to the Doktor."

"The one we agreed on?" Lynx inquired.

Blade nodded. "The same one you gave when you destroyed the Biological Center in Cheyenne."

Lynx grinned contentedly. "That'll do it! I can't wait to get my claws on the bastard!"

"We have a lot of preparations to make," Blade announced. "I want Bertha, Rudabaugh, and Orson to cart these bodies into one of the buildings. We don't have time to bury them. Hickok, I want you and Geronimo to round up the good citizens of Catlow and assemble them in the town square. See if you can get some of them to tend to the wounded soldiers and have them moved to a house on the north side of town. Lynx, I want you to scout around. See how many vehicles there are in town. Also look for any supplies the garrison might have had stashed, especially weapons or explosives." He paused. "Okay! Hop to it!"

All of them moved off except Bertha.

"Something the matter?" Blade questioned her.

"Do you really think it's gonna work?" she bluntly asked.

Blade shrugged. "It might."

"We could all be killed, you know," Bertha mentioned.

Blade didn't answer.

"Why didn't we use the SEAL today?" Bertha queried.

"We're saving it for the Doktor," Blade divulged.

"Figured as much." She gazed around the square. "I must be as wacko as you boys are to go through with this! But there's something I wanted you to know."

"What's that?"

Bertha fondly glanced at Hickok and Geronimo, then at Blade. "I couldn't die in better company."

"We're all going to live through this," Blade disputed her. "You'll see."

Bertha laughed cynically. "I ain't much for fairy tales, so don't try and jive me, sucker! Besides, I got me a . . . a feelin' about this."

"What kind of feeling?"

"I don't know how to put it into words," she said.

"Your intuition could be wrong," Blade remarked. "I think we have a fair chance of coming out of this in one piece."

Bertha started to leave, chuckling. "You just keep thinkin', Blade! That's what you're good at!"

Blade walked toward the SEAL, troubled. Bertha's intuition had better be wrong, because he didn't relish the thought of dying in Catlow, a town he'd never heard of until a couple of weeks before when Yama had returned from his spying mission to Cheyenne with Lynx. After several long talks with Lynx, Plato had formulated his plan. He had picked Catlow because it was one of the northernmost towns in the Civilized Zone, had a relatively small garrison, and was close to South Dakota, the Cavalry's stamping grounds. Speed was imperative, with Plato insisting they achieve their objectives before the heavy snows began. Well, the first step had been taken.

The next move was up to the Doktor.

7

Joshua reined in his horse and stared at the road only five feet in front of him. U.S. Highway 85. He had made it! He glanced in both directions; there was a hill to the north and a plain to the south. He turned the horse to the north and slowly followed the road. If his calculations were correct, he should be five to ten miles south of Catlow.

Perfect.

Just perfect.

His long brown hair blew in the wind as his brown eyes surveyed the surrounding terrain, a panorama of sparse vegetation and essentially flat fields punctuated by a periodic low hill, like the one in front of him. His lean frame was garbed in a green shirt and faded brown pants. Moccasins covered his feet. Hanging on a chain draped around his neck was a large gold cross.

Joshua patted the saddlebags. If he consumed his rations in moderation, the jerky and other food should last a week or longer. He had brought two canteens, more than enough for his purposes if he drank sparingly. Unless Blade and the rest ran into unexpected trouble, a week should be more than sufficient. He could only pray the Doktor arrived on schedule.

The Doktor.

Joshua couldn't really pinpoint when the idea had first occurred to him, but he did know it was shortly after hearing Plato disclose the plans for eliminating the Doktor and conquering the

Cheyenne Citadel. Several of the Warriors had been enjoying their supper near a roaring fire, and Joshua had joined them.

Hickok had been one of the Warriors.

As expected, the gunman had been in a jovial mood and eager to commence the campaign against the Doktor. Joshua had chided him for being so anxious to take more lives, to add to his growing reputation as one of the deadliest men alive. Hickok had indignantly retorted that his reputation had nothing to do with it. The gunfighter had sworn that the only way to deal with someone like the Doktor was to kill him. Joshua had then disagreed, claiming the power of love could be as effective as a bullet.

The Warriors had burst out laughing.

Joshua smarted at the recollection. It wasn't the ridicule, primarily. It was the ongoing dispute between Hickok and himself over which way was better: the gun or spiritual love. Ever since his trip with Alpha Triad to Thief River Falls, Joshua had been arguing with Hickok over the gunman's predilection for shooting first and asking questions later. As one of the Family's more spiritual members and its youngest Empath, Joshua fervently believed that all men and women should be treated as brothers and sisters. If you extended your hand in friendship to others, he reasoned, they would reciprocate in kind.

It was one of the fundamental laws of spiritual relationships. Love others as you would have them love you. Better yet, love others as you believe the Supreme would love them.

Joshua frowned at the memory of his experiences on several of the runs made by Alpha Triad. All of the killing, all of the slaughter, had rocked him to the core of his soul. After a while, he had become desensitized to the violence, and had even begun accepting Hickok's philosophy as valid.

But it couldn't be!

If the gunfighter were correct, it rendered all of Joshua's heartfelt truths invalid.

Joshua refused to accept such an idea.

So, in a stroke of inspiration, he had hidden aboard one of the convoy trucks leaving the Home, then mixed in with the Moles, and later the Cavalry, as they had trekked across the country on their rendezvous with destiny. He doubted the Cavalry would miss the horse he'd stolen; they owned thousands. Which meant no one, absolutely no one, knew his whereabouts or his intention.

Jushua smiled, satisfied at the impending completion of his task. He was going to wait at the base of the hill ahead and, when the Doktor appeared enroute to Catlow, intercept the Doktor's forces and prevail upon the Doktor to accept a treaty of peace.

He could do it!

He had done it once before, in the Twin Cities. He had been responsible for achieving a truce between the warring parties there. If he could do it in the Twin Cities, he could do it now—between the Family and the Doktor.

He would show everyone!

But especially Hickok! He liked the gunman. He truly did. But Hickok had to be shown the truth. Love was the greatest power in the universe of universes, not a pair of Colt Pythons.

Joshua began humming "Day By Day," one of his personal favorites from the extensive music section in the Family library. The Spirit was smiling on his enterprise. Not once during his entire time in the saddle had he been molested by a mutate or an animal. It was all coming together, just as he knew it would.

8

It seemed as if a sea of faces were staring up at him.

"Is that all of them?" Blade demanded.

"All we could find," Geronimo replied.

Blade, perched on the top of the SEAL, glanced down at the 340 or so people thronging the town square. The SEAL was parked in front of the command post.

Bertha, Rudabaugh, and Orson had spent several hours lugging the bodies of the slain soldiers to a house two blocks from the square. A dozen of Catlow's residents had assisted in conveying the injured to a house on the northern outskirts. Hickok and Geronimo had gone from house to house, rounding up the inhabitants. Owning a firearm was illegal for civilians in the Civilized Zone, and since the military had long since confiscated all privately owned weapons, resistance had been nonexistent.

And now, after having climbed the metal ladder attached to the rear of the transport to permit access to the solar collectors on the roof, Blade was prepared to address the assembled citizens. Hickok, Geronimo, Bertha, Lynx, Rudabaugh, and Orson stood near the SEAL, their respective weapons at the ready. Lynx was there too, but he disdained guns and relied exclusively on his pointed claws.

"People of Catlow!" Blade began, raising his arms to attract their attention. "We mean you no harm! We require your cooperation, and if you do as we say, no one will be harmed! Do you understand?"

No one said anything.

"As all of you undoubtedly know," Blade continued, "we wiped out the garrison this morning. Why we did it, I can't say. Who we are, I can't say. But I can say we are enemies of the Doktor! I can say we want to bring freedom to the Civilized Zone! We want you to become masters of your own lives, to live without the Government telling you how to do everything! Think of it! How would you like to be free? How would you like to set up a new Government, one where the people have the power and not a dictator?"

Blade paused to gauge their reaction. Most were gaping at him in stark bewilderment.

"My friends and I came here for several reasons," he resumed. "One of them concerns a man named Toland."

There was a faint stirring among the crowd.

"Let me explain!" Blade shouted. "We know there are many in the Civilized Zone who are unhappy with the way things are! We know many want to change the status quo! The Government calls these people rebels! We call them freedom fighters! A friend of mine took a paper from the Doktor when he visited the Citadel recently. This paper was classified. It told us about rebel activity in this area and about one man in particular, a rebel leader called Toland. This report said Toland was born in this town, in Catlow. It said he is believed to be hiding here, but the Government troops haven't been able to ferret him out. Well, if he is here, we want to talk to him. Toland! If you can hear me, come forward! I give you my word you will not be hurt! Don't be afraid! The future of the Civilized Zone hinges on what you do!"

"How do we know this isn't a trap?" a man yelled.

"What? We attacked the garrison just to flush Toland out into the open?" Blade retorted.

"We wouldn't put anything past the Doktor," a woman cried.

"So you suspect we're in league with the Doktor?" Blade asked. He put his hands on his hips and glared at them. "We hate the Doktor as much as you do!"

"Prove it!" a man demanded.

All eyes were on Blade.

"That's easy enough!" Blade declared. "I take it all of you have heard about what happened at the Cheyenne Citadel? How the Biological Center, the Doktor's headquarters, was destroyed by a thermo?"

"Yeah, we know," a woman called out. "So what?"

"So do you know who is responsible for doing what the rebels were unable to do in a hundred years?" Blade queried.

"None of us know how to use a thermo!" a man shouted by way of justification.

"So who did it?" Blade challenged them. "Who did have the know-how? Who's responsible?"

Several voices responded in unison, "Lynx!"

Blade grinned. "That's right! Lynx! I understand some of you have seen pictures of Lynx in the news. He's probably the most famous rebel in the entire Civilized Zone." Blade straightened to his full stature and swept his right hand up and down, pointing at the furry man-thing below him. "Take a good look! Who is he? Take a good look, and then tell me we're in league with the Doktor!"

The gathered citizenry began milling about, as those farthest from the SEAL pressed forward to catch a glimpse of the smallish creature. Some of them recognized him, and there were gasps and startled countenances galore.

Lynx, Blade noticed, ate up all the attention, standing with his arms casually folded and an imperious expression on his feline face.

Minutes passed.

Finally, a tall man with black hair and blue eyes, attired in a denim shirt and old jeans, moved through the assemblage and stood in front of Lynx.

"What do you want, buster?" Lynx demanded.

"So you're Lynx?" the man questioned.

"What's it to you, bub?"

The man extended his right hand. "I am Toland."

Lynx, ever suspicious, slowly offered his own hand.

Toland shook, smiling. "I am pleased to meet you. We have heard so much about you and your escapades, I expected to meet a giant ten feet tall!"

Lynx smiled. "That's the price of fame, I guess."

Toland glanced up at Blade. "Whoever you are, you must know they will send more soldiers. You should leave while you still can."

"We're counting on them sending more soldiers," Blade said.

"Yeah," Lynx chuckled. "I can't wait to see the Doc again!"

"The Doktor!" Toland exclaimed. "The Doktor is coming here?"

"If all goes well," Blade affirmed. "Which is why we need your help."

"I will do what I can," Toland offered, "but I must tell you my people are too scared of the Doktor to fight him."

"I don't want you to fight for us," Blade

elaborated. "I need your assistance in another respect."

"What can I do for you?"

"How many rebels like you are there in the Civilized Zone?" Blade inquired.

"Thousands and thousands," Toland stated. "And for every one willing to resist the tyrant Samuel the Second and the Doktor, there are two or three more who would join our cause if they thought they had a chance of winning. There are far more than the authorities suspect."

"Do you have any way of contacting them?" Blade asked.

"We have a communications network," Toland answered. "It's crude, but effective."

"Could you get in touch with the other rebel leaders within, say, the next week?" Blade queried.

"I might be able to do so," Toland said warily. "Why are you asking all of these questions?"

Blade crouched and stared into Toland's eyes. "Because in a week the Doktor will be dead and the Cheyenne Citadel, or what's left of it, will be in our hands. Two weeks after that, we will take Denver and oust Samuel the Second. We could use your support."

Toland's mouth parted in slack amazement. He shook his head, as if doubting the testimony of his own ears. "Kill the Doktor? Depose Samuel the Second?" He looked around. "Just you seven?"

Blade laughed. "Think of us as the bait laid out for a marauding bear. Once the bear takes the bait, we spring the trap we've set. I can't supply the details, but there are many, many more of us. We are called the Freedom Federation and we have declared war on the Civilized Zone. We have no ambition to conquer the Civilized Zone and subjugate its inhabitants. We only want you to install a new, free Government. It will then be up to you whether you enter our Federation."

Toland seemed to be in a daze. "Can it be?" he muttered. "All of our dreams come true? All of our prayers answered?"

"Will you aid us?"

"Any way I can," Toland vowed.

Blade nodded. "Good. You must get your people organized and ready to leave Catlow as soon as possible. We don't want them here when the Doktor arrives—"

"I can see why," Toland interrupted.

"We've found two jeeps and two trucks behind the command post you can use," Blade went on. "You'll have to carry as many provisions as you can. We'll give you enough firearms and ammunition from the garrison's stores to adequately defend yourselves."

"Where could we go?" Toland wanted to know.

"Have your people travel north and wait," Blade said. "In two or three days it should all be over, one way or the other, and they can return to their homes. They can take the injured soldiers with them." He paused. "As for you, take whomever you need and begin contacting the other rebel leaders. I will detail what I want you to tell them."

"This is to good to be true!" Toland remarked.

"It's true," Blade assured him. "It may be the only opportunity you will ever have to throw off the oppressive yoke of totalitarianism."

Hickok glanced up at Blade, a sour look on his face. "Gee, pard, you're gettin' worse than Plato when it comes to using those ten-syllable words!"

"Where do you think I first heard it?" Blade rejoined. "So! Do we have a deal?" he asked Toland.

"We have a deal," Toland confirmed.

Blade started down the ladder. He stopped on the third rung and stared at the rebel leader. "Before I forget, there is one thing you must not do under any circumstances. Don't allow any of your people to head due south along U.S. Highway 85."

Toland glanced over his left shoulder in the direction of the highway. It went completely through the town, but bypassed the town square three blocks east of where they stood. He nodded his comprehension. "The Doktor will be coming from the south."

"Exactly," Blade agreed. "And I would imagine he won't be in the best frame of mind. Considering his homicidal tendencies, I wouldn't want to be the one to come between him and Catlow."

9

The small, wiry man with the Oriental features placed his right hand on the hilt of his prized katana, his brow knit in thought. He wore a black martial-arts uniform fashioned by the Family Weavers. "Are you certain one of your horses is missing?"

"Positive," the tall, muscular man in buckskins stated.

"But you have so many," the man in black noted.

The man in the buckskins pursed his lips. His clear blue eyes were focused on the Warrior in front of him. He ran his right hand through his light brown hair, hair streaked with gray. "You're from the Family, Rikki," he said. "Wouldn't you know it if one of the Family turned up missing?"

Rikki nodded. "Of course. But the Cavalry has so many horses, Kilrane," he reiterated.

Kilrane stared at the column below them, stopped for the midday meal at the foot of a ridge. The 510 Cavalry riders were divided, with half at the head of the column and a like number bringing up the rear. Following the first half of the Cavalry, all robust plainsmen garbed in buckskins like Kilrane, came the 14 trucks, troop transports that Alpha Triad had taken from soldiers in the Twin Cities. Because some of them could drive, members of the Clan were handling the chore of navigating the trucks over the rugged South Dakota landscape. The troop transports could accommodate over 500 passengers; consequently,

there was ample room for the 200 fighters from the
Clan, 150 Moles, and all of their supplies and spare
gasoline. "Our horses are our life," Kilrane said to
Rikki. "Every man knows his horses as well as he
knows his wife." He turned and motioned to a
balding man in buckskins below him on the slope of
the ridge. "Come here."

The man hurried up to them, obeying his leader.

"This is Vern," Kilrane said, introducing the
Cavalryman. "Vern, I'd like you to meet Rikki-
Tikki-Tavi. I know he's got a strange name, but he's
the head of Beta Triad and as such, with Blade in
Catlow, is in charge of this here expedition."

"Howdy," Vern said.

"I understand one of your horses is missing,"
Rikki stated, getting right to the point. Plato had
placed an awesome responsibility on his slim
shoulders, commanding the Freedom Federation's
forces until such time as Blade took over, and he
intended to discharge his duties as efficiently as
feasible.

"Yes, sir," Vern confirmed. "Kilrane told each
of us to bring along an extra mount, just in case. As
you know, the spare herd is following 'bout five
miles back of the main column. Every so often some
of us ride back and bring up some fresh horses.
When I went back last night, I couldn't find my
horse, my spare mare."

Rikki thoughtfully ran his left hand through his
short black hair. "Is it possible you misplaced your
animal in so large a herd?"

Vern shook his head. "No, sir. I'd know her anywhere."

"When you are around horses all the time,"
Kilrane added, "you are able to tell 'em apart as
easily as you can tell the difference between two

people. No two horses are alike. Their build, markings, and even their behavior is distinctive."

"Could another Cavalry rider be using your steed?" Rikki inquired.

Vern snorted. "No one else had better be riding my horse, if they know what's good for 'em! That'd be the same as stealin', if they didn't ask my permission. Besides, our guys ridin' guard on the herd know better."

"And you don't think the animal might have slipped from the herd undetected and is roaming around somewhere?" Rikki asked.

Kilrane and Vern exchanged grinning glances. "Lose a horse?" Kilrane queried, and both Cavalry-men laughed at the suggestion.

"If the mare isn't lost, and you didn't overlook it," Rikki said to Vern, "then it can only mean one thing. The horse was stolen," he deduced.

"My thinking exactly," Kilrane stated. "Which is why I brought it to your attention."

Rikki-Tikki-Tavi took several steps along the ridge, studying the encampment below. "Are any of the men missing?"

"None," Kilrane answered.

"You've checked the Clan and the Moles as well as your own riders?"

"Of course," Kilrane said, a touch indignantly, resenting the implication he might be derelict in his duty.

Rikki sighed. This massive operation entailed making so many decisions daily, and necessitated being in such a constant state of readiness, he found the whole experience more trying and stressful than he'd anticipated. Dear Spirit, how he longed for a refreshing interval of meditation to deplete his sapped reserves! Life was so much simpler when he had only two other Warriors to command, Yama and Teucer. He was kept so busy overseeing the campaign, he didn't even have time for his daily workout and routines. For a dedicated, consummate martial artist like himself, this was the hardest burden to bear.

"There is one thing," Kilrane mentioned.

Rikki glanced at the Cavalry leader. "What?"

"Didn't we count everybody, twice, before we left the Home?" Kilrane queried.

"You know we did. Why?"

Kilrane scratched his prominent chin. "You're gonna think this is crazy, but we may have left the Home with one more man than we thought we had."

"Explain."

"Well, the second night we were out, one of the Mole captains was making his bed check of the men in his truck. He counted one more man than he should have."

"Why wasn't this reported?" Rikki demanded.

Kilrane shrugged. "He didn't think much of it at the time. After all, we're concerned about losing someone, not gaining another fighter. It was late, and all the other men were sleeping, so he didn't bother waking them up. He decided to wait until morning. Funny, though."

"What?"

"The very next morning, when he counted again, he had exactly the number of men he was supposed to have in that truck."

"We gain a man and lose a horse," Rikki said, reflecting.

"Do you think it could have been a spy from the Civilized Zone?" Kilrane asked.

"Anything is possible," Rikki declared, "but I doubt it. Would a spy draw attention to his or her activities by stealing one of our mounts? Why would the spy leave now, before ascertaining our des-

tination? Remember, only you, Yama, Teucer, and
myself know where we're headed. Plato, Zahner, and
Wolfe know, but they stayed behind with their
people. I think some of the other Warriors were
informed but, again, they're not here."

"It's strange, isn't it?" Kilrane opined.

Rikki nodded. "Post extra guards at night until
we reach our assembly point, just to play it safe."

"Will do."

"And there is one more thing you can do for
me."

"What is it?" Kilrane questioned.

"Watch the camp for awhile." Rikki pointed at
some boulders 20 yards off. "I'm going to go behind
them and spend some time in communion with the
Spirit."

"No problem," Kilrane commented.

Rikki started to walk off.

"Say . . ." Kilrane said.

Rikki paused and glanced over his shoulder.

"Mind if I ask you a question? If I'm being
nosy, just tell me to take a hike."

"Ask," Rikki urged him.

"I've been meaning to ask one of you Warriors
about this." Kilrane patted the Mitchell Single
Action revolver on his right hip. "You Warriors are
fighters. I've got a rep as being something of a
fighter myself. What I don't get, and what I'd really
like to understand, is how you guys can be so good
at what you do and be so . . . religious . . . at the
same time."

Rikki smiled. "You see a contradiction there?"

"It just puzzles me, is all," Kilrane said. "I
mean, I believe in God. I may not know what God is
like, but I'm smart enough to know there is one. But
you Warriors! You're something else! Everybody—the Moles, the Clan, and my people—all

believe the Warriors are the deadliest folks alive.
Yet, at the same time, I've never met anybody as
religious as you Warriors. Your whole Family is the
same way. What gives?"

"Can you read?" Rikki inquired.

"Yep. My parents taught me. I own some
books," Kilrane said proudly. With the demise of
civilization outside the Civilized Zone, public
education had become a thing of the past. Being
able to read had become a badge of social
distinction.

"Have you ever read any books on the
philosophy of the samurai?" Rikki asked.

"The what?"

Rikki opted for another tack. "Ever read the
Holy Bible?"

"Parts of it," Kilrane disclosed.

"The parts about Samson or David or any of the
other warriors mentioned in the Old Testament?"

"Wasn't David the dude with the slingshot?"
Kilrane queried.

"David was the dude," Rikki affirmed. "Well,
the members of my Family, and in particular the
Warriors, subscribe to a philosophy very similar to
David's and Samson's."

"I don't follow you," Kilrane confessed.

"Let me put it this way," Rikki said. "Imagine
there are two groups of people left in the world. One
group is very savage. They kill everyone else they
meet. They want to conquer the whole world. The
other group is composed of kind, loving people.
They are friendly to everyone they meet. Now, I ask
you, of the two groups, which one is the better
group? Which one has the higher ideals? Which one
would prefer peace to violence?"

"The second group," Kilrane answered.

"But what will happen to this second group if

they won't defend themselves? What will happen to this second group if they offer their hands in friendship to the first group?''

Kilrane's brow furrowed. "I'd say the first group would kill off the second group or enslave them.''

"Without a doubt," Rikki stated. "The lesson learned is this: those who would practice the Golden Rule must be prepared to protect themselves, their children, and their higher culture, their ideals and their liberties, from those who do not live by the Golden Rule. All the members of my Family, from infancy, are impressed with the wisdom of perceiving the reality of our Spirit Maker. We also know what the world outside the walls of our Home is like. If we do not defend ourselves, we will be wiped out. We can't permit that to happen. The Warriors are pledged to insure it never does. We would give our very lives to preserve our Family. Do you understand now?''

"I think so," Kilrane said.

A man with an awesome physique approached them from below. He was dressed all in blue, in a unique seamless garment with an ebony silhouette of a skull stitched on his broad back. He had short silver hair and a drooping silver mustache. In his right hand was a Wilkinson "Terry" Carbine. Under his left arm was a Smith and Wesson Model 586 Distinguished Combat Magnum; under his right was a Browning Hi-Power 9-millimeter Automatic Pistol. Strapped to his waist was a curved scimitar.

"Yes, Yama?" Rikki inquired, knowing what was coming.

"The meal is completed," Yama reported in his deep voice. "The horses are well rested, and the oil and gasoline levels in the vehicles have been checked. We are ready to depart whenever you are.''

Rikki sighed. So much for his meditation! "Then let's get going," he said. "We don't want to be late. The consequences to our friends in Alpha Triad could prove fatal." He stared toward the west. It wouldn't be long, now. Not long at all.

10

Plato couldn't believe what he'd just heard. "You are certain of this?" he demanded.

The woman standing in front of him nodded. She was a redhead with a ruddy complexion, an oval face, and calm hazel eyes. Although short in stature, she conveyed an impression of dignity and inner serenity. She wore a loose-fitting yellow dress in immaculate condition. Her name was Hazel, and she was the chief Family Empath, one of the six Family members blessed with psychic capabilities.

"There is no doubt," Hazel said in her soft voice. "Joshua has left the Home."

They were conversing only 15 feet from the drawbridge located in the middle of the western wall to the Home. This drawbridge was the only means of entering and leaving the 30-acre compound short of scaling the walls.

"Why would Joshua leave?" Plato asked. "Where would he go?"

Hazel's maternal features became downcast. "We attempted to take a reading on him, without much success. We believe he is far to the southwest of the Home."

"And his parents have no idea where he went?" Plato inquired.

"He apparently left without confiding in them or leaving a note," Hazel replied. "It's most uncharacteristic of him," she noted.

"I agree," Plato said. He nervously chewed on his lower lip. If only he hadn't been so preoccupied with this Doktor business! He might have noticed Joshua was missing sooner! Spartacus had even mentioned something about it, hadn't he?

"Don't blame yourself," Hazel said.

"Can you read my mind?" Plato asked, grinning.

"No," Hazel responded. "We're not able to do that. Yet. I didn't need to read your mind to determine what you were just thinking. All it took was one look at your worried face."

Plato turned and gazed fondly at the dozens of Family members, many of them children, playing in the open area between the concrete blocks to the east of the drawbridge. "I'm their Leader," he remarked. "It is my responsibility to safeguard them from harm."

"It would be impossible for you to keep track of all of them at all times," Hazel commented.

"Why would Joshua do such a thing?" Annoyed, Plato smacked his right fist into his left palm. As if he didn't have enough problems without Joshua pulling a stunt like this!

"Will you send someone to search for him?" Hazel inquired.

"I can't," Plato replied. "I can't spare any of the Warriors to go after him. Six of them are off, about to engage the Doktor, if my strategy has attained fruition. The remaining nine Warriors must stay here to defend the Home should an emergency arise."

Hazel could readily discern the turmoil raging in Plato's soul. "Don't fret over Joshua," she said to calm his emotional upheaval. "The Spirit will guide him in whatever he is doing."

"I should have seen this coming," Plato said berating himself. "He was so quiet and reserved after his last trip to the Twin Cities. I should have realized he was upset and endeavored to discover the reason."

"Joshua will be okay," Hazel stressed.

"I hope so," Plato declared. "I'll never forgive myself if something happens to that boy."

"What could happen?"

11

Joshua's ears detected their coming long before he saw them.

He was seated at the base of the hill, near the highway, his body in the lotus position, his hands formed into a pyramid in his lap, worshiping. The mare was in the sagebrush behind him.

The faint roar of powerful engines carried on the wind. Dozens of them, traveling north on U.S. Highway 85.

Joshua slowly opened his eyes and gazed up at the blue sky overhead. The bright sun was well up; it was midmorning on the day after his arrival at the highway. The Doktor hadn't kept him waiting long! To be expected, he told himself. The Cheyenne Citadel was only 170 miles or so south of Catlow. No more than a four- or five-hour drive, once the Doktor was aware Alpha Triad had taken the town.

The noise of the approaching vehicles was growing rapidly louder.

Joshua rose and walked to the mare. He unfastened her bridle and saddle and dropped them to the dry ground. "Thanks for the ride, girl," he said to her. "Now get out of here! I don't want you to be hurt." He pointed her to the north and slapped her on the rump. "Get going!" he shouted. "Go!"

With a toss of her tail, the mare bolted.

Joshua watched her go for a moment, then stepped to the road, to the very middle of U.S. Highway 85, and sat down, assuming the lotus position again, his hands folded in his lap. He bowed his head and closed his eyes, praying.

The breeze picked up.

Joshua struggled to compose his tingling nerves; he felt an almost overwhelming impulse to flee before it was too late. He steadied his surging emotions, focusing instead on his consciousness of the Spirit, requesting guidance and strength to endure the ordeal ahead.

The ground seemed to vibrate as the vehicles drew nearer. A raucous tumult ruptured the tranquil Wyoming countryside.

Joshua knew a vehicle was bearing down on him at great speed, but he refused to budge. He had to demonstrate his resolve, to show them he wasn't afraid, to earn their respect.

The sound of the first approaching vehicle abruptly altered, its racing engine slowing, as simultaneously there arose a grinding screech, the result of brakes being prematurely applied at great speed.

The clamor grew in volume, reaching deafening proportions.

For an instant, Joshua thought he was going to be run over.

The screeching suddenly ceased.

There was a ringing in Joshua's ears. He knew the first vehicle had stopped mere feet from his position.

Footsteps padded on the pavement.

Joshua heard someone grunt, and a moment later hot breath fell on his face. He opened his eyes, expecting to see a soldier.

He was wrong.

The thing leaning over him was one of the Doktor's genetic mutations. It must have stood close to seven feet in height and weighed several hundred pounds. Its body was covered with a fine coat of brown hair; its only clothing was a brown leather loincloth. The most striking feature about the creature was its apelike face: it had a sloping forehead, protruding, bushy brows, deep-set, beady brown eyes, prominent cheeks, and full pink lips. It took a step backward in alarm, hefting the sledge-hammer held in its massive right fist.

"Hello," Joshua greeted it, smiling.

The mutant cocked its head from side to side, evidently extremely perplexed by the man in the center of the road.

"Thank you for not running me down," Joshua said. There was a jeep parked not five feet away, its motor still running.

The thing leaned down toward Joshua. "What are you doing here?" it inquired in a throaty, gruff tone.

"I would like to see the Doktor," Joshua stated.

The creature straightened, exposing its formidable fangs. "The Doktor?" it hissed in surprise.

"Yes," Joshua verified. He noticed a thin metallic collar encircling the creature's squat neck, and recognized it as one of the collars the Doktor utilized to keep his creations in line. Each collar contained sophisticated transistorized electronic circuitry, enabling the Doktor to monitor the where-abouts of his creatures and, if necessary, compel compliance with his edicts by means of a jolting electric shock.

Other vehicles, jeeps and trucks and even a half-track, were slowing to a halt behind the first jeep. Figures detached themselves from the convoy and came forward to ascertain the cause for the delay.

Joshua found himself surrounded by a veritable menagerie: dozens upon dozens of the Doktor's genetically engineered offspring. All were bipedal,

but beyond that basic trait all resemblances ended.
Some were quite tall, others were very short. Some
were on the reptilian side, while others were
decidedly mammalian. All of them were freakish
aberrations, monstrous living monuments to their
demented creator.

The creatures, whispering and muttering,
suddenly grew silent and parted, opening an avenue
between the vehicles and the man in the road.

Joshua saw two beings walking toward him.

On the left was another genetic deviate, this one
a female. She was oddly beautiful, despite her
serpentine features, her narrow lavender eyes, and
her yellow skin, complimented by her flowing oily
black hair. She was wearing fatigues.

On the right strode an imposing man with a
commanding presence, and without being told
Joshua knew the man's identity.

This was the Doktor.

The madman was as tall as the ape-thing with
the sledgehammer. A dark mane of shaggy hair
enhanced the impression of height. His eyes were
black pools and seemed to radiate an inner light. The
man was imbued with a unique aura of raw power.
He wore a black shirt and pants, and black boots.
His broad shoulders and back were covered by a
flowing black cloak or cape. He raked Joshua with
his probing eyes. "What have we here?" he
demanded, his voice resonant and booming.

"He said he wants to see you," the ape-thing
said.

The Doktor's eyebrows narrowed. "Oh, he does,
does he?" He grinned, revealing curiously thin,
pointed teeth. "Now, why would he want to see me,
Thor?"

"Don't know, Doktor," Thor hastily replied.

"Send a patrol out," the Doktor directed.

"Insure he is alone."

"I am alone," Joshua stated.

The Doktor squatted in front of Joshua and examined him from head to toe. "Now, why should I believe you?"

"Because I do not lie," Joshua declared.

"Did you hear him?" The Doktor glanced at the woman. "He claims he doesn't lie! Why, he must be perfect then! What an honor for us, to be in the presence of perfection!"

The woman and several of the other creatures snickered or chuckled.

"There hasn't been a perfect man on this planet for thousands of years," the Doktor said, and Joshua had the feeling the Doktor was toying with him. "Now let me see! What was his name again?"

"Jesus," Joshua stated.

"Ahh, yes! The noble carpenter. Are you telling me, boy, you are as perfect as Jesus? Or, perhaps, you *are* Jesus, risen from the dead? Again?" The Doktor laughed, a bitter, brittle sound. "Who are you, boy?"

"I am Joshua."

The Doktor swept to his feet, glaring down at Joshua. "You! Here?" He appeared to be startled by the news. "Why?" He scanned the nearby fields.

"What is it, Doktor?" the woman anxiously inquired, lisping.

"I don't know, Clarissa," the Doktor replied. He unexpectedly reached down, grabbed the front of Joshua's shirt, and hauled him to his feet. "This brat is from the Family!"

"The Family!" Clarissa repeated, and there were murmurs among the creatures.

Joshua noticed some soldiers had joined the group.

"Talk to me, boy!" the Doktor snapped. "I

know who you are. We haven't spied on your
accursed Family for years for nothing! Talk to me!"

"That's why I'm here," Joshua said.

"What?" The Doktor released Joshua, studying
him.

"I came to talk with you," Joshua explained.

The Doktor looked at Thor. "What are you
waiting for? I told you to send out a patrol!"

Thor cringed and hurried away.

"It isn't necessary," Joshua said. "I'm alone."

"So you say." The Doktor began stroking his
pointed chin with his right hand. "Isn't this an
interesting development, Clarissa? First, I receive a
report Lynx is in Catlow. And now, enroute to
smash that furry lowlife into the dust, we stumble
across Joshua here, one of the Family, an Empath if
my memory serves. How very interesting!"

"I came alone to talk with you," Joshua assured
him.

"What could we possibly have to talk about?"
the Doktor said arrogantly.

"Peace."

The Doktor's eyes seemed to blaze fire. "Do you
take me for a buffoon, boy? Would you have me
believe you traveled all this distance merely to
converse with me concerning peace?"

"Yes."

The Doktor fell silent, his features inscrutable.
No one else moved or spoke.

"I believe you, Joshua," the Doktor said at last.
"Very well. You shall be granted your opportunity
to present your case." He draped his right arm over
Joshua's slim shoulders and led him away from the
others. When they were 20 feet from Clarissa and
the rest, he stopped and crossed his arms, a slight
grin tugging at the corners of his thin mouth.
"Proceed."

"Right here?" Joshua objected. "I was hoping we could relax, break bread together, and get to know one another."

"Regrettably, Joshua, I am pressed for time. I must complete my business in Catlow promptly and travel to Denver to oversee the construction of my new headquarters." The Doktor paused. "I assume you're aware of what Lynx did in Cheyenne?"

"I know he destroyed your headquarters," Joshua admitted. "It was called the Biological Center, wasn't it?"

The Doktor frowned. "Yes. My life's work. All of my equipment and notes. The labor of a century, gone." He snapped his fingers. "Just like that! All thanks to Lynx and . . ." He stopped, as if he couldn't recall the name he wanted.

"Yama," Joshua finished for him.

"Yama, yes." The Doktor grinned. "Thank you."

"But you don't need to continue on to Catlow," Joshua mentioned.

"I don't?"

"No. Turn back, now, before it's too late. We can establish a truce, right here and now, and end all of this bloodshed and violence. Don't you see?" Joshua said, gesturing with enthusiasm. "The future is in your hands! War or peace, it's all up to you. Armageddon or a millennium of tranquility. Why should we continue to fight, when we could work together in harmony toward the betterment of both our peoples?"

"Tell me, Joshua," the Doktor urged, "does Plato know you're here?"

"No one does," Joshua divulged. "I told you, I came alone."

"Remarkable."

"Plato wouldn't have let me come," Joshua

said. "His paranoia would have gotten the better of him."

"Plato isn't too fond of me, is he?" the Doktor inquired.

"Plato believes you are his enemy," Joshua elaborated. "He thinks the only way to deal with you is with brute force."

"And what do you think of me?"

"I think of you the same as I do of all men and women," Joshua stated. "All of us are children of the Divine Creator. We are all brothers and sisters, in a spiritual sense. We must learn to love one another, or our world is doomed. Didn't World War Three teach us anything? Here we are, on the verge of another war! When will we learn our lesson? How long must violence be the norm instead of brotherhood? Why can't humankind see the light?"

The Doktor was staring off into space. "Do you really believe peace on earth is possible?"

"Of course!" Joshua exclaimed, excited, sensing victory. "All it takes is two people, two sides, two nations, whatever, reaching out in friendship, extending a helping hand to one another in place of mistrust and animosity." He paused. "We could do it! The Family and the Civilized Zone! We could sign a peace treaty and end all this needless suffering and misery. Don't you agree?"

The Doktor didn't respond.

"Don't you agree?" Joshua goaded him.

"No." The Doktor sighed, a protracted, peculiarly sad sound, and faced Joshua. When he spoke his voice was softer, tinged with regret. "No, I don't. While I admire your youthful idealism, and I honestly do, I find considerable fault with your wisdom. You see, Joshua, I was an idealist once. Decades ago. Over one hundred years ago, to be precise. I took a long, hard look at this paltry planet

of ours, and I came to many of the same conclusions
you did. I saw a world embroiled in petty conflicts,
where hatred was the rule and greed the motivating
factor in civilization—"

"We can change all that—" Joshua began.

The Doktor held up his left hand for silence. "I
thought the same thing at your age. I wanted the
nations of the world to desist with their foolish
notions of national sovereignty. This is one planet
and we all one people. But I knew the various
Governments would never willingly unite. So I
reached one of the major decisions in my life. I
decided to devote my recognized intellect to
insuring that one nation could dominate all the
others, thereby ending the ceaseless bickerings and
wars for all time. My scientific genius was responsible for the regenerating chemical clouds and
resultant mutates, as you call them. I—"

"What?" Joshua interrupted, astonished.
"You're responsible for the mutates?"

"Unintentionally," the Doktor replied. "I was
developing a new form of chemical warfare, a
gaseous mixture capable of dissolving human tissue
and bone. The acidic agents are specifically
attracted to the human metabolism. Mutates result
because the complicated chemical elements in the
clouds do not leech successfully on animal
metabolisms. Their physiology goes haywire
instead. I never intended to use the gas in this
country. Samuel the First insisted on doing so after
the war, as a means of further disrupting outlying
communities and distracting them from the
business of restablishing a new Government."

"You . . . unleashed . . . the clouds?"

"One of the least of my accomplishments," the
Doktor stated. "My masterpiece is my work in
genetic engineering. I, and I alone, discovered the

technique for editing the genetic instructions encoded in the chemical structure of molecules of DNA. My original purpose was to produce a master race of perfect humans." He glanced behind him at the clustered creatures. "Obviously, I haven't quite attained my goal, but I am close. At least, I was, until my laboratories were destroyed." His features clouded.

Joshua could only gawk, stupefied.

"Nothing ever works out quite the way we expect it to, does it?" the Doktor went on. "Did I tell you I constructed the very first thermo? A potent, portable thermonuclear device. I was certain they would guarantee that we won the war. I was wrong."

Joshua felt a chill creep into his body.

The Doktor looked at Joshua. "Do you have any idea how old I am?"

"Plato told me you are one hundred and twenty-seven years old," Joshua answered.

"How does he know that?" the Doktor inquired in surprise.

"It's all in your notebooks," Joshua explained.

The Doktor's eyes narrowed and his arms dropped to his sides. "Plato . . . has . . . my . . . notebooks?"

Joshua's mouth suddenly went dry.

"A delightful bonus! I'll have them back soon," the Doktor cryptically stated. "Yes. I am one hundred and twenty-seven years old, thanks to my rejuvenation process. And do you know what my years of experience have taught me?"

Joshua shook his head.

"There is no God—"

"But there is!" Joshua protested.

The Doktor's right hand lashed out and slapped Joshua across the face. "Don't interrupt me again!

God does not exist! Where are your brains, boy? Look around you. How could a loving God allow all the anguish and distress in this world to persist? How could a compassionate God permit us to know pain?"

"But God isn't responsible—" Joshua began.

The Doktor backhanded him on the mouth. "I warned you! You mindless jackass! How can any sane person propose a brotherhood of humankind? Humans are cattle, boy! Nothing more, nothing less than dimwitted cattle. How can they see the light when the only motivation they appreciate is the crack of a sturdy whip? Why do you think I wanted one nation, our nation, to dominate the globe? Because I knew I would then be the one cracking the whip, or controlling those who did! Why do you think I influenced the leaders of our military-industrial complex to provoke the Soviets into initiating the war?"

"You did what?" Joshua asked, horrified by the transformation now contorting the Doktor's facial features. His eyes were wild and unfocused, his nostrils were flaring, and his lips were trembling.

"It was I, boy!" The Doktor suddenly cackled. "In the entire history of this planet, my genius has never been surpassed! Einstein was a mental midget compared to me! What Beethoven was to music, and Tesla was to electricity, I have been to the art of war! The ancient Greeks were right in worshiping a god of war, because there is a god of war, boy, and . . ." The Doktor paused and glared at Joshua. "I . . . am . . . he!"

Joshua inadvertently recoiled, shocked by the sheer madness reflected on the Doktor's visage.

"I am the only god you will ever know," the Doktor stated.

"But you're not a god!" Joshua said, disputing

him. "You're a man, just like me! The Spirit of God indwells us, but this indwelling doesn't make us gods."

"Oh?" The Doktor's right eyebrow arched upward. He grinned and reached out with his right hand, gripping Joshua by the throat. "Do you know that if I had slapped you with all my strength a moment ago, your head would be rolling in the ditch?" He began squeezing Joshua's neck, slowly, enjoying himself, savoring the hint of fear in Joshua's eyes. "You dare babble to me about God? How old are you, boy? Twenty-five? Certainly not over thirty. Compare your age to mine. Which one of us do you think is the wiser?"

Joshua was attempting to break the Doktor's steely clamp on his throat, without success. He smashed his fists again and again on the Doktor's arm and hand, but it was like striking a tree trunk; it hurt his fists and the Doktor gave no indication he felt a thing.

The Doktor's tone lowered, returning to normal after his unprovoked outburst. "Believe me, Joshua, when I tell you there is no God. I learned the truth at an early age, when my parents were killed by a hit-and-run driver. A beneficent Supreme Being would hardly allow such calamities to transpire. Ergo, the Supreme Being does not exist. Circumstance and probability are the rule of the cosmos."

Joshua's face was turning red, his efforts to free himself growing weaker by the second and his lungs desperate for air.

"Don't worry, boy," the Doktor told him. "You won't die. Not yet, anyway. I have a special treat in store for you when you awaken. You'll thank me for the honor I will bestow upon you."

Joshua gasped once and went limp.

"I really should thank *you*," the Doktor said,

and released his hold.

Joshua tumbled to the road and sprawled on his stomach.

Clarissa and Thor approached the Doktor.

"Is he dead?" Clarissa inquired in her strangely sibilant tone.

"Not yet." The Doktor smiled. "We owe this moron a debt of gratitude, and you know I always repay my debts."

"Gratitude?" Clarissa repeated, puzzled.

"The fool revealed critical information," the Doktor explained. "He confirmed my suspicions about the Family and Lynx. I knew Lynx had required assistance in escaping from the Biological Center and stealing the thermo unit, but I couldn't imagine who possessed such audacity. Several witnesses reported that a man had helped Lynx. One couple even claimed Lynx had given them a message to deliver, something about Lynx and someone else 'sending their love.' Unfortunately for them, they weren't able to accurately recall the name of the other party. The husband said it was Dama, while the woman maintained it was Lama. Imbeciles! I knew better!"

"Who was it?" Clarissa wanted to know.

"Yama, one of the Warriors from the Family."

"A Warrior entered the Citadel!" Clarissa said, marveling. "You were right, then, and Samuel was wrong."

The Doktor snorted derisively. "Samuel may falsely believe he rules the Civilized Zone, but the simpleton couldn't locate his rectum in broad daylight without a diagram of his anatomy! I warned him, repeatedly, the Family should be eliminated. But no! He knew better! The Cavalry comes first, he said! So there we were, preparing for our march on the Cavalry, with most of our military hardware lined up like sitting ducks outside the Biological Center, and what happens?" he demanded rhetorically.

"Yama and Lynx blew it up," Thor commented, and immediately regretted it. He saw the Doktor's jaw muscles tighten and feared a raging outburst.

Amazingly, the Doktor smiled. "Yes, they did, leaving Samuel with a skeleton force at his disposal. Thanks to them, we'll have minimal opposition when we reach Denver and dethrone Samuel." He chuckled. "I happen to think I'll make an outstanding ruler. Don't you?"

"Of course," Clarissa agreed.

"Yes, Doktor," Thor concurred.

The Doktor nudged Joshua with his right toe. "Thanks to him, I know Plato has my notebooks. It's too bad the boy won't be around in ten days when my little surprise is unleashed on the Home. I'll get my notebooks back and my revenge on Plato and the Warriors at the same time!" The Doktor laughed and laughed. "I can hardly wait! It's lamentable we must attend to business in Catlow first, but I wouldn't consider depriving the fools of the chance to spring their trap on us."

"You know it is a trap?" Clarissa asked. "Yet we walk into it anyway?"

"I suspected an ambush," the Doktor declared. "Joshua's presence confirms the likelihood. Don't worry! The Warriors and Lynx may be working in concert, but what can they do against two hundred and thirty-five primary members of my Genetic Research Division and one hundred soldiers from our Auxiliary?"

"If only we knew what they were up to," Clarissa remarked.

The Doktor stared northward. "I was aware they were up to something when our last monitoring patrol sent to the Home didn't return. But it really doens't matter. There is nothing they can do against our superior force."

"Why not use a thermo on Catlow?" Thor queried.

"Because we don't have any left," the Doktor said, frowning. "The units were obliterated with the Biological Center, although the possibility exists Lynx and Yama absconded with one or two."

"You owe the Family for a lot," Clarissa noted.

"Yes, I do," the Doktor growled, clenching his fists. "And I vow to repay them for every insult, starting with him." He pointed at the unconscious Empath.

Thor extended his sledgehammer. "Do I finish him?"

"No," the Doktor responded. "Fetch some wood."

"Wood?"

"Yes. Two lengthy planks will do. Strip a pair of floor planks from one of the trucks if necessary."

"Yes, Doktor." Thor departed.

"Why wood?" Clarissa questioned the Doktor.

He indicated the sagebrush-covered fields adjacent to the highway. "Because there is nary a tree in sight, dear girl. Two planks will suffice adequately."

Clarissa licked her lips. "Will there be much blood?"

The Doktor nodded. "Yes, but we can't linger while you quench your thirst."

"On to Catlow?"

The Doktor's expression hardened. "On to Catlow!"

12

"It sure is quiet around here with everybody else gone," Bertha commented, cradling her M-16 in her arms.

"I like the quiet," Rudabaugh said. "I never was much for city life."

The sun was hovering above the western horizon and the air was becoming a bit chill.

"Why do you think the Doc ain't hit us yet?" Bertha asked, keeping her eyes trained on the surrounding countryside. They were at the extreme southern edge of Catlow, alongside U.S. Highway 85. Rudabaugh had dug a hole in the ground and was carefully planting a bundle of dynamite in the hole.

"Maybe he couldn't decide what to wear," Rudabaugh said.

Bertha chuckled. "That's a good one." She watched him place dirt on top of the dynamite while holding the fuse to one side. "Say, where'd you learn to use this stuff?"

"The dynamite? The Cavalry has a lot of it. Some of the ranchers hoarded it after the war. I learned how to use it from my paw, and he learned from his. Some of it is real unstable." He completed hiding the bundle and aligned the fuse to one side.

"How do you mean?" Bertha asked.

"When it gets real old, sometimes it'll go up if you just drop it or bump the crate it's in," Rudabaugh explained.

"Lordy! You mean to tell me we rode out here

with two crates of that stuff and it could of went ka-
blewy if somebody sneezed?''

"I checked it before we left," Rudabaugh said.
"I know what I'm doing."

"And I know what I'm doing," Bertha stated.
"I ain't sleepin' in the SEAL tonight!"

"There isn't any in the SEAL," Rudabaugh
informed her. "This is the last of it."

"We got it all set up?"

"Yep. All I have to do is unwind this line back
to the detonating point," Rudabaugh responded.

"How's this stuff work?" Bertha inquired.

"You really want to know?"

"I asked, didn't I?" Bertha retorted.

Rudabaugh grinned. "Okay. From what I
learned, dynamite was used a lot before the war.
They used it for things like construction projects
and in quarries—"

"What are quarries?" Bertha queried.

"A quarry is a big hole in the ground," Rudabaugh informed her.

"You're puttin' me on."

"No, I'm not."

"Why would anyone want a big hole in the
ground?"

"They were blasting for stones they could
use in their buildings," Rudabaugh elaborated.
"Dynamite is wrapped in waxed-paper cylinders we
call cartridges. These cartridges come in all different
sizes, depending on the size of the job. The older
dynamite was made up of something called nitro-
glycerin, mixed in with inert materials. Before the
war, they used a lot of ammonium nitrate instead of
nitro. Normally, the charge is pretty safe, because
you need a blasting cap, or detonating cap, to set it
off. We use the cap and one of two types of fuses,

safety fuses or detonating fuses. A safety fuse has
black powder in it. It burns real slow and gives the
dynamiter time to get away before it blows. A
detonating fuse, on the other hand, has explosive in
the core. I like to use a special kind of cap sometimes, called an electric blasting cap. I hook it up to
that box you saw earlier, the one with the plunger.
All I have to do is press the plunger, and it sends an
electric current through the line to the charge.
Boom!"

"Wow! You sure do know a lot about this
dynamite," Bertha complimented him.

Rudabaugh stood and began unraveling his line.
"It's one of the reasons Kilrane wanted me to
volunteer."

"You got yourself a main squeeze?" Bertha
asked.

"A what?"

"A fox, fool."

"I owned a dog once," Rudabaugh said, "but
I've never owned a fox."

"Are you serious?"

"I never owned a fox," Rudabaugh assured her.

Bertha shook her head. "You people from the
sticks sure do talk weird!"

"And you don't?" Rudabaugh rejoined.

They were nearing a brick wall as Rudabaugh
continued to unstring his line.

"The Doc is gonna be in for a big surprise when
he gets here," Bertha stated.

"Mind if I ask you a question?" Rudabaugh
inquired.

"What?"

"Why'd you volunteer for this mission?"

Bertha shrugged. "I didn't have nothin' better
to do."

"What's the real reason?" Rudabaugh pressed

her.

"I like to travel," she defensively replied.

"Would your reason have anything to do with Hickok?" Rudabaugh queried.

"Ain't you heard? Hickok's married."

"I know that," Rudabaugh stated. "But I couldn't help but notice the way you look at him sometimes."

"You don't know what you're talkin' about," Bertha said.

"I know what I saw," Rudabaugh disputed her. They reached the wall and he climbed over it to the other side. A wooden box with a handle on top was resting on the ground.

Bertha, eager to change the subject, pointed at the line. "Won't they see that and figure out what we're up to?"

"I'll cover it with grass and leaves, just like I did the others," Rudabaugh told her.

"How many of those charges do you have set up?" Bertha asked.

"Enough." Rudabaugh knelt and began attaching the line to the box. "How come you didn't answer my question?"

"What question was that?"

Rudabaugh smirked. "You do like him, don't you?"

"You shouldn't butt your big nose in where it don't belong," Bertha advised him.

"I'm just curious, is all," Rudabaugh explained.

"Well, you know what curiosity did to the cat," Bertha reminded him.

"I like Hickok," Rudabaugh commented. "I'd heard about his reputation before I met him. They tell stories about him, you know. About the gunfights he had in Fox, Thief River Falls, and the Twin Cities. They say he's greased lightning with those

122   David Robbins

Colts of his."

"If you knew he's so fast," Bertha said, "why'd you challenge him to a shootin' match?"

"I wanted to see for myself. I'm no gunfighter, mind you, but I'm right handy with my pistols. I wanted to set up some targets and see how good Hickok really is." Rudabaugh stood, brushing some dirt from his clothes.

"It wouldn't be the same," Bertha remarked.

"I don't follow you."

"I've seen Hickok target shoot," Bertha detailed, "and it ain't the same as the real thing. When White Meat's in action, there ain't nobody like him!" she said proudly. "I saw him in Thief River Falls and the Twin Cities. He was beautiful!"

"You see?" Rudabaugh said, grinning. "The look on your face right now is the one I'm talking about."

"I used to like you," Bertha snapped, "before you became such a know-it-all! If you..." she began, and abruptly stopped speaking, gazing over Rudabaugh's left shoulder.

Rudabaugh turned, his hands dropping to his pistols.

Hickok was strolling toward them, his Henry in his left hand, his right thumb hooked in his belt buckle. "Are you done yet?" he inquired. "Blade sent me to get you. He wants to palaver by the SEAL."

"He wants to what?" Bertha queried.

"Talk, Black Beauty," Hickok stated.

Rudabaugh's Winchester was leaning against the brick wall. He scooped it up and faced the Warrior. "We're finished here," he said.

"Good. Let's mosey on back to the town square." Hickok led the way. "I hope the Doktor gets here soon. I'm itchin' for some action."

"From what I hear, you see a lot of it," Rudabaugh mentioned.

"How about you?" Hickok inquired. "Have you seen a lot of action?"

"Some," Rudabaugh replied.

"Are you hitched?" Hickok asked.

"No."

"Where do you hang your hat?"

Rudabaugh glanced at the gunfighter. "What is this, an interrogation?"

"Just want to get to know you, is all," Hickok said. "I already know a lot about Orson. He doesn't have a wife, either—"

"Who would marry Potbelly?" Bertha quipped.

"—and he comes from a big family and has seven brothers and sisters," Hickok went on. "I gather Wolfe, the leader of the Moles, couldn't find any volunteers 'cause everybody reckoned this trip would be suicide, so he kind of twisted Orson's arm to make him join up."

"How'd you find out Orson ain't married and about his family and all?" Bertha questioned. "I didn't think you two was on speakin' terms."

"Geronimo and Orson had a talk last night," Hickok disclosed, "while they were pulling guard duty. Geronimo told me about it this morning. He thinks we've been a mite hard on Orson."

"Oh, the poor baby!" Bertha cracked sarcastically.

"So how about it, pard?" Hickok said to Rudabaugh. "Where do you live?"

"I have a small ranch about thirty miles north of Pierre," Rudabaugh answered. "I run about two hundred head of cattle, and I handle the dynamiting chores for anybody who needs some blasting done."

"Who watches your ranch while you're gallivanting around?" Hickok asked.

"My younger brother. One day he'll be getting a spread of his own, and it's good experience for him," Rudabaugh stated.

They were only one block from the town square.

"How many brothers and sisters have you got?" Hickok inquired.

Rudabaugh grinned at the mention of his family. "Two older sisters and my younger brother. My sisters are married and they keep nagging me to tie the knot."

"Typical," Hickok declared. "Women are never happy unless they're tellin' a man what to do."

"Oh, really?" Bertha said. "You get married, and all of a sudden you're an expert on women, huh?"

"No man can be an expert on women," Hickok opined.

"And why's that?" Bertha pestered him.

Hickok nudged Rudabaugh with his left elbow and winked. "It's because females are such contrary critters, no man could ever make sense out of 'em."

"I'll be sure and tell your wife you said that the next time I see her," Bertha commented.

They rounded a building and saw the SEAL still parked in front of the command post. Blade and Geronimo were standing near the driver's door, conversing. Lynx was leaning against the vehicle, listening. Orson was visible on top of the command post, peering through the binoculars. The concrete command post was rectangular in shape with a flat roof. Access to the roof was gained via a flight of metal stairs attached to the western side of the structure, only 20 feet from the northwestern corner. The front door faced due north, and there was another exit in the eastern wall, about halfway along the building.

"We're all here, pard," Hickok said as they

reached the transport.

Blade turned from his discussion with Geronimo. "Okay. We have a few things to talk about." He gazed up at the roof. "Orson, can you hear me up there?"

Orson's bearded countenance appeared over the rim of the roof. "Loud and clear."

"Good. Give a listen to what I'm about to say, but keep your eyes peeled for any sign of movement on U.S. Highway 85," Blade directed.

"Will do," Orson replied.

Bertha grinned. Orson had obeyed Blade's every command since the incident with Hickok the other night.

"The Spirit has smiled on us so far," Blade said to them, "but the worst is yet to come. We're as ready as we're going to be for the Doktor. I'm surprised he hasn't shown up yet, but his delay has worked to our advantage, allowing us the time to prepare our little surprises." He paused, glancing at each of them in turn. "You all know what we're doing here. We're to stall as best we can. Somehow, some way, we're to hold out here for two days."

"Why two days?" Bertha asked.

"The Doktor will be expecting an ambush," Blade stated. "He's not stupid. He'll have patrols scouting this area. If all of the Freedom Federation, all of the Cavalry and the Clan and the Moles and ourselves, were waiting for him here, he might decide to avoid a conflict and return to Cheyenne. Or he might elect to use a thermo on Catlow and wipe us all out—"

"What's to stop the Doktor from using a thermo on our Home?" Geronimo interjected.

"I doubt the Doc would waste a thermo on the Family," Lynx declared. "There weren't too many thermo units still functional. If they have any left,

you can bet the Doc and Sammy will save 'em for
something special."

"As I was saying," Blade resumed, "we want to
draw the Doktor in, deceive him into believing we're
alone. If our main column stays miles from here, if
the Doktor doesn't know we have a well-armed army
of our own, he'll become overconfident. He'll throw
everything he has at us, and the longer we can hold
out, the more convinced he'll be that we're by ourselves. He'll concentrate on us and his perimeter
security will lapse. Two days should do it. Two days
after the fighting starts, Rikki-Tikki-Tavi and
Kilrane will lead their forces in a combined assault
on the Doktor's flanks and defeat him."

"We hope," Hickok muttered.

"Wait a minute," Rudabaugh said. "This plan
of yours has a couple of holes in it. How do we know
how big the Doktor's force will be?"

"We don't," Blade replied.

"And what if his army is bigger than ours?"
Rudabaugh queried.

"Rikki and Kilrane will attack unless they feel
their column would be slaughtered if they did. In
which case, it has already been decided they should
retreat," Blade explained.

"Leaving us high and dry." Rudabaugh stated
the obvious.

"Now you know why this was a volunteer
mission," Blade commented.

"One more thing," Rudabaugh remarked. "How
will Rikki and Kilrane know when to attack? How
will they know when the fighting begins if they're
off in the distance somewhere? And what happens if
we need them sooner, if we can't hold out for two
days?"

"Already taken care of," Blade disclosed. "One
of Kilrane's most trusted men should be watching

us at this very second. He's under orders to keep
Catlow under surveillance, evade the Doktor's
patrols, and report to Kilrane and Rikki on the
double if we need them sooner than anticipated."

"Hey!" Orson called down from the roof.

Blade looked up. "What is it?"

"Did Wolfe know all of this?" Orson asked.

"Every stage. He was in on all the planning
sessions. Why?" Blade responded.

"He never told me all the details," Orson
complained. "All he said was whoever came here
might not come back."

"We didn't want to divulge the entire scheme,"
Blade informed him. "Who knows where the Doktor
might have spies?"

"There's one thing I'd like to know, chuckles,"
Lynx mentioned.

"What?"

"Why just seven of us? Why not ten? Or
twenty?"

"Seven was the most we could comfortably
cram into the SEAL," Blade answered.

"Speaking of the SEAL," Rudabaugh stated,
"I've heard you guys mention it has some
armaments. What type of weapons, exactly?"

Blade reached out and patted the door. "The
SEAL has already been battle tested, and we can
vouch for its reliability. Our Founder, Kurt Carpenter, had two fifty-caliber machine guns hidden in
recessed compartments under the front headlights.
There is a flamethrower hidden in the center of the
front fender. The SEAL has a rocket launcher
positioned in the middle of the front grill. And,
finally, we have a miniaturized surface-to-air missile
mounted in the roof above the driver's seat. The
weapons systems are activated by a bank of four
toggle switches installed in the dash. You also know

the body is shatterproof and bulletproof. The SEAL will be our ace in the hole, so to speak.''

"So we might be able to boogie out of here if things get too hot," Bertha said.

"Yes and no," Blade declared.

"Uh-oh." Bertha frowned. "I don't like the sound of that. What do you mean by yes and no?"

"Yes, we could boogie, as you put it, and we'd probably stand a good chance of breaking through the Doktor's lines. But no, we won't do it because I don't intend to let the Doktor know we have the SEAL here."

Bertha's brow creased. "I may not be too bright sometimes, but even I can figure out you don't intend to use the SEAL in our fight with the Doktor, do you?"

Blade shook his head. "Not during the first two days. We'll hide it in the big shed behind the command post."

"Hey!" Orson yelled down from the roof again.

Blade glanced up. "What?"

Orson pointed to the south. "We've got company!"

Everyone tensed.

"What do you see?" Blade asked.

Orson had the binoculars pressed to his eyes. "A lot of vehicles coming over a low hill about a mile south of town. Ten, twelve, fourteen..." Orson looked down at Blade "A hell of a lot of 'em!"

"Keep watching!" Blade ordered. He stepped up to the transport and grabbed the door handle. "I'm going to hide the SEAL in the shed. You all know where your posts are. Remember, each of you is to take an M-16 and as much ammunition as you can carry from the collection we took from those dead soldiers. It's piled inside the command post, in the first room to your left."

Hickok patted his right Python. "I'm partial to these, pard."

"We've already covered this," Blade reminded him. "Save your favorite weapons until you really need them. Use the M-16s as much as you can. We have ample ammunition for them." He grinned at each of them. "Hop to it!"

Lynx watched Blade climb into the SEAL and drive the transport around the western corner of the command post.

Rudabaugh started into the building to claim an M-16. "Do you want me to get one for you, Lynx?" he offered.

Lynx shook his head. "Thanks, chuckles, but I don't go in for firearms."

"Then what're you gonna fight the Doktor with?" Bertha inquired. "Spitballs?"

Lynx chuckled and raised his right hand. One by one, he extended his fingers and thumb, revealing the tapered nails, in reality iron-like claws, on the end of each digit. "These little beauties will do just fine, thanks."

"Your claws against guns?" Rudabaugh queried doubtfully.

"If the Doc has brought his G.R.D.'s with him," Lynx said, "it'll be even-steven, 'cause us genetic misfits don't go in much for guns. And as far as the soldiers are concerned," Lynx said confidently, "if you don't think I have a chance against guns, why don't you walk over to the fountain and tell that to Captain Reno? I'm sure he'll be tickled pink at the news."

Rudabaugh had seen the gory remains of the hapless officer. "No, thanks. I get the point."

Lynx clicked his nails. "So will they, bub! So will they!"

13

The Doktor waited until the next morning to launch his assault on Catlow.

The night was cold, with the temperatures dropping down into the upper 30s. A stiff breeze blew in from the northwest. Geronimo, huddled in a blanket at his post behind a wooden fence in a yard just to the southeast of U.S. Highway 85, spent the long hours reflecting on his wife, Cynthia Morning Dove, and the likelihood of his being able to continue the family tree given his present situation. He thought of Plato, and Joshua, and Rikki, and all of his other close friends and loved ones in the Family, and wondered if he would ever experience the joy of seeing them again. Toward morning, when the first tinge of pink suffused the eastern horizon, he roused himself and placed the blanket on the ground.

It would be soon.

He could feel it in his blood.

Geronimo peeped between the slats in the four-foot-high wooden fence, which was painted white and badly in need of repair, and gazed southward. U.S. Highway 85 was to the west of his position, running north and south. North of the yard it entered Catlow, making a beeline through the town. In the center of Catlow, to the west of 85, was the town square. Blade had scattered the seven of them at strategic locations designed to maximize their concerted firepower.

South of Catlow, the highway proceeded for

about 500 yards in a straight line and then traversed a small rise.

Had something moved near the top of the rise?

Geronimo squinted, scanning the rise. He held an M-16 in his hands; his FNC Auto Rifle was slung over his right shoulder. The Arminius was snug in its holster under his right arm, and his tomahawk was angled under his belt.

Figures were slowly advancing over the rise.

Geronimo flattened, keeping his eyes on the approaching forms. He counted at least two dozen, even more.

Surprise! Surprise!

They all appeared to be troopers.

What gives? Geronimo mused. Surely the Doktor had brought some of his genetic horrors with him. So why would he send in ordinary soldiers? Geronimo could think of only one reason: the Doktor was saving his G.R.D.'s, and the patrol coming in now was sent to test the defenses the Doktor would have to face.

The troopers were cautiously heading toward Catlow, strung out in two lines on either side of the highway, their weapons at the ready.

The eastern sky was rapidly brightening.

Geronimo could see their faces, their intent expressions and worried eyes. Many of them were young, and he felt a twinge of sorrow for the families they had left behind. Mourning a dearly beloved was a devastating experience, and he didn't wish it on anyone. He vividly recalled his own grief when his parents had died; such misery should be kept to an absolute minimum.

The soldiers were halfway across the straight stretch.

Geronimo glanced to the west. He was in the

southwestern corner of the fence, two yards from
the road. Orson was supposed to be on the other side
of U.S. Highway 85, waiting at the upstairs window
of a green frame house.

Would the Mole pull his weight when push came
to shove? Orson had performed admirably during
the fight in the town square, but they had—

Wait!

Two of the soldiers had detached themselves
from the patrol and were racing toward Catlow at
top speed.

The point men.

Geronimo inched forward and squinted between
two of the slats. This would complicate matters. He
would have to let the two point men pass his
position.

Would they spot him?

Geronimo froze, immobile, holding his breath,
as the two soldiers came abreast of his station. They
were nervously looking in every direction, their
fingers on the triggers of their M-16s.

Geronimo could see their legs and boots as they
passed by. There was less than a half inch of space
between each wooden slat, and it was unlikely they
would detect his presence unless they gazed directly
at him. Otherwise, his prone body, dressed as it was
in dark green, would simply appear to be part of the
shadows at the base of the fence.

The point men entered Catlow and kept going.

Geronimo shifted his attention to the patrol.
They were 30 yards out and closing. His nose began
itching, and he suppressed an impulse to sneeze.

Then it was 20 yards.

Geronimo risked a hasty glance to his right, at
the dilapidated home the fence was attached to, calculating the distance he would need to cover once
the firing began.

Ten yards.

He mentally debated the wisdom of opening up as soon as they neared the fence, or waiting for some or all of them to go on by. If they went past, he would be shooting them in the back, and he found the idea morally distasteful. Hickok would have no qualms about doing it, he knew, but he wasn't Hickok.

Thank the Spirit!

His dilemma was rendered moot by Orson.

The burly Mole abruptly appeared, framed in the second-floor window of the house on the other side of the highway. His M-16 burped, shattering the glass in the window, and three of the first soldiers in line went down.

Almost immediately, the patrol swung their automatic rifles on the window and started firing.

Orson disappeared from view as the window, the sill, and the wall enclosing it were riddled with holes.

That idiot!

Geronimo jumped up, his M-16 pressed to his shoulder, unable to afford the luxury of a choice thanks to Orson's stupidity. He let them have it, his bullets ripping into their backs and exploding from their chests, spraying crimson and flesh over the highway. They fell like the proverbial flies, seven, ten, and more, before the rest realized they were under attack from the rear.

Some of the troopers spun, firing at the stocky form in green.

Geronimo moved, sprinting toward the house, still firing as he ran, taking down two, three, four more, and then he reached the porch and dodged for the door, slugs from the soldiers hitting the porch all around him.

Something nicked his left thigh.

Geronimo slammed into the door.

It didn't budge!

Five of the troopers ran up to the fence, blasting away.

Geronimo dove, landing on his elbows and knees on the porch, as the wall above his body was perforated by bullets.

The firing near the highway rose in volume, as if others were joining the fray. More soldiers were falling. The five near the fence turned to face some unseen foes and were promptly cut to ribbons in a hail of gunfire. Several more on the other side of the road dropped.

Those remaining broke and ran.

Geronimo crawled to the edge of the porch. He glanced down at his thigh. The bullet had only torn his pants and broken the skin; the wound was bleeding, but it wasn't serious.

Blade and Hickok appeared at the fence.

"You okay, pard?" Hickok called out.

Geronimo nodded and rose to his feet. He could see eight soldiers sprinting toward the rise to the south as rapidly as their legs would carry them.

Orson emerged from the house across the highway.

Geronimo walked to the fence.

"You've been hit," Blade commented as Geronimo approached.

"It's nothing," Geronimo assured him. "I've been hurt worse."

Hickok gazed at the bodies of the fallen troopers. "I reckon we've just ruined the Doktor's day."

"We fall back to our next positions and wait for their next move," Blade stated. "It won't be as easy the next time."

"How'd I do?" Orson eagerly inquired as he reached them.

Geronimo opened his mouth, about to rebuke the Mole for his carelessness, but he changed his mind. Orson, he deduced, hadn't seen much combat, and it wouldn't do to discourage the Mole so early in the conflict.

"From what I saw," Blade said, "you did just fine, although you may have jumped the gun a bit."

"I'm sorry," Orson apologized, frowning.

Hickok patted Orson on the back. "Don't fret it! We all get the jitters now and then."

"Let's fall back," Blade suggested.

Geronimo hurried to a gate set in the middle of the southern section of fence, exited the yard, and walked around to the others.

"How long do you reckon the Doktor will wait before he tries something else?" Hickok casually inquired as they headed deeper into town.

"Not long," Blade predicted.

14

Blade was right.

Bertha saw them coming first. She was posted behind a tree in the backyard of a residence 50 yards west of U.S. Highway 85, and she was extremely annoyed because she hadn't been able to render assistance when the initial patrol had advanced on Catlow. She had seen them approach, but when the shooting had begun there were several buildings interposed between her position and the fire fight and she couldn't get a clear shot at the soldiers. Blade had ordered her to stay put until he notified her to the contrary, and it had taken all of her self-control to comply with his command.

So when the jeep with a piece of white cloth affixed to its antenna roared over the rise and streaked across the field directly toward her, instead of using the highway, she was immensely pleased.

"Will you look at this!" she exclaimed to herself, raising her M-16 to her shoulder. "Are these dummies in for a surprise! Come to momma, sucker!"

There were four figures in the topless vehicle.

Bertha deliberately sighted on the driver, a hideous reptilian monstrosity, and waited, biding her time, wanting to be sure when she pulled the trigger.

Someone grabbed her elbow.

Startled, Bertha twisted around.

Blade stood behind her. "What do you think you're doing?" he demanded.

"Where'd you come from?" she blurted.

"I was making my rounds of our perimeter," Blade replied, gazing at the speeding jeep. "Do you see their white flag?"

"I see it," Bertha answered.

"And you were going to shoot them anyway?" Blade asked her.

"I wanted to sight in my gun," Bertha quipped.

"You're getting worse than Hickok," Blade told her.

Bertha beamed, taking the statement as a compliment. "Thanks!"

The jeep slowed to a stop approximately 30 yards from the tree and slightly to the left.

"You, in the town! Can you hear me?" bellowed a deep voice. The speaker was a tall, apish mutant bearing a sledgehammer in his huge right fist. He stood on the front passenger seat, surveying the nearest homes and other buildings.

"Cover me," Blade directed Bertha.

"You ain't goin' out there!" Bertha protested.

Blade nodded.

"It's your funeral," Bertha mumbled.

Blade stepped from behind the tree. "I hear you!" he shouted, and walked toward the jeep, an M-16 at the ready, his Commando over his left arm, the Vegas in their holsters, and the Bowies on his hips.

The ape-like mutant swiveled to face the Warrior.

Blade walked to within ten yards of the vehicle. "What do you want?"

"I am Thor," the creature announced. "And you must be Blade."

"I am," Blade confirmed.

"I bring a message from the Doktor," Thor

said.

"What is it?"

"It's for Lynx," Thor revealed.

"You tell me," Blade stated, "and I'll relay the message to Lynx."

"My message is for Lynx," Thor insisted, "and only Lynx."

Blade noticed all four of the occupants of the jeep were mutants. "Why didn't the Doktor deliver this message in person?"

"He told me to do it," Thor replied.

"Could it be the Doktor's afraid to show his miserable face because he knows what we'll do to it?" Blade said, taunting the creature.

"The Doktor knows best," Thor responded. "Now get Lynx!"

"Give me your message," Blade declared.

Thor put his knobby left hand on top of the windshield and leaned forward. "I won't tell you again!" he growled. "Get Lynx!"

Blade's eyes narrowed. "How would you like me to take that sledgehammer and shove it up your ass?"

"I'd like to see you try!" Thor angrily retorted. "Are you going to get Lynx or not?" he stubbornly persisted.

"I told you already," Blade said flatly, "I'll relay the message to Lynx."

Thor seemed to be mulling the issue. "All right," he said at length. "You can give Lynx the Doktor's message. Tell Lynx the Doktor is only interested in him. If Lynx will surrender to the Doktor, the Doktor will allow the rest of you to leave here alive."

"That's the message?" Blade demanded.

"That's it," Thor confirmed.

Blade chuckled. "And you expect us to believe the Doktor will keep his word?"

"Of course he will," Thor said blandly.

"Bet me," Blade rejoined. "Tell the Doktor no deal."

"You refuse to turn Lynx over to us?" Thor queried.

"For someone, or should I say some*thing*, with the brains of a turnip, you're pretty bright!" Blade said, mocking him.

Thor glared at the Warrior. "I will tell the Doktor." He paused. "We will meet again."

Blade rested his left hand on the hilt of his corresponding Bowie. "I'll be looking forward to it."

Thor nudged the driver, and the jeep spun out, turned a tight circle, and made for the rise.

Blade wheeled and headed for the tree.

Bertha stood to the right of the trunk, watching the departing jeep. "Someone here to see you," she remarked.

Lynx walked around the left side of the tree. "I heard what you said," he told Blade.

"Why aren't you at your post?"

"Hey, I was being a good kitty," Lynx replied, "cooling my heels on top of the command post, like you wanted. I saw the jeep coming and recognized Thor and got curious about what Granite Head wanted. So I came for a look-see."

Blade stepped up to the genetic deviate. "Don't ever desert your post again!" he warned. "You're no different than Orson. When I give a command, you're to follow it. Understand?"

Lynx's lips curled backward, exposing his pointed teeth. For an instant, it appeared as if he were going to launch himself at the huge Warrior.

"Lynx!" Bertha exclaimed.

Lynx glanced at her, then at Blade. He visibly
relaxed. "Sorry, dimples. I don't usually let anyone
talk to me the way you just did."

"You agreed I was to be in charge," Blade
reminded the feisty feline.

"That's the reason I didn't just rip you to
shreds," Lynx said. "That, and what you told Ape
Face."

"You're one of us," Blade stated. "We don't
betray our own."

Lynx averted his eyes. "Yeah, I gotta admit
your Family treated me real nice when I was stayin'
at your Home. It can grow on you, thinkin' you
belong somewhere."

"What do you think the Doktor will do next?"
Blade inquired.

"He won't pussyfoot around," Lynx stated.
"He'll send in his shock troops."

"His what?" Bertha asked.

"His G.R.D.'s," Lynx elaborated. "The things
from his Genetic Research Division, like Thor and
me."

"He'll try to overwhelm us in one fell swoop,"
Blade deduced.

Lynx nodded. "If I know the Doc, and unfortunately I do, that's exactly what the prick will do."

Blade gazed at the rise. The jeep had disappeared over the crest. "Do you think he'll send
them in from every which way, or straight on?"

"Straight on," Lynx responded. "He must
know by now there aren't too many of us. The Doc
will want to get it over with. He's a real stickler for
not wastin' time."

Blade scanned the field and the nearby homes.
"Okay. Lynx, return to the command post and stay
there, no matter what you hear or see."

Lynx jogged off.

"Bertha," Blade said, "give a yell if you see them coming over that rise. I'll be right back."

"Where are you goin'?" she wanted to learn.

"To get the others," Blade replied. "I'm going to redeploy them in a skirmish line to your right and left. We'll hold Lynx in reserve, and I'll have Rudabaugh redistribute some of his special surprise packages."

Blade left.

Bertha leaned against the tree trunk. She hoped Blade would put Hickok somewhere close to her, so she could keep an eye on him. She didn't want any harm to come to White Meat. The realization troubled her. How could she allow herself to still care for Hickok? She knew the gunfighter loved another woman. She knew he was married. But she cared, anyway. And Rudabaugh had been right earlier. She had volunteered because she knew Hickok was coming on this trip.

Look at this! she mentally berated herself.

She was in love with a married man!

And she wanted to be near him so much, she was about to take on a horde of crack-brained freaks!

Yes, sir!

There was no doubt about it!

If she wasn't a glutton for punishment, *nobody* was!

15

Rudabaugh rested his hands on the plunger, his muscles inadvertently tightening, as he spotted some commotion on top of the rise south of Catlow.

The attack would come soon.

From his vantage point on the roof of a garage 75 yards from the field, he could see most of his companions. Bertha was at the edge of the field, behind a tree. Hickok was about 20 yards to her right, crouched in a shallow depression in the ground. Geronimo was approximately 30 yards to the left of Bertha, waiting at the rear of a yellow frame house. In the next yard to the left of Geronimo, Orson was squatting behind a large, tumbledown doghouse. Blade wasn't anywhere in sight, and Lynx was to Rudabaugh's rear, atop the command post.

"You all set up there?" a voice called out from below.

Rudabaugh inched to the edge of the sloping roof and gazed down.

Blade smiled up at him. "Are you all set?" he repeated.

"I'm ready," Rudabaugh acknowledged.

"Good. Remember what I told you. Don't do anything until I give you the signal, and then let them have it!"

"Will do," Rudabaugh said. "Say, do you think they saw me placing the charges?"

"Did you follow my instructions and keep the dynamite out of sight?" Blade questioned him.

"Yep. I kept the charges tucked under my shirt, and when I buried them I angled my body between the rise and the hole so they couldn't see what I was up to," Rudabaugh detailed.

"Then I doubt they know what we've done. How many charges did you relocate?"

"Seven. I thought I'd give them a present from each of us," Rudabaugh replied.

"I like your sense of humor," Blade stated.

Rudabaugh heard a loud noise in the distance and looked up at the rise.

It was swarming with movement.

"Here they come!" Rudabaugh yelled down.

Blade took off, running around the ramshackle garage and racing for the tree screening Bertha.

Rudabaugh elevated his head above the top of the roof. The garage contained a few pieces of furniture and a lot of dust; it evidently hadn't been used to shelter a vehicle in ages. It was a detached structure; the house it belonged to was ten yards behind and to the left of Rudabaugh.

Dozens upon dozens upon dozens of figures were cresting the rise and pouring over the field.

Rudabaugh remembered the binoculars dangling from the black strap around his neck. Blade had seen fit to leave the binoculars with him, saying he would need them the most. He raised them and focused on the wild throng sweeping across the field. His eyes widened in disbelief.

There were hundreds of them! They came in all shapes and sizes, but they shared one dominant characteristic: they were all members of the Doktor's Genetic Research Division. Hairy, scaly, horrid creatures, possessed of ghastly aspects and relatively few human attributes. Few were armed, and even fewer wore any clothing except for a

scanty loincloth. Some resembled common animals,
like dogs or cats, while others looked like bizarre
combinations of humanity and savage beasts. They
shrieked and howled, bellowed and roared as they
closed on Catlow.

Rudabaugh saw Blade reach the tree and say
something to Bertha. She shook her head,
apparently disagreeing, but Blade wasn't listening.

The Warrior rounded the tree and charged the
G.R.D.'s!

Rudabaugh marveled at the man's courage.

Blade was running all out, his Commando in his
right hand and the M-16 in his left. He was about 15
yards from the tree when he abruptly dropped to his
knees, cradling the two automatics in his muscular
arms, and opened up.

The nearest G.R.D.'s were cut down in droves.

Blade swept the Commando and the M-16 in
small arcs, emptying the magazines into the onrushing mass.

Bertha, Hickok, Geronimo, and Orson began
shooting, providing covering fire for Blade.

Rudabaugh saw Blade toss the empty M-16
aside.

The Warrior hastily ejected a spent magazine
from the Commando and replaced it in a smooth,
practiced motion. He rose and backed up, the
Commando chattering, felling the G.R.D.'s closest
to him.

Rudabaugh lost all track of how many foes
Blade killed. Two dozen. Three. And still they came
on, hungry for his flesh, anxious to crush him to a
pulp!

Blade whirled and ran toward the tree. He was
five yards from it when he suddenly clutched his left
side and sprawled to the ground.

No! Rudabaugh screamed in his mind. Get up!

Get out of there!

Bertha dodged out to support Blade. She was almost to him when she too was hit, and went down on one knee.

No!

The G.R.D.'s were screeching in triumph and rapidly narrowing the gap.

Blade rolled onto his side, firing from his prone position.

The fastest G.R.D.'s stumbled and collapsed as the heavy 45 slugs ruptured their vital organs and severed their veins and arteries, splattering the ground with splotches of blood and gore. Undeterred by the carnage, the rest of the G.R.D.'s continued coming.

Rudabaugh gripped the binoculars so hard his knuckles were white. There was no way Blade could hold them all off!

Bertha was trying to stand and go to Blade.

Move! Rudabaugh wanted to shout. He caught a movement out of the corner of his right eye.

Hickok was running toward Blade and Bertha, his M-16 spitting death. He wasn't more than ten yards away when the M-16 went empty and he threw it away in disgust. Instead of unslinging his Henry from his left shoulder, Hickok drew his Pythons.

Rudabaugh had never seen anyone draw so swiftly. One instant the gunfighter's hands were empty, and in the next the Pythons were out and up.

Hickok fired as he ran, blasting a lizard-like deviate about to pounce on Blade.

Blade's Commando was empty again!

Hickok reached Blade's side, his Colts cracking, and two more G.R.D.'s died, one of them clutching at a reddish hole in its hairy forehead. A creature with the facial features of a weasel rushed up from the right, and was met by a bullet in the brain.

Geronimo darted from cover, the FNC in his hands, heading for his friends.

Bertha was on her feet, helping Blade to rise.

Hickok was blasting G.R.D.'s with ambidextrous accuracy.

The G.R.D.'s in the center of the field, the ones bearing the brunt of the conflict, were beginning to hold back, unwilling to needlessly risk their lives confronting the Warriors and Bertha.

Rudabaugh noticed the G.R.D.'s on the flanks were still advancing. The ones on the left were bearing down on Orson, who was picking them off from behind the doghouse. The G.R.D.'s on the right, without any effective opposition, were the nearest to Catlow. They were rushing in toward the middle of the field, trying to sweep around and close on Bertha and the three Warriors from the rear.

Rudabaugh glanced down at his feet. There were seven sets of wires lying near the wooden box. He scooped up one set and quickly attached them to the proper connections.

The G.R.D.'s on the right were sweeping toward the center, flowing over a line of backyards, clamoring for blood.

Rudabaugh waited, keeping his eyes on his marker, a rusted swing set in one of the backyards.

The G.R.D.'s reached the backyard in question and swarmed around the swing set.

Now!

Rudabaugh drove the plunger down.

Six sticks of dynamite detonated with a resounding explosion, blowing dirt and dust and tangled metal, along with torn limbs and ravaged torsos, into the air. The noise was deafening.

The G.R.D.'s in the middle and on the left slowed, taken completely unaware by this development.

Hickok, Blade, Geronimo, and Bertha were sprinting toward the garage, taking advantage of the momentary lull.

Orson left the cover of the doghouse and jogged to join them.

The G.R.D.'s on the left spotted Orson leaving and renewed their onslaught.

Rudabaugh removed the first set of wires and applied the second.

The G.R.D.'s on the left were about 30 yards from the doghouse.

Then 20.

Then ten.

Rudabaugh depressed the plunger, and six more sticks of dynamite blew countless genetic mutations to kingdom come.

Two charges expended—five to go!

Rudabaugh stripped the second set of wires and affixed the third.

Bertha tripped and fell. Hickok was at her side in a flash, yanking her erect and propelling her toward the garage.

Blade, reloaded, was protecting his friends. He unleashed a rain of death on any G.R.D.'s foolhardy enough to get within range of his Commando.

Geronimo's FNC was equally as efficient in dispensing ruinous mayhem among the furious creatures.

Orson caught up with the others and added his M-16 to their firepower.

The G.R.D.'s were fanning out, the flanks deploying in uneven lines, evidently intending to encircle the defenders and finish them off.

Rudabaugh knew he would need to time this just right. He gripped the plunger, observing the left flank as it swung wide of the area near the doghouse. He hastily counted at least 20 of the brutes in the desired tract and leaned on the plunger.

Another gigantic explosion rocked Catlow.

His nimble fingers flying, Rudabaugh replaced the third set of wires with the fourth. An instant later, he pressed the plunger.

The G.R.D.'s on the left flank received the same destructive treatment as their counterparts on the right.

The cool air was now filled with billowing dust, literally choked with clouds of pulverized dirt.

The Warriors, Bertha, and Orson reached the garage.

Blade, his left hand pressed against his side, the Commando in his right, looked up at the slanted roof. "Rudabaugh!"

Rudabaugh peered over the edge.

"Fall back!" Blade ordered. "We can't hold them!"

Rudabaugh waved them on. "Keep going! I have three more surprises to set off!"

Blade hesitated, reluctant to leave one of his men behind.

"Go!" Rudabaugh urged him. "I'll catch up!"

The others started toward the command post. Blade nodded once and took off.

Rudabaugh turned to survey the field.

The dust was beginning to disperse. Bodies covered the field and the backyards of many of the homes. The remaining G.R.D.'s were congregating in the center of the field, gathering their forces for an all-out assault.

Rudabaugh calculated his tactics. The final three charges were planted in a line between the garage and the field. The first was 60 yards from the garage; the second, 40; and the third, only 20. If the placements were to be utilized to their peak advantage, he would need to insure that the

G.R.D.'s came directly toward the garage. He attached the set of wires for the first charge, grinned, and stood up.

Some of the G.R.D.'s spotted him, and with a mighty din they advanced on the garage.

Rudabaugh stayed erect. He knew he was taking a great risk, because some of the creatures were armed, but he wanted them to concentrate on him to the exclusion of all else.

The G.R.D.'s reached the tree Bertha had hidden behind, surging forward, game for the battle despite their heavy losses.

A bullet smacked into the roof to the right of Rudabaugh.

Not yet! he told himself.

The leading line of creatures approached the vicinity of the first charge.

Not yet!

Something buzzed by Rudabaugh's head to the left.

They were now at the 40-yard point and still coming.

Not yet!

He wanted the expanse of ground between the garage and the field to be crammed with the fiends when he detonated the trio of charges.

The G.R.D.'s sprinted onward, and the fleetest of them arrived at the 20-foot mark.

Rudabaugh started to bend over, to reach for the plunger, when a scorching, searing pain shot through his left shoulder, wrenching his body sideways and causing him to totter, lose his balance, and fall on his right side as his feet dropped out from under him and he endeavored to catch himself before he slid off the garage roof.

He'd been hit!

He couldn't afford to waste precious seconds

examining the wound. His left arm was tingling,
strangely unresponsive and useless, so he lunged for
the plunger with his right.

The 60-yard charge exploded.

Frantically, Rudabaugh took off the wires for
the spent charge and replaced them with the set for
the next bundle.

There was a peculiar scraping noise coming
from the other side of the garage.

Rudabaugh depressed the plunger and the air
vibrated with the concussion of the 40-yard charge.

Hurry! his mind screamed.

Hurry!

In a twinkling, he had the third set of wires
fastened to the contacts.

The odd scraping was louder.

Rudabaugh fell on the plunger.

Only 20 yards from the seventh charge, the
garage was buffeted by the tremendous blast, its
walls shaking and swaying. For a moment, it
seemed as if the building would collapse. Dirt, rocks,
and tiny pieces of mushy flesh showered from the
sky.

Rudabaugh grimaced as a large stone glanced
off his temple. His left shoulder felt cold and
clammy, and he backed up, scrambling down the
roof. He looked up at the box, regretting he had to
leave it behind, and the act saved his life.

Perched on the top of the garage roof was one of
the Doktor's genetic deviates. Decidedly reptilian,
this one had bulging red eyes and scaly green skin.
Instead of four fingers and a thumb, the creature
had three abnormally long digits, each capped by a
razor-like claw. It hissed and leaped.

Rudabaugh went for his right pistol, his draw
impeded by his awkward position. He managed to
clear leather, but not before the G.R.D. slammed

into him, driving him backward, both of them hurtling from the roof and falling to the ground.

Rudabaugh twisted as they fell, hoping the creature would bear the brunt of the impact, but they both landed on their left side. A lancing spasm racked his body, and he forced himself to respond, to roll away from the G.R.D. before it could recover. He lurched to his knees and brought the 45 automatic up.

The thing was already on its feet.

Rudabaugh fired, the 45 booming, the bullet catching the deviate in its chest and jerking it rearward. But it recovered almost immediately and sprang, snarling, its claws outstretched. He fired again and again, each slug stopping the creature in its tracks, but each time it kept coming. His fingers abruptly became weak as a wave of dizziness washed over him.

The G.R.D. towered above him, its fangs gleaming.

Rudabaugh attempted to use his pistol, but his sluggish body refused to respond to his commands. He flinched, expecting the claws to slash into him, to rend him apart, but instead a volley of lead crashed into the creature and flung it against the garage.

"Hang on!" someone exclaimed.

Rudabaugh felt an arm encircle his waist and he was forcibly hauled to his feet and half-carried, half-dragged in the general direction of the command post. He turned his weary head, anticipating he would see Blade or Hickok or Geronimo.

It was Orson.

"Hang on!" the Mole reiterated, casting frequent glances over his shoulder to ascertain if they were being pursued. "We'll make it!"

Rudabaugh nodded once, then blacked out.

16

Blade gazed up at the late afternoon sun, then down at Rudabaugh.

"How long was I unconscious?" the Cavalry-man inquired. He was lying on a green Army blanket, which Orson had placed on the ground outside the concrete command post, to the right of the front entrance. His legs were pointed toward the town square.

Bertha answered his question. She was sitting with her back to the wall, only two feet away from Rudabaugh to his left, resting her injured right leg. "You've been out for hours, honey," she informed him.

"What happened?" Rudabaugh queried. He couldn't remember anything after Orson came to his rescue.

"Those explosives of yours did the trick," Blade stated. "They broke and ran after the last three. We haven't heard a peep out of them since." He glanced up at the roof of the command post. "Anything?" he yelled. "Hey, Lynx! Do you hear me?"

Feline features popped into view. "I hear ya, dimples! Don't you think I'd let you know if I see somethin'? There's no sign of 'em!" He vanished from sight.

Blade frowned. "I don't like it! It's been too quiet!"

"Haven't you had enough fun for one day, pard?" Hickok asked. The gunman was leaning on the door jamb.

Geronimo stood to his right.

Orson was squatting on the ground about four feet behind Blade, absently tugging at his black beard.

"Any orders?" Geronimo asked.

"There's not much we can do except wait," Blade replied. He looked at Rudabaugh. "You did ring the town square and the command post with charges like I told you to do?"

Rudabaugh nodded. "Yesterday afternoon."

"Then we're all set at your end," Blade said.

"Not quite," Rudabaugh corrected him.

"What do you mean?" Blade queried.

"I do have nine charges left," Rudabaugh mentioned, "but they won't do us much good if I have to detonate them all by hand. We'll need to dig them up and replace the caps."

"But what about your electric blasting caps?" Blade inquired.

"They only work with my little box," Rudabaugh answered, "and I lost it."

"Lost it?"

"Actually, I left it on the roof of that garage," Rudabaugh elaborated.

Blade nodded at Hickok. "Go get it."

"On my way, pard," the gunfighter responded, unslinging his Henry.

"I'll go with him," Geronimo offered. "He'll need a boost onto the garage roof."

"Stay alert," Blade advised them.

The two Warriors ran around the northeastern corner of the command post.

Rudabaugh carefully examined the wound in his left shoulder. Someone had cleaned it and applied a bandage while he was unconscious. "Who do I thank for this?" he questioned the others.

"Thank Bertha," Blade said. "She took care of you and me before she tended to herself."

"Thanks," Rudabaugh said to Bertha.

"It's a clean hole," Blade went on. "The bullet missed the bone. Bertha took a hit in her right thigh, but it's stopped bleeding and it isn't broken."

"What about you?" Rudabaugh pointed at Blade's left side.

Blade opened his black leather vest, displaying a crude bandage consisting of white strips torn from a sheet in the command post and wrapped around his broad torso. "As near as I can determine," Blade commented, "the slug penetrated low on my back, deflected off one of my ribs, and exited shy of my sternum."

"It must hurt like hell!" Rudabaugh observed.

"It does keep you on your toes," Blade admitted.

"Speakin' of stayin' on our toes," Bertha interjected, "shouldn't we have someone patrollin' the outskirts of this dump?"

Blade shook his head. "We can all use a short breather, and Lynx will spot them if they make a move."

"What's *our* next move?" Bertha asked.

"We'll eat and bed down in the command post," Blade answered. "We'll rotate guard shifts tonight so everybody can catch some shut-eye."

"I'll take the first shift," Orson volunteered.

"You?" Blade was pleasantly surprised by Orson's eager-beaver attitude.

"Sure. I'm a Mole, ain't I? And we're used to living underground, which means I can see real good in the dark. I'll relieve Lynx when you give the word," Orson said.

Blade scrutinized the Mole's bearded visage.

"You weren't too keen on this mission a couple of days ago. What changed your mind?"

Orson glanced at Bertha. "The other night, when all of you were picking on me. It got me thinking. I saw I was being the world's worst pain in the ass. You're right, Blade. I don't want to be here. But I am here now, and there's nothing I can do about it. I'm pissed off at Wolfe for making me come along, but there's no reason why I should take it out on all of you." He paused and chuckled. "Besides, if I don't fall in line Hickok just might put a bullet between my eyes, and the last thing I need is another hole in my head."

Blade smiled. "Welcome aboard."

"Hey! Mighty Warrior!" Bertha chimed in.

Blade faced her. "What?"

"Do you still think we can hold out for two days?" Bertha inquired.

"I don't see why not."

"You don't see!" Bertha sputtered. "Take a look around you! In case you hadn't noticed, three of us have had our wings clipped. We came awful close to gettin' racked today."

"Racked?" Blade repeated quizzically.

"Yeah. Racked. Wasted. Dead, dummy!"

Blade shrugged. "We hold out for as long as we can."

"I was afraid you'd say that," Bertha declared.

Blade stared at the western horizon. "It'll be nightfall soon. You'll feel better after a good rest."

"Bet me!" Bertha retorted.

Blade grinned and cupped his hands around his lips. "Hey, Lynx!"

Lynx appeared on the roof. "I ain't seen nothin' yet!"

"It's not that," Blade said. "You know the

Doktor better than any of us. Will he try anything
before daylight."

"It's hard to outfox the Doc," Lynx replied.
"He took a real beatin' today, and he may sulk all
night and try again come morning. Then again, he
may send in some of his pets after dark to
assassinate us."

Blade placed his hands on his Bowies and began
pacing. If he were the Doktor that's exactly what
he'd do: send in some of his best men, or things, to
quietly slit a throat or three and reduce the
opposition. To be forewarned was to be forearmed,
so what action could he take to negate the threat?
There was only one logical recourse. "Except for the
guard on the roof, we're going to spend the night in
the SEAL," he announced.

"Why the SEAL?" Orson asked.

"Several reasons," Blade answered. "The
Doktor doesn't know we have the transport here,
although he may suspect we do. The SEAL's im-
pervious plastic body will shield us from a would-be
assassin's bullet. Even if one of them stumbled on
the transport in the shed, they can't see inside. We'll
be safer in the SEAL than we would be in the
command post."

"If we're so safe in the buggy," Bertha remarked, "why bother having a guard on the roof?
Wouldn't it be best if everybody was in the SEAL?"

"We can't shut ourselves off from the outside
completely," Blade explained. "If the Doktor
should be foolish enough to launch a mass assault at
night, we'd need to know about it."

Rudabaugh had a question. "Did Kilrane say
who it was who'd be out there keeping Catlow under
surveilance?"

"Nope," Blade said. "Just that it would be

someone he could trust, and he'd get word to their column if we were in trouble."

"How many do you think we killed today?" Bertha inquired.

"A lot," Blade guessed.

"I'd estimate somewhere between seventy-five and a hundred," Rudabaugh commented.

"That many?" Bertha marveled.

"Maybe more," Rudabaugh said.

"And not one of us was racked!" Bertha stated, shaking her head in wonder.

"But three of us were hurt," Blade pointed out. "We were fortunate today, but only because the Doktor didn't know we had the dynamite. Tomorrow will be a completely different story. He'll be more cautious. He'll probably come at us from all sides."

"Which is why we need my magic box," Rudabaugh joked.

As if on cue, Hickok and Geronimo came around the northeastern corner of the command post, their arms empty except for their weapons.

"Where's the box?" Blade demanded.

"Gone," Hickok laconically replied.

"Gone? Where?"

Hickok leaned against the wall, catching his breath. Geronimo and he had jogged both ways. "How should I know?" he rejoined. "We got there and I took a look-see on the roof. No box."

"One of the G.R.D.'s must have taken it," Rudabaugh speculated.

"What about the charges you placed around the town square?" Blade asked.

"We'll have to dig them up," Rudabaugh said. "I can't detonate them remotely without the box. We'll dig them up, and I'll attach different caps and

fuses. Each of us can take a couple of bundles of
dynamite, and when the time is right, you just light
the fuse, throw your bundle, and run like hell.''

"But you said you only have nine charges left,"
Blade noted.

"Each charge consists of a bundle containing
six sticks of dynamite," Rudabaugh detailed. "I'll
break down the bundles and make them smaller, say
four sticks apiece.''

"Are you certain you're up to it?" Blade
queried.

"I can manage," Rudabaugh assured him.

"Okay. Tell us where they're buried and we'll
dig them up for you," Blade offered.

"I didn't count on handling dynamite," Orson
mentioned. "Isn't it dangerous? I mean, what
happens if we light a bundle and don't toss it far
enough or drop it at our own feet?''

Rudabaugh grinned. "Believe me, you'll throw
them far enough.''

"How do you know?" Orson asked skeptically.

"I know.''

"How?''

"Because when you're holding a bundle of
dynamite in your hand," Rudabaugh said, "and the
fuse is lit, you'll want nothing more at that
particular moment than to put as much distance
between the dynamite and you as humanly
possible.''

"Good point," Orson conceded.

17

He stood on the rise south of Catlow, the wind whipping his black cloak and disheveling his dark hair. Overhead, the stars were bright pinpoints of light.

Footsteps sounded behind him.

The brooding figure turned. "What do you want?" he brusquely demanded.

"I thought you might like some company, Doktor," Clarissa said. "And it was cold in our cot without you to warm me."

The Doktor stared at Catlow, his lips a tight line.

"What's bothering you?" Clarissa ventured to inquire.

"I miscalculated today," the Doktor stated. "I made serious blunders."

"For instance?"

"For instance, I should never have sent in the Genetic Research Division en masse," the Doktor remarked.

"You were unaware they had explosives," Clarissa stated in justification of his maneuver.

"Still, I should have considered the contingency," the Doktor reprimanded himself. "I'm slipping."

"You are not," Clarissa disputed him.

"I tell you I am," the Doktor disagreed. "My mental lucidity is strangely impaired. If I didn't know better, I'd swear I'm suffering from the same premature senility I inflicted on the Family by poisoning their water supply."

"But you haven't consumed any of their tainted water," Clarissa said. "And even if you did, you have the antidote. You're merely fatigued."

"Do you really think so?"

"Of course," Clarissa asserted. "You haven't enjoyed a good night's sleep since the Biological Center was destroyed."

The Doktor's shoulders slumped. "How can I sleep? For the first time in decades, I'm facing the specter of my own demise."

"But you can't die!" Clarissa objected, striving to cheer her lover and creator, the man she practically worshiped.

"No, I couldn't die," the Doktor muttered, "as long as I had access to my laboratory, to my equipment and chemicals, and to a constant source of fresh infant blood. But it's gone! All gone! Thanks to them!" He shook his right fist in the direction of Catlow, his voice rising in mounting fury. "They'll pay for what they have done!"

Clarissa wisely remained silent. She recognized the symptoms: the Doktor was working himself up into one of his periodic frenzies.

"Those imbeciles have meddled in my affairs for the final time! I'll grind them underfoot as I would a common slug! I will show them why my name is feared far and wide! They shall see!"

Clarissa heard the Doktor take a deep breath, evidently seeking to control his raging emotions.

"I'll play on their nerves tonight," he said in a softer tone. "They're probably anticipating an attack, but there won't be one. Let them stay awake all night, dreading an assault! Then they'll be tired, come morning, and we'll defeat them easily."

"We will crush them," Clarissa vowed. "And

then we will travel to Denver and establish a new laboratory. Locating healthy babies will be simplicity itself. Once you've synthesized your rejuvenation complement, you'll be as good as new."

"Thank goodness I'd had a transfusion shortly before the Biological Center was demolished," the Doktor said. "Otherwise, I might be dead by now."

Clarissa couldn't comprehend all this talk of dying. It was utterly uncharacteristic of the Doktor. Her feminine intuition was tugging at her mind. "What's really bothering you?" she asked, reaching out and touching his right elbow, reassuring him of her concern and affection.

The Doktor glanced at her, his black eyes probing. "Can you read my mind then?"

Clarissa didn't respond.

The Doktor sighed. "I would expect no less from my masterpiece. The majority of the others are so primitive, so savage. But you! You're unique! You give meaning to my life and provide hope for my future accomplishments! You're beautiful, and intelligent, and I wouldn't be surprised if you're telepathic as well."

She wasn't telepathic, but saying so would simply depress him further.

The Doktor gazed at the stars, his stature seemingly diminished by their majestic grandeur. "Did you see his face?" he asked in a hushed whisper.

"What?"

"Did you see his face?"

"Whose face?" Clarissa had no idea whom he was talking about.

"The boy's," the Doktor said quietly, "when he was nailed to the crossbeam."

"Joshua? The one from the Family?"

"Who else?" the Doktor snapped, glaring at her.

Clarissa recoiled in shock and amazement. "Is that what's bothering you? What you did to Joshua?"

The Doktor turned and looked off into the distance. "Did you hear him? Did you hear what he said to me when we hung him up?"

"No," Clarissa responded. She had been conversing with Thor when the youth mumbled several words to the Doktor.

"He stared into my eyes with this pitifully sad expression," the Doktor said, relating the incident, "and told me . . ." The Doktor paused, his voice fading. "I was forgiven."

Clarissa threw back her head and laughed. "Forgiven! He—" Her sentence was abruptly cut short as the Doktor whirled and grabbed her by the front of her fatigue shirt.

"Are you laughing at me, my dear?" he demanded. "You may be my favorite, but you know I will not tolerate anyone ridiculing me!"

"Doktor! Please!" Clarissa put her hands on his arm. "You're hurting me!"

The Doktor slowly released her, his features troubled.

"I don't understand," Clarissa stated. "You've killed so many during your lifetime. Why is this one affecting you so much?"

"Didn't you see his eyes?" the Doktor replied. "There was something about them, an ineffable quality of . . . compassion. I've never beheld eyes like his."

"I can't believe you let him get to you," Clarissa remarked.

The Doktor studied the firmament. "Is it possible he was right?"

"About what?"

"Is it possible there is a God after all?"

Clarissa was alarmed by the Doktor's erratic behavior. He was a confirmed atheist and had been ever since she'd known him. Why was he doubting his beliefs? What motivated this peculiar discussion? Had the loss of his laboratory unhinged his mental equilibrium? "But you've told us time and time again there is no God," she reminded him.

"What if I was wrong?" he queried in a melancholy tone. "Look at all those stars! Ponder the infinity of the universe, and observe how everything, from the grandest galaxy to the minutest microbe, has a functional purpose to perform." He paused. "What if I was wrong?"

Clarissa gently took his right hand in hers. "Doktor, get a hold of yourself. You are not wrong. You are never wrong. Oh, you may commit a small error every now and then. We all do. But your genius, your mighty intellect, is unequalled. Your wisdom is beyond reproach. Your accomplishments are unparalleled. Men and women tremble at the mere mention of your name. You are the greatest man this planet has ever seen."

The Doktor slowly nodded. "Yes, I am, aren't I?"

Clarissa grinned. She was getting through to him, nipping this morbid introspection in the bud. "What was Joshua compared to you? He was an insignificant gnat. Will his name be remembered? No. Yet yours is legend. Why let the memory of a gnat upset you so?"

The Doktor straightened, smiling. "You are correct, of course. I apologize for this rare display of weakness. I haven't quite been myself since Yama and Lynx obliterated my Biological Center." He stared at her and laughed. "Do you know what I've been thinking about lately?"

"No, what?"

"Dying."

"You? But you're immortal."

"I know," he said with conviction. "But the loss of my Center caused me to begin to doubt myself. It shook my confidence. I've been troubled by a sense of impending doom, and disturbed by my seemingly fragile fallibility. Can you imagine!" He laughed at his childish fears.

Clarissa impulsively embraced him.

The Doktor leaned down and kissed her on her scaly forehead. "Thank you for restoring me to myself."

"Could I do any less for the man I love?"

He sighed and held her close. "Sometimes I experience an urge to go away somewhere, just the two of us. We could locate a secluded spot and forget all of our cares and woes. How does that sound?"

"It sounds wonderful," Clarissa said happily.

"We'll do it, then."

"We truly will?"

"Absolutely," the Doktor confirmed. "After our business here is finished, and after I deal with Samuel in Denver, we'll let Thor run the Government while we enjoy a much-deserved vacation. Would you like that?"

"I'd love it!" Clarissa declared. "But can Thor be trusted to direct the Government in your absence?"

The Doktor snorted. "Bureaucratic Government, my dear, is an organic sociopolitical mechanism. Whether controlled by a dictator or a so-called democracy, any Government can function independently of the personal presence of its leader. Thor will perform admirably. He's already proficient in the primary rule of successful governing."

"Which is?"

"Eliminate the opposition by whatever means necessary."

Clarissa giggled. "I can hardly wait for our vacation to begin! It's a marvelous idea!"

The Doktor grinned. "You see? Rumors to the contrary, I'm not such a bad person after all!"

18

"And you say Blade sent you?" Rikki-Tikki-Tavi asked.

The column was halted at the western edge of the Black Hills National Forest in South Dakota, only 15 miles from the Wyoming border and about 23 miles from Catlow.

"How else do you think we found you?" the Indian responded. "Blade gave us explicit directions. He said you would be waiting here for word on when you should attack the Doktor."

"And your people are willing to fight, Red Cloud?" Rikki inquired.

"We will gladly join you against those who enslaved us!" Red Cloud stated earnestly.

Rikki glanced at the two troop transports and the jeep parked in the field ahead. Dozens of Indians were clustered near the vehicles. "How many are with you?"

"Forty-eight," Red Cloud answered. "We all want to fight," he added proudly.

"You'll get your chance," Rikki promised him. He glanced over his left shoulder. The Freedom Federation's fledgling army was encamped in a wide meadow near the forest, awaiting the signal to march on Catlow. The volunteers from the Clan and the Moles occupied the center of the meadow, positioned next to the 14 trucks. The Cavalry riders encircled the meadow, serving as a mobile buffer, prepared to take the field at a moment's notice.

Five yards to Rikki's right stood three stalwart

figures: Kilrane in his inevitable buckskins, Yama in his blue "death shirt," and Teucer, the third member of Beta Triad, a lean, rakish Warrior attired in a green shirt and pants. Teucer's hair was blond, his locks secured in a ponytail, and he cultivated a neatly trimmed blond beard on his chin. He carried a compound bow in his left hand, and a quiver full of arrows was attached to his brown leather belt and slanted across his right hip. Like every other Warrior, Teucer had a preference in weaponry based on his natural aptitude and ability. As the Family's best archer, Teucer preferred a bow and arrows. Hickok, by virtue of his uncanny skill with handguns, was entitled to possess the Colt Pythons. Blade, because of his expertise at knife fighting, carried the Bowies. And Rikki, in honor of his position as the Family's supreme martial artist, could claim the only katana in the Family's armory. The Founder of the Home, Kurt Carpenter, had stocked an incredible array of arms including hundreds of guns as well as more exotic weapons. Family members, even the Warriors, could not automatically assume ownership of a particular firearm or other weapon; they first had to prove themselves worthy of such a distinction.

"May I ask you something?" Red Cloud ventured.

Rikki nodded.

"Why are you so far from Catlow?" Red Cloud inquired. "Wouldn't it be wiser to be closer?"

"We don't want to alert the Doktor to our presence," Rikki explained. "If we were any closer, we would risk detection by one of his patrols."

"But how will you know when to attack?"

"We have a man watching Catlow," Rikki detailed. "He has one of our fastest horses. If he determines Blade and the others require our assistance, he will ride and warn us. If not, he is under orders to notify us on the evening of the second day after the battle has begun."

Red Cloud slowly shook his head, his shoulder-length black hair waving. "It sounds too dangerous to me. Blade and his companions could be killed before you got there."

"It's a chance we have to take," Rikki said. "We want the Doktor so involved with defeating Blade, he won't realize we are here until it is too late."

"Are you a close friend of Blade's?" Red Cloud questioned.

"I am," Rikki stated.

"Then I hope, for his sake, you know how to pray!"

19

The Doktor strode from his tent and stared at the pair in front of him. One was Thor. The other was a short man, standing slightly under five feet in height, who was covered with a coat of light brown hair. His body was well proportioned and muscular, but his face was a startling contrast to his physique. His nose was circular and protruded at a slant above his large oval mouth. Beady brown eyes were focused on his creator in abject fear. The corners of his mouth tended to chronically droop, exposing his oversized teeth.

The sun was just clearing the eastern horizon.

"What is it, Thor?" the Doktor demanded impatiently. "I told you not to awaken me unless it was absolutely necessary."

Thor bowed deferentially. "I'm sorry, Doktor, but I felt this was important."

"What is it?"

Thor extended his right arm. Clutched in his furry right hand was a bloodstained buckskin shirt.

The Doktor took the shirt and examined the fabric, noting the back of the garment had been torn to shreds. "What is this?"

Thor glanced at the one to his left. "Tell him, Boar."

Boar went to speak, but hesitated.

Thor hefted the sledgehammer in his left hand. "Tell him!" he bellowed.

"Do you know where this shirt came from?" the Doktor asked in a calm tone of voice, smiling at the terrified Boar.

"Y . . . y . . . yes," Boar stuttered.

"Tell me," the Doktor coaxed him.

Boar began wringing his hands together. "You promise you won't get mad?"

A steely gleam flickered across the Doktor's features. "Mad? Why should I get mad?" He walked up to Boar and placed his right arm around his underling's shoulders. "Tell the Doktor all about it."

Boar took a deep breath. "I was going to tell you myself, really! Thor didn't need to bring me."

The Doktor held up the bloody shirt in his left hand. "I'm waiting."

"I was going to tell you about it this morning," Boar said nervously.

"When I saw him," Thor interjected, "he was trying to bury it."

"Oh?" The Doktor stared into Boar's eyes. "Are you open to some unsolicited advice?"

Boar's head bounced up and down.

"Talk to me, Boar," the Doktor urged softly. "Talk to me right this instant and explain to me where you got this shirt."

"I took it from the man," Boar hastily blurted. "Last night I was assigned to patrol the area northeast of the town. I heard this sound, like someone coughing, and when I went to check I found a man hiding in a ravine. There was a horse with him."

"What happened then?" the Doktor prompted.

"I tried to capture him, to take him alive for questioning," Boar said. "But during our struggle I accidentally killed him. The horse ran away." Boar paused.

"Where is this man now? Did you bury his body?" The Doktor suppressed an impulse to laugh;

he already knew the answers to his questions.

"I . . . I . . . d . . . didn't bury him," Boar stammered.

"Oh? What did you do with him?"

"You've got to understand!" Boar whined. "We've been on short rations since we left the Citadel. I was hungry. No one else was around. What harm was done?"

"You still haven't told me what you did with the body," the Doktor said, toying with him.

Boar mumbled some words.

"What was that?" The Doktor grinned. "I'm afraid I didn't quite catch what you said."

Boar started trembling. "I ate it."

"You ate the body?"

"Yes, Doktor."

"And when Thor spotted you," the Doktor deduced, "you were burying the evidence."

"I brought one of his arms back with me wrapped in the shirt," Boar said. "Sort of a snack."

"Sort of a snack," the Doktor said, mimicking him.

"Are you mad at me?" Boar asked, dreading the answer.

"No."

"You're not?" Boar brightened. "You're really not?"

The Doktor smiled. "No, I'm not mad at you, but . . ." His right hand fell from Boar's shoulder, then streaked upward, his fingers clamping on Boar's throat. He squeezed and heaved, lifting Boar bodily from the ground.

Boar attempted to break the Doktor's iron grip. He kicked and punched, to no avail.

"But although I'm not mad at you," the Doktor went on, as if he were giving a lecture instead of

strangling someone, "I am upset with you. Don't
you want to know why?"

Boar was gasping for air, his chest heaving.

"I can't abide liars," the Doktor commented.
"And you are a liar. Don't you want to know how I
know?"

Boar gurgled and thrashed.

"Look at this shirt." The Doktor held the buckskin shirt aloft. "Take a good look at it."

Boar's eyes were bulging from their sockets.

"Notice the back of the shirt," the Doktor
directed. "The man wearing this shirt was jumped
from behind. You jumped him from the rear, didn't
you? You didn't give him a chance to defend himself
or surrender, did you?"

Boar wheezed, blood flowing from his nostrils.

"You never tried to take him alive for
questioning," the Doktor said. "You were hungry.
You thought you could kill him and eat him and no
one would be the wiser. Am I right?"

Boar's body was convulsing and quaking.

"Of course I'm right," the Doktor stated. "If
Thor hadn't found you with the shirt, you wouldn't
have said a word. Correct?"

Blood was now running from Boar's mouth,
down his chin, and dripping on the Doktor's hand.

"Well, you don't disagree," the Doktor
remarked. "No, Boar, I'm not mad at you for con-
suming an impromptu meal. I might have satisfied
my appetite too, given a similar set of circumstances. Had you only confessed the truth, I would
have pardoned your monumental stupidity. But I
can't pardon a liar. When a person lies to another,
it indicates a lack of respect. I'm saddened, Boar, to
discover the low esteem in which you hold me."

Boar's eyes were glazing.

"I can't trust a liar," the Doktor said. "Whether predicated on respect or fear, trust is essential to any relationship. Without trust, there can't be a mutual rapport. Without trust, how could I possibly rely on you? And if I can't rely on you, then I don't have any further need of you, do I?" The Doktor sighed. "You can see I'm right, can't you?"

Boar was limp in the Doktor's grasp.

"Our relationship, therefore, is officially severed," the Doktor stated, and released his hold.

Boar's lifeless body sank to the hard ground.

"Why didn't you just fry the turkey?" Thor asked, referring to the slim metal collar around Boar's neck. All of the Doktor's genetically engineered offspring wore the collars; it was his infallible technique for insuring obedience. Thor had seen a number of malcontents subjected to the electrocution treatment over the years, their flesh crisped from the neck up by the collars.

The Doktor was inspecting the buckskin shirt. "Applying the personal touch always boosts one's morale. I needed that."

"Who do you think the guy was Boar ate?" Thor queried.

"There's no way of telling from this," the Doktor replied, waving the shirt in the air. "Buckskins are commonplace apparel outside the Civilized Zone." The Doktor thoughtfully stroked his chin. "Are you still sending out regular patrols as I ordered?"

"Every quadrant is covered at least once every four hours," Thor responded.

"And they haven't seen anything?"

"Not a sign," Thor verified.

"How odd," the Doktor commented. "And yet Boar finds a man with a horse hiding in a ravine.

Why? What was this man doing there?"

"Maybe," Thor suggested, "this guy was
passing through and had bedded down for the night
in the ravine."

"A possibility," the Doktor said doubtfully.
"But why was he so close to Catlow? Surely he
heard the battle waged yesterday."

"Maybe he came to see what all the racket was
about."

"Another possibility," the Doktor acknowledged. "But I can't accept his presence as a mere
coincidence. Was he a messenger of some sort?
If so, was he carrying a message to the defenders in
Catlow? Or was he taking a report from them to
someone else?"

"Does it matter?" Thor asked. "Either way, the
message didn't get through. And today we'll finish
off those bastards in Catlow."

"I find it difficult to believe there are only six of
them," the Doktor mentioned.

"I saw Blade myself," Thor mentioned, "and
some woman behind a tree. From the descriptions
given by some of our troops, we know Hickok and
Geronimo are in Catlow too. Two others were also
seen. Some fat guy with a beard and another one
who wears all black."

"But there was no sign of Lynx?"

"No one reported seeing him."

"What are they trying to pull?" the Doktor
mused aloud. "Why hasn't Lynx shown his face? If
Lynx is in Catlow, that still means there are only
seven of them. Where are the rest?"

"The rest?" Thor repeated quizzically.

"Use your brain, Thor," the Doktor said testily.
"Blade isn't a moron. He wouldn't place himself and
the others in jeopardy without a sound reason.

Catlow is obviously a trap. The question remains: why haven't they sprung it?"

"There could only be the seven of them," Thor stressed.

The Doktor glanced at Thor and sighed. "I can see where she was right. Leaving you in charge would be a grievous mistake."

"What?"

"Never mind. Suffice it to say there must be more of them. Reinforcements must be nearby."

"Why haven't our patrols seen any sign of them?" Thor asked.

"How far afield have our patrols been ranging?"

"About two or three miles in every direction," Thor said.

The Doktor ran his right hand through his shock of dark hair. "Logic would dictate reinforcements be close to Catlow so they could assist Blade as promptly as possible. But if the reinforcements are beyond the three-mile limit, they couldn't hope to reach Catlow before we . . ." The Doktor's face brightened and he snapped his fingers. "Of course!"

"What?" Thor inquired.

"That must be it!" The Doktor started laughing.

"What?" Thor persisted.

"It's the classic fencing ploy! The feint and thrust!"

"The what?" Thor's confusion was evident.

"Catlow is a feint," the Doktor said. He saw the consternation on Thor's features and decided to elaborate. "In fencing, in boxing, or in any type of combat, you feint when you make a move in one direction, hoping your opponent will concentrate on that move, when all the time you were simply setting up your foe for the real thrust. The Warriors initiated a foray into the Civilized Zone by taking Catlow. But the move is a feint, designed to draw me out so they can launch their main thrust. That's what the rider was doing hiding in the ravine.''

"The rider?"

"Certainly. He was the one who would contact the reinforcements at the proper time. There's no other rational explanation!"

Thor pondered the Doktor's words.

The Doktor laughed triumphantly. "The fools! They have unwittingly played into our hands! Without their messenger, they are stranded in Catlow. They are at our mercy!"

"I don't know how you do it," Thor complimented the Doktor. "I would never have figured it out."

The Doktor's chest puffed outward. "This is a valuable object lesson. Remember it always. The Genetic Research Division wouldn't last two seconds without me at its helm."

"I will always remember," Thor promised, "and be loyal to you."

The Doktor placed his hand on Thor's shoulder. "I appreciate your devotion. It's why I made you my second in command."

"Do we attack soon?" Thor asked eagerly.

"After my breakfast."

"Can I lead the charge today?" Thor requested.

"No."

"But you didn't let me lead it yes—" Thor began, and then caught himself before he aroused the Doktor's volatile temper.

"I did not allow you to participate yesterday because I wanted to observe their defenses before committing my best men," the Doktor elucidated.

"I held you and the twenty-four members of my personal guard in reserve. Today, though, everybody goes in. All of my G.R.D.'s and the Auxiliaries."

"Why can't I lead?" Thor inquired, pouting.

"Somebody else will be leading today," the Doktor said.

"Who?" Thor questioned, peeved, annoyed at the prospect of the Doktor favoring someone else over him.

"I am personally commanding our troops today," the Doktor revealed, grinning. "You will ride with me in the half-track."

"We will crush them!" Thor enthusiastically cried.

The Doktor gazed in the general direction of Catlow. "I hope Blade is enjoying a hearty morning meal. It's the last one he will ever eat."

"Where the blazes are they?" Hickok demanded impatiently.

"They'll be here," Geronimo stated. "What's your rush?"

"They should have been here by now," Hickok groused. "The sun was up hours ago."

"Why is it," Geronimo philosophized, "the white man is always as ready to get into trouble as he is to get out of it?"

They were standing at the corner of a brick house located on the western outskirts of Catlow. Blade had divided the defenders into pairs, leaving Lynx behind again at the command post. Blade and Bertha were somewhere in the southeastern part of the town, while Rudabaugh and Orson were watching to the north.

"Hey," Hickok retorted, miffed, "the white man doesn't go looking for trouble, pard. We're peaceable folks at heart."

"Tell that to Custer," Geronimo quipped.

Hickok opened his mouth to speak, but stopped, staring to the west over Geronimo's left shoulder.

Geronimo turned.

Over a dozen forms were moving toward the town, slowly advancing across a sagebrush- and weed-covered field.

"Looks like we got us some company," Hickok declared.

"Astute observation, eagle-eye!" Geronimo said. "Do we fall back or take them here?"

"I ain't one for running," Hickok stated. "Let's take 'em right here."

Geronimo hurried to the other end of the house so they could cover both flanks. He cautiously peered around the northern corner of the home, spotting more of their adversaries coming toward Catlow, noting the assault force was composed of G.R.D.'s and soldiers. He looked down at the light green pillowcase dangling from his belt, the pillowcase containing his 2 bundles of dynamite. After Rudabaugh had prepared the 14 charges, 13 of them comprised of 4 sticks of dynamite and the final one including only 2, he had distributed them among the others. Blade, meanwhile, had entered the command post and emerged shortly thereafter bearing seven pillowcases taken from the cots the garrison had slept on. He had dispensed the pillowcases and a pack of matches to each of them. The matches had been taken from a drawer in the command post kitchen. Geronimo decided he wouldn't use the dynamite until it was absolutely necessary. He glanced up.

A trooper was within 25 yards of the brick house, inching forward on his hands and knees.

Geronimo sighted the FNC, his fingers on the trigger.

Hickok's Henry suddenly boomed, and in the distance there was a loud shriek.

Geronimo fired, the FNC recoiling against his shoulder.

The soldier jerked backward and flipped over, then lay still.

That should stir them up! Geronimo conjectured.

He was right.

A hail of lead tore into the brick house.

Geronimo ducked back as a bullet bit into the corner of the building and a brick fragment dislodged and whizzed past his eyes.

Hickok's Henry thundered again, and once more.

Geronimo crouched and risked a hasty look-see.

The G.R.D.'s and troopers were rushing the house.

Geronimo shot twice, downing two foes, and then looked at Hickok.

The gunman waved to him, motioning for them to retreat.

Geronimo jogged to his friend, and together they ran 20 yards to a white frame house and swerved behind it.

None too soon.

Soldiers and G.R.D.'s poured around both corners of the brick home.

"How about a little cat and mouse?" Hickok whispered.

Geronimo grinned.

"Hold this," Hickok said, and handed his Henry to Geronimo. He drew his Colts, winked at his partner, and stepped out into the open, his Pythons leveled.

One of the troopers saw him immediately and attempted to bring his M-16 to bear.

The Pythons blasted two, four, six times in rapid succession, and with each shot an opponent dropped, felled by a slug to the head.

Unnerved, the remaining soldiers and G.R.D.'s raced to the rear of the brick house and disappeared.

Hickok jumped from sight and twirled the Colts into his holsters. "Piece of cake," he said.

"Let's play some hide and seek," Geronimo recommended, giving the Henry to Hickok.

"Lead on," the gunfighter said. "You've always been better at gettin' lost than I have."

Geronimo recognized a cut when he heard one, but deferred retaliating for the moment. Instead, he led the way as they ran through several yards and reached a two-story structure with a stone foundation on the bottom and brown siding on the top. There was a large window in the middle of the second floor with a balcony on the outside.

"Do you see what I see?" Geronimo queried.

"I sure do, pard," Hickok said, then reached out and grabbed Geronimo's right elbow. "Listen!"

Geronimo heard it too. Sporadic gunfire splitting the morning air.

"Let's do in these wimps so we can go lend a hand to the others," Hickok suggested.

Geronimo nodded. He hurried to the back door and tried the knob. To his surprise, the door opened. Together, the two Warriors entered and Geronimo closed the door behind them. They found a flight of stairs at the other end of a narrow kitchen and ascended to the second floor.

"I kind of like this spread," Hickok commented. "It's a lot bigger than the cabins us hitched types get to live in at the Home."

Geronimo hastened to the window he wanted. He discovered a latch in the center of one side and slid the window open.

In unison, the Warriors dropped to the carpeted floor and crawled out onto the wooden balcony. They eased to the railing and peeped between the rails, which were spaced about six inches apart.

There was no sign of pursuit.

"Where are they?" Geronimo inquired in a soft tone.

"Maybe they're takin' a potty break," Hickok

replied.

Geronimo reached down and removed a bundle of dynamite from his pillowcase. "I'll do the honors. We might be able to get them all at once."

"Here they come!" Hickok warned.

Geronimo looked up. He began counting, but gave it up when he reached 31. There were more of them than he had thought! They were moving forward very slowly, searching every nook and cranny, their eyes alertly scanning the terrain.

But very few of them were bothering to glance up.

Geronimo extracted his pack of matches from his right front pants pocket. He studied the bundle of dynamite. Rudabaugh had instructed them in its proper use, and had cautioned them they would have about half a minute between the time they lit the fuse and the charge going off.

Not much time.

Hickok nudged Geronimo.

The troopers and G.R.D.'s were only 15 yards from the balcony.

Geronimo quickly lit one of the matches and applied the flame to the fuse. It sputtered and crackled as it caught on fire.

Move! his mind screamed.

Geronimo rose and threw back his right arm, intending to lob the charge directly at the group nearing the house.

Hickok, on his stomach at Geronimo's feet, detected a motion out of the corner of his left eye. He twisted, surveying the yard below, and even as he did he heard the crack of an M-16.

There was a trooper not more than five yards from the house!

Geronimo felt the bullet rip into his left

shoulder, and he was slammed backward by the impact, crashing into the window and tumbling to the balcony.

Hickok aimed the Henry and fired, putting a slug into the soldier below.

The other troopers began shooting at the balcony.

Geronimo, his senses swimming, gaped at the charge in his right hand. The fuse was continuing to crackle and sparkle.

Dear Spirit!

Geronimo struggled to rise, to get rid of the dynamite. His body refused to cooperate with his dazed mind.

Hickok was conducting a raging gun battle with the enemies below.

Geronimo shook his head to clear it, and managed to laboriously lift himself to his knees. The strain of his exertion prompted a surge of dizziness to engulf his consciousness. Unable to control his equilibrium, he pitched forward, the fuse over half gone.

21

"Lordy! What in the world is that thing?" Bertha exclaimed in alarm.

Blade, squatting alongside of her behind a low stone wall not far from U.S. Highway 85, recognized the vehicle from photographs contained in several of the military history books in the Family library. "It's called a half-track," he told her.

"I ain't never seen nothin' like it!" Bertha declared nervously.

"The Doktor's pulling out all the stops," Blade commented.

Bertha was gawking at the green half-track. "I think we'd best go get the SEAL!"

The armored half-track was slowly proceeding north on U.S. Highway 85 toward Catlow. Its rear caterpillar treads were clanking and creaking. At least six soldiers were riding in the open back section, one of them manning a mounted machine gun.

"We'll try and take it out with our charges," Blade stated.

Dozens of troopers and G.R.D.'s were following the half-track on foot.

"It ain't gonna be easy," Bertha predicted.

"You never know until you try," Blade declared.

The stone wall was 20 yards to the west of the highway.

Bertha removed a bundle of dynamite from her pillowcase. "It's kind of far to throw one of these suckers, isn't it?''

Blade frowned. She was right. The bundles weren't very heavy, but they were ungainly and would be difficult to pitch any great distance with any degree of accuracy. What else could they do? He stared at the half-track, at least 400 yards from their position.

"I still think we should get the SEAL," Bertha stressed.

Blade gazed over his right shoulder. A yellow wood frame house was 15 yards behind them. He shifted his attention to the north. There were two more homes between the stone wall and the downtown business district of Catlow, a collection of a dozen or so brick buildings including a small store, a pharmacy, a clothing establishment, and other retail enterprises.

The small store caught his eye.

The structure was two stories tall, with the bottom half devoted to perishable foodstuffs and the upper portion, according to a large sign on the building, a hardware emporium with the "greatest selection in Catlow." Of course, the sign neglected to mention it was the *only* hardware selection in Catlow.

"Follow me," Blade directed. Keeping low, stooped over at the waist and ignoring the agony lancing his left side, Blade ran in the direction of the business district.

"Not so fast!" Bertha complained. "You know I got a bum leg!"

Blade mentally chided his stupidity and slowed.

"That's better," Bertha whispered. "You don't want me to get any madder at you than I already am!"

Blade waited until they were out of sight from

the highway and moving down an alley behind the stores before he asked the obvious question. "Why are you mad at me?"

Bertha snorted. "Don't play innocent with me, turkey! You knew I wanted to pair off with White Meat! But, no! I get stuck with you!"

Blade grinned. "You have only yourself to blame for not being with Hickok right now."

They reached the rear of the establishment Blade had been heading for.

"How do you figure?" Bertha challenged him.

There was a wooden door before them.

Blade drew up his right leg and lashed out with his foot, striking the door near the doorknob. The oak splintered and shattered and the door swung open several inches. He pushed the door aside and walked into a dark hallway leading to the front of the building.

"How do you figure?" Bertha repeated.

Blade moved along the hall until he came to a flight of stairs leading up to the second floor. "We're friends, Bertha," he said as he started up the steps. "I don't want to see you killed."

"Oh? I'd have a better chance of gettin' racked with White Meat than I do here with you?" Bertha asked, disputing him.

"Yes," Blade stated frankly.

"How so?"

They reached the top of the stairs and found aisle after aisle of merchandise.

Blade gazed at the ceiling, wondering if the structure would have the feature he required.

It did.

In the middle of the room was a trap door to the roof.

Blade hurried toward it. "Bertha," he said over

his shoulder, "I've seen the way you look at
Hickok—"

"Brother! First Rudabaugh and now you!"
Bertha said interrupting him. "Does everybody
know?"

"Probably," Blade replied. "You don't exactly
hide things well."

"I don't believe in beatin' around the bush,"
Bertha said.

"We know it," Blade assured her. "I can
imagine how you feel about him. I don't think
you've accepted his marriage, and possibly you
never will. But that's rightfully none of my
business—"

"You bet it ain't, sucker!" Bertha snapped.

"Unless it falls within my province as a Warrior
and the head of this mission," Blade elaborated. "If
I sent you out with Hickok, and the two of you came
under fire, you'd be so worried about protecting
him, about making certain he wasn't hurt, you'd undoubtedly fail to watch out for yourself."

"I would not," Bertha protested, but her tone
lacked conviction.

"And I was born yesterday," Blade cracked.

They reached the aisle under the trap door. A
piece of rope about a foot long was attached to a
handle in the door.

Blade jumped up and caught the rope in his
right hand. He yanked, and the trap door swung
open.

"How we gonna get up there?" Bertha wanted
to know.

There was a four-foot space between the top of
Blade's head and the opening.

The Warrior glanced around the room and spied
a display of stepladders two aisles over. "Wait

here." He jogged to the rack and returned with a six-foot ladder.

"What are we gonna do once we're up there?" Bertha inquired as he quickly unfolded the step-ladder.

"Play it by ear." Blade began climbing the ladder.

"I was afraid you'd say that," Bertha mumbled, staying on his heels.

The roof was flat and rectangular. A large metal antenna was situated a few feet north of the trap door. The surface of the roof was coated with a peculiar sticky black substance.

"What is this?" Blade asked, noting how the coating stuck to his hands and fingers where he touched the roof.

"Beats me," Bertha responded.

A brick rim, standing about twelve inches high, completely encircled the roof.

Blade, his body crouched over, ran to the front of the building and dropped to his hands and knees.

Bertha joined him, muttering something about "this damn sticky stuff!"

Cautiously, Blade peered over the rim and looked to the south.

The half-track and its deadly entourage were approximately 100 yards from Catlow.

"It's not too late to get the SEAL," Bertha remarked hopefully.

"Will you forget the SEAL?" Blade urged her.

"So let me hear your great plan for takin' that thing out," Bertha said, watching the rumbling half-track.

"Simple," Blade declared. "You light your charge and we drop it on the half-track as it drives by below."

"What if one of those boys in green spot us and begin blastin' away?" Bertha inquired.

"That's the chance we take," Blade mentioned.

The vehicle was 50 yards from the town and closing.

"Do you have your matches?" Blade asked.

Bertha fished in her pants pockets and withdrew a pack of matches. "Got 'em."

"Then get set," Blade directed.

The half-track had passed the stone wall.

Bertha giggled. "Are they in for a big surprise!"

The half-track was abreast of the intervening homes between the stone wall and the business district.

In the distance, from the west, came the crackle of gunfire.

Bertha shut the noise from her mind, knowing it meant Hickok and Geronimo were engaging some of the Doktor's forces.

"After you blow the half-track," Blade was saying, "I'll let the infantrymen have it."

Bertha glanced at the half-track, her stomach muscles involuntarily tightening.

"When I give the word," Blade instructed her, then abruptly exclaimed, "What the—"

One block south of the business district, the half-track took a left on a side street, heading westward.

Bertha couldn't believe it. "What the hell are they doin'?"

"They're heading for the town square," Blade guessed. "Come on!"

Together, they descended from the roof and raced to the rear of the store. Blade peeked out the door, looking south, and saw several of the soldiers pass the mouth of the alley.

Damn!

Blade was angry at himself. Bertha and he had crossed the side street to enter the alley, and it had never occurred to him the half-track might take it instead of using U.S. Highway 85.

"What now, bright boy?" Bertha asked.

There was only one feasible recourse. Turn right up the alley until they reached the next side street, one paralleling the street being used by the half-track. Then they would need to outrace the lumbering vehicle and get ahead of it.

"Is your leg up to some serious running?" Blade questioned her.

"I'll keep up with you," she vowed.

Blade smiled reassuringly and bolted from the building, hugging the wall, his eyes on the mouth of the alley to the south as he bore due north.

The troopers and G.R.D.'s were still passing the alley, but none of them gave it more than a cursory examination.

Deep in the alley, partially concealed by the shadows, Blade and Bertha ran to the next side street, designated as Lexington by a street sign. They darted to the left, sticking to the sidewalk, their legs pumping as they gathered speed.

Blade's left side was aching miserably before they reached the end of the first block. He stoically suppressed the discomfort, hoping his exertions wouldn't cause the wound to start bleeding again. At the junction of Lexington and Hamilton he paused, prudently inching to the edge of the sidewalk and glancing to the south.

Several troopers and G.R.D.'s were one block away to the south, as they continued their advance toward the town square, now only two blocks off to the west.

Blade frowned, frustrated. There was no way they could outrun the half-track in their condition. They needed to do something to turn the half-track around, to divert it from the town square. He had geared his entire defensive stratagem on utilizing the town square as the penultimate battleground. He wanted to draw the Doktor as far into the town as possible, but not until he was ready.

"What's the holdup?" Bertha asked. She was bent over, her hand on her injured thigh, and breathing heavily.

"We need to do something to get their attention," Blade told her.

"Oh? Is that all?"

Before Blade could restrain her, Bertha limped to the middle of Hamilton and, facing south, cupped her left hand to her mouth. "Hey! You ugly bozos! Your momma wears combat boots!"

Bertha giggled and hurried to Blade's side. "How's that?"

"Your momma wears combat boots?" Blade repeated, puzzled.

"I'll tell ya' later," Bertha promised. "Right now, we'd best split!"

They began jogging, retracing their footsteps to the mouth of the alley. As they reached it, Blade peered over his shoulder and spotted four troopers just arriving in the intersection of Lexington and Hamilton. One of the four gave a loud yell, and they charged after the Warrior and his companion.

"What now, big brain?" Bertha queried.

Blade led her down the alley to the back door of the food-and-hardware store.

"We goin' up on that roof again?" Bertha asked, holding up her right hand. It was covered with the tar-like substance coating the roof. "This icky gunk could ruin my beautiful complexion!''

Blade grinned and hurried into the structure and along the hall. Instead of turning to take the stairs to the second floor, he proceeded straight ahead until he came to a large chamber containing racks of food and other items.

The front door was directly ahead.

"Are we gonna break for lunch?" Bertha joked.

"Nope." Blade moved to the front door, unlatched the lock, and opened the door. He pointed at a rack of produce to their left. "Get out of sight."

Bertha limped to the rack, chuckling. "You sure are sneaky, you know that?"

Blade moved behind a rack filled with tin cans. He squatted and verified the Commando was fully loaded.

A minute passed in silence.

From the rear of the building came the sound of muffled voices and the dull tramp of boots on the floor.

Blade tensed, his finger on the trigger of his Commando.

There was a brief commotion at the back of the room. Someone shouted, "Out here! The front door is open!"

Footsteps pounded on the floor, nearing the front door.

Blade waited until he was certain they were clustered close to the front door, and then jumped up, the Commando stock snug against his right shoulder.

Three soldiers were huddled at the door, one of them framed in the doorway as he peeked outside.

Blade shifted the barrel in a short arc as he fired, his bullets tearing into them from a distance of only ten feet.

All three were flung from their feet by the brutal impact of the Commando's slugs. Miniature bright red geysers erupted from their backs as they were propelled forward and slammed to the floor or, in the case of the trooper in the doorway, to the sidewalk beyond.

Blade caught a motion out of the corner of his left eye, but before he could pivot to confront this new threat, Bertha's M-16 chattered.

A fourth soldier had just entered the chamber when Bertha's burst caught him in the head. His eyes and nose disappeared in a crimson spray and he toppled to the floor.

"Let's go!" Blade directed her. He ran to the front door and stepped out, glancing to his right and left.

At both ends of the block, soldiers and G.R.D.'s came into view.

Blade ducked inside. "Out back!" he yelled.

They were almost to the hallway when the clamor of uplifted voices arose from the rear of the building.

Blade stopped so suddenly Bertha nearly collided with him.

Damn!

The enemy had them surrounded!

They were trapped!

22

"It sounds like the others are already in the thick of it," Rudabaugh commented.

"Should we go help them?" Orson inquired.

Rudabaugh debated the wisdom of deserting their post. They had heard gunfire to the west and shots to the southeast, which meant the Doktor was assaulting Catlow from every direction this time. "No," he replied. "We'll wait a while and see if any of the Doktor's troops show up here."

They were stationed behind a small shed on the extreme northern outskirts of Catlow. U.S. Highway 85 was 11 blocks to the east.

Orson hefted his M-16. "I don't mind telling you," he said nervously, "I'll be glad when this is over."

"So will I," Rudabaugh admitted, leaning against the shed and cradling his Winchester in his arms.

"Can I ask you something?" Orson queried tentatively.

"What is it?"

"Do you think your boss, Kilrane, would mind if I came to live with the Cavalry after this is done?" Orson asked hopefully.

Rudabaugh eyes narrowed in surprise. "You want to come live with the Cavalry?"

"If they'd have me," Orson said.

"Why in the world would you want to do that?" Rudabaugh probed.

"I know I don't want to go back to the Mound,"

Orson stated, referring to the huge subterranean city inhabited by the Moles.

"Why not?"

"Because Wolfe will continue to make my life miserable for me," Orson remarked.

"What's Wolfe got against you?" Rudabaugh inquired.

Orson sighed. "It goes a long way back to when we were kids together. You see, Wolfe always was a bossy bastard, even before he became ruler of the Moles. We had a lot of fights when we were kids, because I was one of the few who wouldn't take his crap."

"And he's held it against you all these years!" Rudabaugh commented. "The man sure knows how to hold a grudge."

"You don't know Wolfe," Orson began. "He's—"

A booming explosion punctuated his sentence, coming from the west.

"Hickok and Geronimo," Rudabaugh mentioned, facing in the direction of the explosion.

A cloud of dust was spiraling into the air.

"They may need us," Orson stated.

Rudabaugh was about to concur, when he glanced at the field to the north of the shed.

It was swarming with troopers and G.R.D.'s, about 200 yards off and closing.

Rudabaugh pulled Orson further behind the shed.

"What is it?" Orson asked.

"Take a look."

Orson did, and immediately drew back, whistling softly. "Uh-oh. I'd say we're going to have company."

Rudabaugh surveyed the buildings to the south,

a collection of brick and frame homes separated by marginally tidy yards and narrow streets, a typical residential neighborhood.

"Are we going to stay here?" Orson wanted to know.

"No, we're not," Rudabaugh answered. "Follow me."

They sprinted southward.

Rudabaugh searched for an ideal spot to make a stand. The homes weren't very practical; they afforded scant protection from a concentrated attack, and he didn't relish the idea of being caught inside a building.

But there had to be something!

Two blocks south of the shed he found what he was looking for.

"What the hell are those?" Orson questioned curiously.

"I don't rightfully know," Rudabaugh confessed, "but they'll serve our purpose."

There was a flatbed trailer parked next to the curb on the north side of the street. Stacked on the trailer, and secured by sturdy metallic lashings, were ten huge concrete pipes or culverts.

Rudabaugh abruptly recalled a visit to Pierre many years before, and a construction site he had seen. The Cavalry, because of its reliance on horses as its mode of transportation, wasn't particularly concerned with maintaining the highways and roads constructed prior to the Third World War, except in the cities where chronic flooding produced by intermittent heavy rains was a problem. "I think they're called drainage conduits," he speculated. "Come on!"

They ran around the trailer and started ascending the pile of pipes.

"What's your plan?" Orson asked.

Rudabaugh was finding the climbing extremely difficult, what with his left shoulder hurting every time he moved. "We'll get to the top," he said, "and wait for them to catch up."

Orson reached the apex of the stack first. He leaned down and extended his right hand to Rudabaugh. "Here."

Rudabaugh hesitated for an instant, his masculine pride balking at accepting assistance.

"Hurry it up!" Orson urged him.

Rudabaugh took Orson's hand and allowed himself to be pulled to the top. The concrete pipes were arranged in the shape of a pyramid, with four on the bottom layer, three in the middle, and two forming the point, placed snugly side by side. Although the conduits were circular in form, they were large enough to accommodate a person lying prone on the summit with extra room to spare. Each pipe was four feet in diameter.

Orson took the conduit on the left.

Rudabaugh lay down on the pipe on the right and unfastened his pillowcase from his belt. He took out his pair of charges and his matches.

Orson was doing likewise.

"Would you do something for me?" Orson whispered.

"What?"

"If something should happen to me," Orson said, "would you send word to my mom for me?"

It was the last thing Rudabaugh would have expected Orson to ask. "Nothing's going to happen to you."

"Just in case," the Mole persisted, "get word to my mom. Tell her I was thinking of her at the end." He paused. "We've always been kind of close."

"Will do," Rudabaugh pledged. He stared northward. "Here they come!"

G.R.D.'s and soldiers were moving through the yards of the residential neighborhood, alert for trouble.

Rudabaugh kept his eyes just high enough to note their proximity. When the nearest troopers were 20 yards away, he lowered his head and prepared to strike a match.

Orson was watching Rudabaugh, awaiting his cue.

Rudabaugh counted to ten, then lit the match and applied the flame to the first charge. He drew back his right arm, and then threw the bundle as hard as he could. Instantly, he curled up, putting his hands over his head.

Orson followed suit.

Seconds later, when the twin explosions came, the flatbed shook and shimmied, and for a moment Rudabaugh thought it would collapse under the stress. His ears felt like they were going to burst. Clumps of sod, dirt, grass, and other debris rained from the sky, pelting his body and stinging his skin, even through the fabric of his wool clothing.

Orson was coughing, choking on the dust.

Rudabaugh looked up, startled to discover a severed human arm lying on the pipe next to his left elbow, the tattered remnant of a green fatigue sleeve clinging to its shredded flesh.

A great brown cloud was hovering over the area.

Rudabaugh rose to his knees, the stock of the Winchester Model 94 Standard pressed against his right shoulder. He detected an indistinct form moving on the ground to his left. The Winchester cracked, and there was a strident screech accompanied by a faint thud as a body toppled to the earth.

"Where the hell are they?" someone bellowed below.

"I can't see them!" another soldier replied.

There was a slight scratching noise from the right.

Rudabaugh turned, his eyes beholding a lizard-like G.R.D. climbing the conduits toward him, its baleful gaze fixed on him with malevolent intent. He aimed and pulled the trigger.

The G.R.D. was struck in the forehead. Its arms flung wide, it was catapulted from the pipes and tumbled to the ground.

The dust cloud was commencing to disperse on the breeze.

Several dark figures were vaguely visible in front of the flatbed trailer.

Orson rose to his knees and cut loose with the M-16, his burst attended by screams and shouts and curses.

"Dammit! Where are they?" a trooper demanded.

Rudabaugh spotted a pair of G.R.D.'s to his left, slinking in the direction of the flatbed. He fired twice, each shot connecting and slamming them to the ground.

"I think I see them!" a soldier cried. "They're up there!"

Rudabaugh hastily slid backward. "Let's go!" he called to Orson.

"Over here!" somebody bawled.

Orson rose and turned, about to clamber over the side of the uppermost pipe.

Rudabaugh, already down to the middle row of culverts, glanced up and saw Orson's right shoulder explode outward as a slug penetrated him from behind. The Mole's head snapped back, and he was propelled from the pile of pipes, his legs and good arm waving frantically as he dropped to the ground.

No!

Rudabaugh released his grip, falling the rest of the way and landing on his feet. He quickly knelt alongside Orson.

The bearded Mole was on his stomach, writhing in torment, his M-16 a few yards away, his shotgun still slung over his left shoulder.

Rudabaugh grabbed Orson's left shoulder. "Orson! You've got to get up!"

Orson glanced at the Cavalryman, his face contorted in pain.

"Can you get up?" Rudabaugh pressed him, looking both ways to insure their foes weren't nearby.

Orson nodded, grunted, and heaved to his feet. He swayed for a moment, but recovered, his right arm hanging useless at his side.

"Hurry!" Rudabaugh led the way, running, bearing due south. Blade's orders had been explicit: engage the enemy at the perimeter, then retreat to the town square.

Orson did his best to keep up.

Rudabaugh adjusted their path, heading a bit to the east. He looked over his right shoulder as they neared a white picket fence.

Soldiers and G.R.D.'s were pouring around both ends of the flatbed trailer.

Rudabaugh was almost to a gate in the middle of the fence. He motioned for Orson to continue, then spun and snapped off a shot at their pursuers.

They ducked for cover.

Rudabaugh whirled and ran for the gate.

Orson was already on the other side, crouching behind the fence.

The troopers near the flatbed darted into view and unleashed a volley from their M-16's.

Rudabaugh was framed in the gate opening when the hail of bullets plowed into the fence, splintering wood in every direction, and something tore through his left calf, sending a sharp spasm up his body and causing his leg to buckle. He sprawled onto his knees and rolled to the left.

He'd been hit again!

The soldiers and G.R.D.'s were charging across the yard toward the picket fence.

His fingers trembling, Rudabaugh removed his second charge from the pillowcase and lit the fuse. He didn't bother counting to ten this time; his only concern was providing them with enough cover to obscure their escape to the town square.

Orson was doubled over and gasping for air, on the verge of hyperventilating.

Rudabaugh tossed the bundle of dynamite with all of his strength. Predictably, the resultant blast sent a cloud of dirt and dust up, shrouding the picket fence and the immediate vicinity in an ambiguous brown haze.

Time to get their butts in gear!

Rudabaugh lurched to Orson and pulled him to a sitting position. "Orson! Snap out of it!"

Orson's eyes were dazed, his mouth slack.

Rudabaugh rudely shook him. "Orson! I've been hit! I need your help!"

Orson blinked his eyes, responding to the plea for aid. "You too?" he mumbled.

"I need you!" Rudabaugh reiterated.

Orson shook his head, striving to eradicate his wooziness. He glanced at Rudabaugh, noting the crimson hole on the Cavalryman's left calf.

"We've got to get out of here!" Rudabaugh urged him.

Orson nodded and stood. He slid his left arm under Rudabaugh's right shoulder and heaved, straining to hold Rudabaugh erect. "I've got you," Orson stated. "We'll make it."

But would they?

Even as Orson assisted Rudabaugh in limping away from the picket fence at a rapid clip, the Cavalryman could hear the pounding footsteps of their foes on the turf behind them.

23

Lynx, alone on the roof of the command post, was mad as all get out! His very genes craved to be in the battle, to be doing what he'd been designed to do: kill and kill again. Gunfire was rising from every direction. It sounded as if a veritable war were in progress.

And here he was, on top of the damn command post, missing all the action!

That idiot Blade!

Stay behind, he had said!

Wait in reserve, he'd said!

You'll get your chance!

That big dimwit!

Lynx was furiously pacing back and forth above the front door, listening to the shooting and the explosions and chafing to leave his post and join in the fun. He stopped and put his hands on the rim of the roof, about to leap over the side.

What was that?

He paused as the roar of a large motor drowned out the uproar of the conflict.

It was coming from the east.

Lynx ducked down and peered over the rim.

Son of a bitch!

A half-track loaded with soldiers was wheeling into the town square.

Lynx grinned.

Happy days were here again!

He laughed and lowered himself completely out of sight. No sense in letting them know he was there. They might turn tail and split before he got in his licks.

The rumble of the engine grew louder, until the building itself trembled. There was the grating squeal of brakes applied rather abruptly, and the motor was turned off.

Lynx peeked over the rim of the roof.

Will you look at this!

The driver of the half-track had parked the vehicle within a few feet of the front door!

Perfect!

Lynx smiled in anticipation. He calculated the angle and jumped, his sinewy muscles lifting him over the rim and down onto the cab of the half-track in one fluid motion. His legs coiled under him as he landed, and he leaped, clearing the cab and plunging into the midst of the shocked soldiers in the rear section.

The advantage was all his.

Packed into the back of the half-track with little space to spare, the troopers were unable to bring their M-16s to bear.

With a flashing swipe of both arms, Lynx dispatched two of the six soldiers by ripping open their throats. He pounced on a third and jammed the sharp claws of his right hand into the man's eyes. Blood spurted from the burst eyeballs and the trooper jerked backward, attempting to escape.

One of the soldiers pulled a bayonet from a sheath in his belt.

Lynx grinned as he bounded onto the joker with the bayonet and sank his pointed fangs into the jerk's neck. He twisted and yanked, and a large portion of the trooper's throat was sheared off in a red geyser of blood and gore.

Four down and two to go!

One of the remaining soldiers was trying to scramble over the tailgate to safety.

Lynx went for the other trooper, who foolishly tried to punch him in the face. In a blur, Lynx dodged under the futile blow and drove his left hand up and in, his fingers and claws rigid, spearing the man in the throat and gouging open a hole the size of his fist.

The final adversary was precariously perched on the edge of the tailgate, prepared to spring to the ground.

He never made it.

A gun thundered, and the soldier was struck in the center of his back, between the shoulder blades, and toppled over the tailgate.

Lynx vaulted to the roof of the cab, ignoring the moaning, thrashing forms on the floor of the rear section. For a second, he believed one of his friends had returned and helped him.

But he was wrong.

Lynx landed on the cab and froze, his hair bristling.

"Surprise, surprise!" said a tall figure in black outside the cab to his left, the man's cape covering his left arm, a 45 automatic pistol in his right hand with tendrils of smoke drifting upward from the barrel.

"Hello, Lynx," greeted the apish hulk outside the cab to his right. "Long time no see."

The Doktor and Thor.

Lynx glanced from one to the other in astonishment. They must have just gotten out of the cab of the half-track!

"What's the matter, Lynx?" the Doktor chortled. "Cat got your tongue?"

Thor laughed and raised his right hand,

revealing his sledgehammer. "Got a little present for you, Lynx," he said baiting him.

Lynx glared at the Doktor. "This must be my lucky day."

"And why is that?" the Doktor queried.

"Because," Lynx growled, "I've been looking to rip you to pieces, and here you are, delivered on a silver platter!"

The Doktor waved the 45 in his hand. "You're forgetting something, aren't you?"

"You think that peashooter of yours will stop me?" Lynx taunted.

"It stopped *him*," the Doktor noted, nodding at the tailgate.

"Why'd you waste your own man?" Lynx asked, stalling.

"I can't abide cowards," the Doktor said, "and he was fleeing."

Lynx started to inch forward.

"Hold it right there!" the Doktor warned, his voice hardening.

"Why don't you shoot?" Lynx teased him. "What are you waiting for?"

The Doktor sneered. "I want to savor this moment. And there are a few things I want to say to you."

"It figures," Lynx quipped. "You're plannin' to talk me to death."

Smiling, the Doktor shook his head. "I'll be brief. First, I want to compliment you."

"Compliment me?" Lynx asked incredulously. "Have you been sniffin' glue again?"

"Do you have any conception of the damage you've caused?" the Doktor inquired. "You have set my work back decades."

"I tried my best," Lynx said.

"I want to thank you for what you've done," the Doktor stated.

Lynx looked at Thor. "What'd you do? Whack him on the head with that hammer of yours?"

"Initially," the Doktor went on, as if Lynx had not spoken, "I viewed the destruction of my Biological Center as a great calamity. It wasn't until last night that I recognized the real significance of what you had done. Certainly, you've delayed the implementation of some of my plans, and you've ruined my laboratory, my precious laboratory!" The Doktor paused. "But, as Clarissa said, I can always rebuild my laboratory. I'll continue to live on indefinitely, so long as I have access to a fresh supply of blood and can synthesize my unique dehydroepiandrosterone sulfate—"

"Yeah, yeah, yeah," Lynx interrupted. "What's all of this got to do with me?"

"Don't you see?" the Doktor replied. "You've taught me an invaluable lesson. I had grown complacent over the years. After ten decades without any resistance or competition, I'd allowed my sense of self-preservation to atrophy. To utilize a quaint colloquialism, what good is it to be king of the hill if there's no one around to challenge your kingship? Do you understand?"

"I understand, all right," Lynx snapped. "I understand that you're looney-tunes! You think the whole world should do what you want it to do. You believe you can do anything you want."

"I can," the Doktor stated smugly.

"And hang the consequences, huh, Doc?" Lynx retorted.

The Doktor appeared puzzled. "Consequences?"

Lynx pointed at his own chest. "Consequences, you bastard! You fiddled with the laws of nature, and look at what you've done! Look at what you've done to me!" Lynx hissed.

"Is that what's bothering your meager intellect?" the Doktor asked. "Is that why you rebelled against me? Because I created you as a special being with exceptional talents?"

"Special?" Lynx exploded. "You made me into a freak! Me and all the rest of your misfits!"

The Doktor sighed. "You fail to see the light."

Lynx leaned forward. "Oh, I see it, all right! I see that you've got to be stopped, no matter what it takes!"

"And you think you can do it?" The Doktor laughed.

Lynx noticed Thor was grinning. "What's with you, lunkhead? Do you like being the Doc's pet monkey?"

The Doktor stiffened. "Thor is my close associate," he said, correcting Lynx.

"Your ass!" Lynx snapped. "Thor is an expendable flunky, just like all the rest of us test-tube freaks!"

"He is not," the Doktor declared indignantly.

"Oh, yeah?" Lynx pointed at Thor. "Tell me you wouldn't kill him in a minute if it suited your demented mind!"

"Don't listen to him," the Doktor said calmly to Thor. "He's raving."

"Am I?" Lynx gazed at Thor. "Think! Use your pitiful excuse for a brain! Do you really think the Doc gives a damn about you?"

Thor glanced from Lynx to the Doktor, his sloping brow furrowed.

"This conversation is terminated," the Doktor said brusquely. "Thor, finish him off."

Thor hesitated.

The Doktor's left arm moved under his cape.

Thor suddenly clutched at the metal collar around his squat neck, his powerful body arching, as a jolting surge of electricity jarred his senses.

The Doktor's left hand emerged from under his cape, his fingers grasping an odd black box about six inches in length and four inches wide. There were a number of silver toggle switches and blinking lights on the upper surface of the black box.

Thor dropped his sledgehammer and fell to his knees, his lips curled back from his prominent teeth, his entire frame quaking.

"When I give an order," the Doktor said, "I expect it to be obeyed.

Lynx was staring at the black box. It had to be one of the portable control units the Doktor was known to secret on his person. Without it, the Doktor would be unable to activate the transistorized electronic circuitry in the collars. Without it, the Doktor would not be able to compel his genetic aberrations to passively submit to his commands.

A crackling sound arose from the metal collar as Thor continued to tremble.

Lynx was thankful his own collar had been removed weeks before, shortly before the Warrior known as Yama had rescued him from the Citadel.

The Doktor was concentrating on Thor, watching his "associate" struggle to resist the collar.

There would never be a better opportunity.

Lynx voiced a strange trilling sound as he launched himself from the cab of the half-track and sprang at the Doktor. His maneuver caught the Doktor unaware. He swung his right arm, knocking the control box from the Doktor's hand, and lunged for the Doktor's throat.

The madman was endowed with incredible reflexes. His right arm swept upward, the barrel of his 45 connecting with Lynx's forehead and sending him sprawling.

Lynx tumbled to the earth, rolling with the blow, and bounded to his feet, his claws clenched, ready to pounce again.

The Doktor was pointing the 45 at Lynx's head. "Before I conclude this fiasco, there is a question you will answer."

"Eat dirt!" Lynx retorted.

"What have you done with the rest of the thermos?" the Doktor demanded.

Lynx did a double take before he understood: the Doktor must believe that Yama and he had stolen several of the thermonuclear devices when they fled the Citadel. Truth was, they hadn't, but there was no reason to let the Doktor know. Lynx grinned. "I'll never tell."

The Doktor's eyes narrowed. "I need those thermos! What did you do with them?"

"Wouldn't you like to know?" Lynx rejoined.

The Doktor frowned. "I really didn't expect you to volunteer the information, but that's all right. I've already deduced their location and have sent a force to retrieve them."

Out of the corner of his eye, Lynx saw Thor stand and rub his bullish neck.

The Doktor caught the movement too. "Are you ready to do my bidding?" he asked Thor.

Thor nodded.

"Then kill Lynx!" the Doktor directed. "Now!"

Thor reclaimed his sledgehammer and moved around the front of the half-track. He looked at Lynx, his features softening. "I'm going to smash you to a pulp for getting the Doktor mad at me!" So saying, he raised the sledgehammer above his head.

24

The thump of Geronimo's body on the balcony next to his own caused Hickok to glance to his right. He saw the bundle of dynamite, its fuse sparkling, drop from his friend's hand. The gunman's reaction was instantaneous; his right hand flicked out and grabbed the charge and heaved it up and out.

Hickok threw his own torso on top of Geronimo's, sheltering him—and none too soon.

The dynamite went off, shattering the windows in the house, cracking its foundation, obliterating the soldiers and the G.R.D.'s below, and ripping the balcony from its supports.

His eardrums stinging from the blast and the subsequent concussion, Hickok felt the balcony give way and plummet toward the turf. The floor of the balcony was still intact, and it absorbed the brunt of the brutal impact when they smacked onto the ground.

Both of the Warriors were bounced and jostled by the severe collision.

A cloud of dust was filling the air.

Hickok shook his head to clear his stunned senses. He gripped Geronimo's shirt and hauled him over onto his back.

Geronimo's left shoulder was all bloody, his eyes closed.

"Pard! Pard!" Hickok shouted in alarm. "Don't die on me!" He slapped Geronimo's right cheek. "Please don't die!"

Geronimo's eyes flicked open and a devilish grin

creased his mouth. "Why, Hickok, I didn't know you cared!"

The gunman leaped to his feet. "You lousy Injun! I should of known you were faking it!"

Geronimo chuckled, despite his agony. "Wait until I tell Blade! The great Hickok got all misty because I suffered a little scratch!"

"Misty my butt!" Hickok leaned over and yanked Geronimo to his feet, careful not to aggravate the wound in his left shoulder. "I just didn't want to have to tell your wife you got yourself killed because you can't even throw a few sticks of dynamite without getting yourself shot!"

"And you could have done better?" Geronimo asked.

Hickok bent down and picked up the Henry and the FNC. "In my sleep," he said when he straightened up.

Geronimo suddenly pressed his left arm against his side and winced.

"How bad is it, pard?" Hickok inquired.

"The collarbone may be broken," Geronimo speculated.

"Here." Hickok placed his left arm under Geronimo's right armpit. "Lean on me."

They started to walk around the ruined house.

"Let me carry one of the guns," Geronimo offered.

"Don't be ridiculous," Hickok countered.

They could distinctly hear the din of gunfire and explosions coming from the north, and more shooting off in the east.

"I hope we get there before the party is over," Hickok commented.

Geronimo glanced over his left shoulder, the movement eliciting a sharp twinge.

No one was behind them.

They hurried as rapidly as possible, given Geronimo's condition.

"I hope Rikki doesn't wait too much longer," Geronimo mentioned at one point.

"Relax," Hickok said. "Rikki won't let anything happen to us."

Geronimo nodded at his injured shoulder. "Oh? What do you call this?"

Hickok made a show of rolling his eyes. "Brother! If you're gonna whine every time you get a teensy-weensy scratch—"

"Teensy-weensy?" Geronimo bristled. "If you were shot instead of me, you'd be screaming for your mommy right about now."

"Is that a fact?"

"It certainly is," Geronimo stated. "Only my superior Indian heritage enables me to bear up as nobly as I am."

Hickok grimaced. "Only your superior Indian heritage makes you such a natural-born bull-shitter!"

"It takes one to know one," was all Geronimo could think of to say in response.

They hastened in silence. The noise of conflict to the north had abated.

"We only have a block to go," Geronimo announced after a few more minutes.

Both of them heard the voice call out, "Hickok!"

They stopped and glanced to the north.

Orson and Rudabaugh were coming toward them, supporting one another. Both appeared to be pretty shot up.

"Glad we found you," Orson said as they approached, his relief reflected on his face.

"They're after us," Rudabaugh stated.

"How many?" Hickok asked.

"Too many," Rudabaugh replied.

Geronimo twisted his head, scanning to their rear. "It looks like we have some company too."

Hickok glanced back.

Another wave of troopers and genetic deviates was headed toward them, the leading figures perhaps a hundred yards off.

"The Doktor is sending them in waves," Hickok conjectured.

"We've got to reach the town square," Rudabaugh declared.

"Let's go," Hickok said, and led the way.

They were nearing the town square from the west, passing homes and a few scattered businesses. Ahead was a house with a low stone wall paralleling the street.

"We'll never make it to the command post before they catch up with us," Hickok stated. "Let's make a stand here."

They clambered over the wall and dropped to the grass on the other side.

"If we can drive 'em back," Hickok remarked, "we'll make a run for the command post." He gave the FNC to Geronimo.

All four of them checked their weapons.

"How do you think Blade is doing?" Orson questioned.

Geronimo scanned the town square. He could see the fountain in the middle and a military vehicle parked in front of the command post. What kind of vehicle was it? he wondered. And was it his imagination, or was there a commotion of some sort taking place on the other side of the vehicle?

"How many charges do we have left?" Hickok queried them.

"I used up mine," Rudabaugh answered.

"I have one left," Orson said.

"I have one left too," Geronimo noted.

"And I have both of mine," Hickok stated. "Four charges and there are four of us. Get them out."

Orson, Geronimo, and Hickok extracted their remaining charges. The gunman gave one of his to Rudabaugh.

"Here's the plan," Hickok informed them. "We'll wait until they're almost on us, then toss the four charges all at once. The explosions should cover our tracks."

"What then?" Orson inquired nervously.

"Make for the fountain," Hickok advised. "From there, we'll try and reach the command post. Blade should be there soon, if he isn't already."

Geronimo nudged his friend and pointed at the command post. "What is that?"

Hickok studied the military vehicle. "I think it's called a half-track," he guessed. "Didn't we have pictures of them in one of the books in the library?"

Geronimo, never one to miss his chance, grinned. "You mean to tell us you can read?"

Orson was peering over the wall. "Here they come!" he declared.

Soldiers and G.R.D.'s were advancing from the north and the west.

"Get ready!" Hickok directed them. "Hold your charges out and I'll light them for you."

"Why should you light them?" Geronimo asked.

"Because I'm the only one with brains enough not to have gotten shot," Hickok quipped. "How are you going to light it with one of your arms out of action?"

Orson extended the bundle in his left hand,

while Rudabaugh and Geronimo used their right.

Hickok peeked above the wall.

The enemy skirmish line was only 15 yards away.

The gunman swiftly lit all four charges. As soon as the last one was lit, which was his own bundle, Hickok nodded and swung his right arm down and up.

Three other arms did the same.

All four men dropped to the ground and tensed.

When the explosions came, the very earth rumbled and shook. The stone wall swayed slightly, but held firm, and the invariable billowing cloud of dust permeated the sky overhead.

"Move it!" Hickok ordered. "I'll cover you." He slung his Henry over his left shoulder and drew his Colt Pythons.

Rudabaugh and Orson took off, Orson helping the Cavalryman as they made for the fountain.

Geronimo balked. "I'm not deserting you."

"Get the blazes out of here!" Hickok yelled.

"I won't leave without you," Geronimo declared obstinately.

"Danged hardheaded Injun!" Hickok muttered. He stood, facing the street and the yards beyond, and spotted several figures rushing in the direction of the wall. The Pythons bucked as he fired, four times in speedy succession, and four vague forms toppled to the ground.

Geronimo was holding the FNC in his good arm.

Hickok backed away from the stone wall. "Let's go."

Geronimo turned and ran toward the fountain.

Hickok waited several seconds, to insure they had deterred their foes. He whirled and sprinted after the others.

Orson and Rudabaugh were close to the fountain.

Geronimo was only a few yards ahead.

There was movement near the half-track, and Hickok's blue eyes narrowed as he tried to see clearly through the swirling dust and refracted sunlight.

Someone was climbing up onto the rear of the vehicle.

The cloud of dust diminished as Hickok continued to race to the fountain, and as his mind registered the scene near the command post he ran even faster.

One of the Doktor's freaks, a huge ape-like thing, had scaled the tailgate on the half-track and was swiveling a mounted machine gun in the direction of the fountain—in the direction of the four defenders!

25

Blade's eyes blazed with an intense inner fury at being hemmed in by his antagonists.

"What are we gonna do?" Bertha cried.

"Stay close to me!" Blade ordered her. He darted from the room and into the hallway beyond.

Three troopers were just entering the back door.

Blade fired into them before they could bring their M-16s to bear, the Commando thundering in the narrow confines of the hallway.

All three soldiers were struck, their bodies dancing and flouncing and thrashing in uncontrollable spasms.

Blade ceased firing and brushed past their crumpled bodies. He burst through the rear doorway and found himself surrounded by four G.R.D.'s. One of them, a furry monster with pink pupils, was directly in front of him. Blade rammed the barrel of the Commando into the thing's stomach and pulled the trigger.

The deviate was almost cut in two by the slugs.

Blade pivoted, going for a scaly horror to his left, but the creature grabbed the Commando barrel and wrenched it aside. Blade released the gun and drew his right Bowie. His huge arm flashed up, then out, and the knife gleamed as it cleaved the air and imbedded itself in the thing's chest.

The creature screeched and attempted to pull the Bowie from its body, but a geyser of blood erupted from its narrow lips and it fell to the pavement.

The third monstrosity leaped on the Warrior from

behind and pinned his arms to his sides.

The fourth, in the act of diving at the Warrior, was hit in midair, Bertha's M-16 chattering from the doorway and puncturing holes in its body from its head to its feet.

Blade swept his head straight back, connecting with the nose of his foe and crushing the cartilage. The hairy arms securing him momentarily weakened, and Blade surged his massive biceps and triceps, exerting his prodigious strength, and broke free. He dove forward and Bertha gunned the thing down.

Blade scrambled to his Commando and scooped it into his arms. Two more G.R.D.'s were rushing up from the south. He cradled the Commando and pulled the trigger. Both G.R.D.'s were bowled over, spurting blood and flesh over the alley.

"Let's get the hell out of here!" Bertha shouted.

Blade bent over the scaly deviate and extricated his Bowie from its chest. The knife made a slurping noise as it came loose. He wiped the gory blade on his left pants leg, then slid the Bowie into its sheath.

"Look!" Bertha yelled.

Soldiers and G.R.D.'s were pouring into the north end of the alley.

Blade and Bertha started running toward the south end, their speed impeded by Bertha's injured right thigh.

Blade deliberately hung back, shielding Bertha. He abruptly spun and fired a few rounds at their pursuers, dropping a few and forcing the rest to duck for whatever scant cover was available.

Bertha reached the south end of the alley and took a right, and a second later Blade was on her heels.

"The town square?" Bertha asked.

Blade nodded.

Voices were heard all around them, as their

adversaries closed in.

Blade and Bertha sprinted westward. A block and a half from the alley Blade spotted a row of metal trash cans lined up alongside the sidewalk.

Not much protection, but they would have to do!

Blade grabbed Bertha's elbow and drew her from the sidewalk. They dodged behind the trash cans and dropped to their knees.

Dozens of their foes were in hot pursuit, maybe a block away.

"Hurry!" Blade directed her, his chest heaving from the strain. "One of your charges!"

They each removed a bundle of dynamite from their respective pillowcases.

Blade risked a quick peek over the trash cans.

"There they are!" the nearest trooper bellowed.

Blade nodded at Bertha, then lit his charge.

Bertha struck a match and ignited her fuse.

"On the count of three," Blade told her.

Both fuses were sputtering and crackling.

"One . . ."

"They're behind the trash cans!" someone bawled.

"Two . . ."

One of the approaching soldiers fired his M-16, and the trash cans pinged as the bullets hit.

"Three!" Blade cried.

Together, they popped up from behind the trash cans and threw their charges.

One of the troopers, faster than the rest, raised his M-16 to his shoulder and snapped off a shot.

Blade heard Bertha grunt as she was struck, but before he could turn to aid her the dynamite detonated. The tremendous concussion from the blast knocked Blade onto his broad back. He swiftly rose to his hands and knees.

Bertha was unconscious on the sidewalk beside

him.

"Bertha!"

A cursory examination revealed a wound on the left side of her head. It didn't appear to be deep, but you could never accurately judge a head injury without an extensive examination.

And there wasn't time for that!

Coughing from the dust as much from the pain in his left side, Blade lifted Bertha into his brawny arms and jogged in the direction of the town square. This fiasco wasn't going well at all. There was no way they could hold out until the end of the day. If Rikki and Kilrane didn't show up soon, they might show up too late.

About 20 yards from the town square, Blade saw a house to his right with its front door wide open. The occupants must have evacuated in a hurry. He angled toward the door and cautiously entered the home.

"Is anybody here?" he called out.

No response.

Blade gently lowered Bertha to a sofa flanking a wall not ten feet from the door.

"Sleep tight," he whispered. He wished he could say more: how very proud he was of her professionalism and courage, how he would be honored to sponsor her for Warrior status if she ever decided to formally join the Family, and how sorry he was her relationship with Hickok hadn't worked out.

Circumstances dictated otherwise.

Blade exited the house, closing the front door behind him. He jogged toward the town square, his left side smarting.

What the—!

He saw the half-track parked in front of the command post. Three figures were near the vehicle. One of them was Lynx, and the diminutive feline was

engaged in fighting an apish brute at least three feet
taller than himself. Standing aloofly to one side,
observing the struggle with a sneer on his lips, was a
big man dressed in black, with a flowing black cape
over his shoulders. His unruly hair was black, and he
was holding a 45 in his right fist.

The Doktor!

It had to be!

Blade had never met the infamous Doktor, had
never even seen him, but he intuitively recognized the
man in black as the nefarious scientist.

The Doktor was concentrating on the fight
between Lynx and the ape-man. The ape-like figure
was striving to bash Lynx's brains in with a sledgehammer, but Lynx was more than holding his own, his
superior speed and agility enabling him to avoid the
ponderous blows.

Blade darted to the left, crossing the street and
zigzagging across a yard. He passed several trees and
a bicycle, running due south, keeping his gaze on the
command post, insuring the Doktor did not look in his
direction. He wanted to put the corner of the
command post between himself and the Doktor, then
sneak up to the building and take the Doktor
completely by surprise.

His left side was throbbing.

Blade suppressed the torment and kept running.

Where were Hickok and Geronimo and the
others? he wondered. Were they faring any better?

Blade realized the Doktor and the half-track had
disappeared from view. The command post was now
blocking his avenue of approach from the Doktor. He
turned, racing to the command post and stopping only
when he reached the east wall of the structure, and
was 15 feet from the northeastern corner.

The Spirit was smiling on him!

He took a moment to catch his breath, and then

cautiously eased toward the corner. If his calculations were correct, the Doktor would be standing ten feet from the corner. Lynx, the ape-thing, and the half-track were five to eight yards beyond the Doktor.

Blade was tingling with anticipation when he paused mere inches from the corner of the building. Their strategy had worked! And with the Doktor eliminated, Samuel II was next!

"Don't toy with him," the Warrior heard the Doktor say. "Get it over with!"

Blade grinned, placed his finger on the trigger of the Commando, and leaped from concealment.

The Doktor was watching the combat, his back to the corner.

"Doktor!" Blade shouted triumphantly.

The Doktor spun around, his dark eyes widening in disbelief.

Blade, relishing his victory, squeezed the trigger.

Nothing happened.

There was a loud click, and that was all.

The Commando was empty!

Lynx had twisted at the sound of Blade's voice, and for the briefest of instants was off guard.

Thor immediately took advantage of the unexpected diversion. He delivered a vicious stroke at Lynx's head.

Lynx sensed the danger, but too late. He twisted, trying to avert the sledgehammer, but it struck him a glancing blow, the stunning impact sufficient to send him hurtling into the half-track. He slumped to the ground next to the front tire.

The Doktor was pointing his 45 at Blade's chest. "Are we having problems?" he asked, grinning.

Blade considered rushing the madman, but discarded the notion as patently stupid. He'd be dead before he was halfway there.

"Drop it!" the Doktor commanded, nodding at

the Commando.

Blade released his weapon and it clattered as it landed.

"Now the pistols," the Doktor directed. "Slowly!"

Blade carefully drew the Vegas from their shoulder holsters and let them fall.

The Doktor seemed to relax slightly. He smiled and studied the knives on the Warrior's hips. "Bowie knives," he said matter-of-factly, and looked up. "You undoubtedly are Blade."

Blade simply nodded.

"So we meet at last," the Doktor remarked.

Thor was standing behind the Doktor, glaring at Blade.

"I truly wish I could prolong our encounter," the Doktor commented, "but I must complete my business here and travel to Denver. Any last words before we wrap this up?"

Blade remained silent.

The Doktor chuckled. "Oh, come now! Not even a few words of spite and malice?"

Blade was praying for a distraction. Something. Anything.

The Doktor, evidently unable to resist the allure of a captive audience, continued to speak. "Come to think of it, there are some words I'd like to say to you. I want to praise you."

"Praise me?" Blade finally asked.

"Oh, not you personally. Your Family. Specifically, the accursed Warriors. You have created more difficulties for me than anyone else in the past one hundred years, and that's quite an accomplishment," the Doktor said.

"I'm flattered," Blade snapped sarcastically.

"Seriously," the Doktor stressed. "Haven't you ever heard that you can measure the quality of a man by the excellence of his competition?" The Doktor sighed. "Believe it or not, I shall be sorry to see you go. You and the rest of the Warriors. There is no place in a society like ours, where peace is promoted at the expense of personal liberties, for Warriors like yourself. You are an anachronism, Blade. You and Geronimo and Hickok and the rest." The Doktor laughed. "Especially Hickok. I've heard of some of his escapades and listened to some of the tapes of monitored Family conversations. Does he use that phony Wild West jargon all the time?"

Blade nodded.

"Remarkable," the Doktor stated. "But then, the Family is remarkable. It has produced an astonishing quantity of outstanding individuals. Plato. Joshua. Your own father."

"My father?" Blade repeated bewildered. "You knew my father?"

"Haven't you ever speculated who was responsible for your father's death?" the Doktor inquired, a wicked gleam in his eyes.

Blade's mouth fell open as he gawked at the Doktor. "You?" he asked in stupefied amazement.

"Who else?" the Doktor said, smiling arrogantly.

Blade's mind spun, his emotions staggered by the revelation. He vividly recalled the day, about four years ago, when the runner had told him his father had been attacked by a mutate while on a hunting trip. At the time, his father was the Family Leader. He had been with two other men from the Family. They had dropped behind while one of them removed a stone from his boot. Blade's father had been 30 yards ahead of them, near a growth of dense brush, when what the men thought was a mutate had charged from cover and attacked him, ripping and slashing with its fearsome claws. Regrettably, Blade's father had passed on to the higher mansions mere minutes prior to his own arrival on the scene. Blade had knelt in the

grass and held his father's hand while tears streaked
his cheeks.

The men with Blade's father had rushed to his aid,
but the mutate responsible for the savage onslaught
had whirled and vanished in the underbrush. Both
men had claimed there had been something unique
about that particular mutate; they had insisted it had
worn a collar, a leather collar.

The collar!

Blade's memory flashed back to the run Alpha
Triad had made to Thief River Falls. He remembered
the ferocious creatures called the Brutes, the bestial
beings the soldiers had used for tracking and guard
duties. Blade had barely survived a fierce fight with
one of them, and *it had worn a leather collar!*

Blade was feeling dizzy. He abruptly recalled an
incident during the trip to Kalispell. What was it the
officer had told him? Yes! Now he recollected what it
was: "That metal collar is how the Doktor controls his
freaks. His earlier creatures . . . just wore leather
collars."

Damn!

Damn! Damn! Damn!

Right in front of his nose the whole time!

"It was necessary to dispose of your father," the
Doktor was saying. "He intended to send out
expeditions to ascertain if there were other survivors
of the war. So long as your Family remained
comparatively isolated, we were content to
periodically send monitoring teams to eavesdrop on
your conversations, using sophisticated electronic
equipment, as we do with all the other outposts of
civilization beyond the borders of the Civilized Zone.
But we couldn't allow your Family to contact the
others. We weren't quite ready to commence
reconquering the United States, and we wanted all
surviving factions to be as disorganized as possible to

prevent them unifying against us. Consequently, I sent in a team with one of my little pets. Your father conveniently left the security of the Home, and the rest you know."

Blade felt an intense fury mounting within him. His fists clenched into compact clubs.

"I would have done the same to Plato," the Doktor revealed, "only he decided to send Alpha Triad out so abruptly we couldn't assassinate him beforehand."

Blade's cheeks were flushing from the passionate rage welling up inside him.

"Killing your father wasn't anything personal," the Doktor commented. "It was strictly business. Killing Joshua, on the other hand, was purely personal."

Blade wasn't sure he had heard correctly. "Joshua?"

"Oh? Didn't I mention it?" The Doktor chuckled. "The foolish pacifist tried to convert me to the path of life and light! Imagine!" He tossed back his head and gave vent to uncontrolled mirth.

Blade's muscles tightened. He no longer cared if the Doktor held a gun. He didn't give a damn if Thor was nearby. He wanted one thing and one thing only: to wring the Doktor's neck!

A gigantic, thunderous explosion erupted from the west end of the town square, sounding as if several charges went off simultaneously.

Both the Doktor and Thor involuntarily glanced in the direction of the cacophonous blast.

It was the moment Blade had been waiting for. He charged, forgetting to draw his Bowies, his arms extended and his fingers rigid.

The Doktor detected Blade's assault out of the corner of his right eye. He turned and fired.

Blade experienced a burning sensation along his

rib cage on his right side, but he disregarded it and leaped the final four feet.

The 45 boomed again, but in his haste the Doktor missed, and before he could aim again the Warrior slammed into him and bore him to the ground.

Thor, about to hasten to the Doktor's defense, saw four forms hurrying toward the center of the town square from the west. He recognized them almost instantly; the fat one with the beard, the guy in black, the Indian Geronimo, and, trailing a few yards behind, the gunfighter called Hickok.

What should he do?

Thor glanced at the Doktor and Blade. The Doktor had landed on his back with the Warrior on top, but he suddenly swept his left knee up and rammed it into Blade's left side. Blade winced and doubled over, releasing his hold on the Doktor.

"Doktor!" Thor yelled. "Hickok and the others . . ." He pointed in their direction.

The Doktor never bothered to look up. "Kill them!" he ordered, scrambling to his hands and knees.

Thor ran to the rear of the half-track and climbed over the tailgate to the mounted machine gun. He pivoted the gun, sighting on the four defenders, and let the sledgehammer fall to the floor.

Blade, his left side in excruciating agony from the Doktor's blow, was lying on his right side. He felt something hard being pressed against his left temple and twisted his head to find the reason.

It was the Doktor, and he was holding the 45 next to Blade's head. "Don't move!" the Doktor hissed.

Lynx abruptly began moaning.

"No one lays a hand on me!" the Doktor snapped at Blade. "No one!" He sounded as if he were on the verge of going off the deep end, his tone strident and ragged.

What was he waiting for? Blade wondered.

The Doktor's face conveyed the fanatical nature of his insanity: his eyes were wide, the pupils distended; his nostrils were flared; his lips were curled upward in a fake grin, exposing his teeth; and his entire countenance seemed to be aglow with a bizarre inner light.

Lynx, unnoticed by the Doktor or Thor, opened his green eyes and rose to his knees, still groggy, his movements unusually slow.

The Doktor inexplicably cackled. "Adieu, Blade!" he declared happily. "It's the void for you!"

Blade, striving to regain control of his limbs, tensed, knowing the Doktor was playing with him and dreading that something would happen.

It did.

Pandemonium erupted.

"Over here, sucker!" a female voice screamed, coming from the east.

Both the Doktor and Blade glanced up.

Bertha was ten yards away, weaving toward them, the left side of her face caked with blood.

The Doktor instinctively swung the 45 at her, not realizing she was unarmed and didn't pose a threat.

Blade drove his right hand, balled into an iron fist, up and around, connecting with the madman's chin and slamming him to the ground. The 45 went flying.

Lynx jumped to his feet.

Blade pushed himself to his knees. "Lynx!" he shouted. "Thor! The half-track!"

The Doktor was trying to stand.

Blade executed a flying tackle, bearing the Doktor to the turf. He kneed the lunatic in the groin, then flicked his fists in a furious combination of brutal punches, smashing his knuckles into the Doktor's face again and again and again.

Thor had turned upon hearing Blade's cry, but he

was too late.

Lynx cleared the side of the half-track in two bounds. His second leap brought him to the top of the side panel, and he added to his momentum by grabbing the upper edge and propelling his body at Thor like a shot out of a cannon.

Thor lunged for his sledgehammer, but his reach was impeded by the machine gun.

Lynx snarled with a feral frenzy as he landed on his foe, his feet raking Thor's massive chest while his hands, his slashing talons, ripped ten crimson furrows in Thor's face.

Thor shrieked and tried to cover his eyes with his hands.

The scent of fresh blood drove Lynx wild. He went berserk, his arms flailing away at Thor's face and neck, as hair and flesh and gore splattered every which way. A shredded eyeball sailed over the tailgate.

On the ground, Blade was grappling with the Doktor, the two of them rolling back and forth as each attempted to gain the upper hand. One of their rolls caused them to collide with the front of the command post, to the right of the door. Blade bore the brunt of the collision, his head banging against the concrete and momentarily dazing him.

The Doktor wrenched free of Blade's grasp, sprang to his feet, and darted through the front door.

Blade shoved himself erect and took off inside in hot pursuit.

26

Hickok saw Lynx pounce on the apish figure in the rear of the half-track. He concentrated on catching up with the others. Orson and Rudabaugh had already reached the fountain and were crouched alongside the basin. Geronimo joined them an instant later.

"Look!" Orson shouted as Hickok joined them.

They could see the other side of the half-track for the first time. Blade and a man wearing a black cape were wrestling on the ground.

Bertha was a few yards from the vehicle, her left hand pressed to her face, staggering.

"Black Beauty!" Hickok cried. He started to run around the fountain to assist her.

"Look!" Orson yelled again.

Soldiers and G.R.D.'s were swarming toward the town square from several directions at once. They appeared to the west, the north, and the east, hollering exultantly as they spied the four men near the fountain.

"This is it," Rudabaugh said, drawing his pistols, forcing his left arm to obey his mental bidding.

Orson quickly unslung his shotgun. "Remember what I told you," he stated, directing his comment at Rudabaugh, grimacing from the pain in his right shoulder.

Geronimo caught Hickok's eye. "I've loved you like a brother," he informed his friend, "which goes to show you how warped my taste is."

Hickok was in a quandry. He couldn't believe what Geronimo had just said, the words only serving to aggravate his confusion. He wanted to aid Blade and Bertha, but he couldn't leave Geronimo.

Some of the approaching troopers opened fire, their rounds smacking into the fountain.

Hickok risked a last glance at the command post. The creep with the cape and Blade had vanished! And Bertha was climbing over the tailgate of the half-track, evidently intending to use the machine gun.

More bullets were striking the fountain.

Hickok raised the Henry and fired, his aim rewarded by the sight of a reptilian G.R.D. taking a slug in the head.

Geronimo downed several antagonists with a burst from his FNC.

Orson began blasting away with his shotgun.

Rudabaugh picked up the lethal refrain with his pistols.

The onrushing throng scarcely slowed.

Hickok emptied his Henry and threw it aside. "Into the fountain!" he bellowed over the noise of the gunfire. The basin rim might afford some shelter from the withering hail of lead.

Orson, his shotgun booming, went to take a step over the rim. His whole body suddenly jerked to the left and he was knocked over the basin and into the water. He fell on his stomach, splashing the water over the sides of the fountain, and didn't move.

"Orson!" Rudabaugh turned and stepped over the rim. He reached down and gripped Orson's flannel shirt.

Hickok leaped over the rim to help Rudabaugh. He distinctly heard a thup-thup-thup, and

Rudabaugh arched his back, gasped, and pitched into the pool.

Geronimo backed up, stepping over the basin into the pool while still firing the FNC. He crouched behind the rim, shooting the closest foes, the gravest threats, as they presented themselves. As he twisted to mow down three G.R.D.'s charging from the west, he realized Hickok was standing and staring at Rudabaugh and Orson.

Enemy gunfire was chipping away at the basin and pockmarking the pool with dozens of concentric ripples.

"Get down!" Geronimo shouted.

Hickok, miraculously untouched so far, looked up, his mouth a thin slit, his blue eyes glaring.

Geronimo abruptly stiffened and toppled across the rim of the fountain, his legs in the water, his head dangling outside.

"*Geronimo!*" Hickok took a step toward him, then stopped. His hands flashed to the Pythons, the barrels glinting in the sunlight as they cleared leather. Heedless of his personal safety, he left the pool, deliberately walking toward the soldiers and the G.R.D.'s. His right Colt cracked, and a furry G.R.D. clutched at a hole where its left eye had been and tumbled to the ground. The left Colt bucked, and a trooper took a slug between the eyes.

A genetic deviate resembling a walking lion bounded up from the west.

Hickok whirled, both Pythons blasting, and the lion-man was flung backwards to crash to the turf.

A bullet creased the gunman's right leg.

Hickok spotted a soldier sighting his M-16 for a second shot, and let him have a bullet in the brain for his efforts.

A monkey-like G.R.D. waving an axe rushed the

gunfighter, gibbering crazily.

Hickok, a twisted smile on his face, let the creature get within three feet before he angled a slug into the G.R.D.'s mouth.

Something stung the gunman's right forearm.

A pack of G.R.D.'s swarmed in from the west, at least ten of them working in concert.

Hickok spun, thumbing the hammers and squeezing the triggers on his Colts with a precision few men could equal. Three, four, five, six of the pack were down, contorted in their death throes, and he was leveling the Colts at a seventh when a hard object struck his right temple, stunning him, jolting his senses and causing him to drop to his knees.

The world was spinning.

Move! he mentally screamed.

Move or die!

He looked up, squinting, as a shadow fell over his face.

A genetic mutation with the canine features of a coyote towered above him, a metallic club grasped in its bony fingers and uplifted for the coup de grace.

What transpired next seemed more like a dream than reality.

Hickok was suddenly aware of a tremendous clamor, of a deafening, confusing din swelling in volume, of constant gunfire.

The G.R.D. with the club glanced to one side and its mouth gaped open in astonishment.

Hickok saw a gleaming sword appear as if from thin air, swooping from above, and the coyote literally lost his head as he was decapitated by the stroke. One second he was intact, and the next his head was flying off trailed by a crimson spray while his body swayed for a moment, then keeled over backwards.

Hickok's senses were clearing. He became aware of a horde of horsemen filling the town square and engaging the soldiers and the G.R.D.'s in savage combat.

Another shadow obscured the sun.

It was a short, agile man dressed in black, astride a brown stallion, a bloody katana held in his right hand. He slid from the horse and landed beside the gunman.

"Are you okay?" he shouted over the racket.

Before Hickok could respond, a soldier with a bayonet affixed to the barrel of his M-16 tried to spear the man in black from the rear. The man twirled around, his katana a streaking blur, and the trooper's head was split open from his forehead to his chin. He was dead before he hit the earth.

"Are you okay?" the man repeated. "It's me, Rikki."

Hickok rose to his feet. He was about to reply when a wave of vertigo engulfed him and everything went dark.

27

Blade halted a few feet inside the front door of the command post, puzzled.

The Doktor was nowhere in sight.

But that was impossible! He had only been a couple of yards ahead!

So where . . . ?

The Warrior cautiously moved toward the first door to his left, the door to the communications room. He peered around the jamb, then froze.

The Doktor was serenely standing about three feet inside the doorway. "Don't be shy," he said, and laughed.

Blade, wary of a trick, edged into the room. The Doktor didn't appear to be armed. What was he up to now?

The Doktor's left hand was hanging loosely at his side, but his right was curled into a fist. He chortled and unfurled his fingers. A silvery ball plummeted to the floor and split open upon impact, releasing a stream of odoriferous white smoke.

Blade recoiled in alarm, suspecting the smoke was a form of deadly gas. The smoke formed a small cloud within the blink of an eye, completely enshrouding the Doktor.

How could the cloud be toxic if the Doktor was immersed in it?

Blade took a step toward the cloud. It must be a wily ruse of some sort. Maybe there was a secret passage and the fiend was escaping under cover of the smoke.

The Doktor hurtled from the cloud and crashed into the unprepared Warrior, sending him flying from the communications room to slam against the far side of the hallway.

Blade's chest was lanced by an acute spasm, but he ignored the agony and lashed out with his right leg, catching the Doktor on the left knee as he closed in.

There was a loud snap, and the Doktor nearly fell, but he recovered and lunged, his immensely strong fingers encircling the Warrior's throat.

Blade grabbed the madman's wrists and tried to pry the fingers from his neck.

"I've got you now!" the Doktor hissed, gloating.

Amazed by the Doktor's display of physical force, Blade released the wrists. He drew back his right hand and, his index finger extended and rigid, drove the stiff digit into the Doktor's left eye.

The Doktor howled and backed away down the hallway, his left hand shielding his injured organ.

Blade leaped, his arms clasping the Doktor around the waist and bearing him to the floor.

The Doktor's right hand disappeared in a fold of his flowing cloak, emerging a second later with a small hypodermic syringe. A tiny red plastic tip covered the tip of the needle. With a flick of one finger, the Doktor removed the tip and stabbed the point at the Warrior's left shoulder.

Blade detected the ploy out of the corner of his eye, twisting his body to avoid the syringe and rolling to his feet.

The Doktor did likewise, the needle held at chest height. His left eye was open but watering, a line of moisture flowing across his left cheek to his chin.

Blade assumed the horse stance and waited for

the Doktor to make his move.

Instead, the demented scientist grinned. "You should see your face!" he exclaimed. "Judging by your expression, your hate for me is unbounded."

Blade, his gaze on the syringe, refused to comment. Talking in the midst of hand-to-hand combat was ridiculous. Total concentration was required in life-or-death situations, and only someone as unhinged as the Doktor would babble inanely while so occupied.

"Why are you amusing yourself at my expense?" the Doktor asked. "I didn't think you had it in you."

What was the psychopath talking about? Blade didn't reply. He waited for that syringe to move.

"Why else haven't you used your knives?" the Doktor calmly inquired.

Despite his reservations, Blade found himself mulling the question. Why hadn't he resorted to the Bowies? Because he wanted to beat the Doktor with his bare fists? Or because he had forgotten about them in the heat of battle, which was utterly unlike him?

"Go ahead," the Doktor said. "Draw your knives. I won't go anywhere."

Blade was thoroughly confused. What was up the Doktor's sleeve? This was insane! There had to be an ulterior motive.

"Tell you what I'll do," the Doktor stated. "I'll make it easy on you." So saying, he tossed the hypodermic syringe to the floor.

Blade was stunned by the action. It was impossible to predict what a murderous lunatic like the Doktor would do next. Why did he throw away the syringe?

The Doktor, smiling, extended his arms, palms up, toward the perplexed Warrior. "See? There's nothing to be afraid of. Use your knives and finish it. I'm tired of living."

Unnerved, Blade debated the wisest move. They were at a stalemate; there was no way the Doktor could get past him to the door, and it appeared unlikely he could best his crafty adversary without a weapon.

"Go ahead," the Doktor repeated, goading him. "What are you waiting for?"

Blade reached a decision. He was tired of these damn games! The Doktor was standing about two feet in front of him. All he had to do was whip out the Bowies and, as he had practiced so many times over the years, sweep the big knives up and out, flinging them point first into the Doktor's torso.

"Well?" the Doktor baited him.

When it came to drawing his Bowies, Blade was almost as fast as Hickok was with his cherished Colts. His hands flew to the handles and the gleaming blades leaped clear of their scabbards. His arms began to swing upward and outward, the razor tips elevating. He was all set to release the handles and let the Bowies fly when the Doktor made his move.

The Doktor's left hand dropped at a 90-degree angle to his forearm and a tiny metallic dart shot from under his sleeve trailing a thin wire behind it.

Blade believed the miniature dart was meant for him, so for the briefest fraction of a second he was relieved when the dart struck the blade on his right Bowie. But instead of striking the steel and being deflected to the floor, the dart *stuck* to the Bowie.

What transpired next was totally unforeseen.

Blade felt a terrific jolt of . . . something . . . lance up his right arm and course through his entire body. The shock to his system was staggering. It was as if he had been kicked in the chest by a bucking bronc. He was lifted from his feet and flung almost to the front door, crashing to the floor on his back and lying there with his breath caught in his throat. His limbs were trembling uncontrollably, although his mind seemed perfectly lucid.

The Doktor's sneering visage came into view directly overhead. "You're still alive? Remarkable. The shock would have terminated any ordinary man," the Doktor said.

No matter how hard he tried, Blade couldn't stop his body from quaking.

"Aren't you the least bit curious about how I did it?" the Doktor inquired.

Blade's feet abruptly ceased shaking.

The Doktor held up his left hand. It held the small dart and several coils of thin wire. "Do you see this? Do you know what it is? Law enforcement agencies once used a crude, cumbersome version of this device. I, of course, have improved on the original design and incorporated many advanced refinements."

Blade's legs stopped their shuddering.

The Doktor nodded at his left forearm. "There's a tube under my sleeve. The dart is fired by means of a compressed gas cartridge."

Blade felt his hips halt their vibrating.

"This insulated wire," the Doktor explained, dangling the wire in Blade's eyes, "runs up my sleeve and over my shoulder to a portable power pack strapped to the small of my back."

Sensation returned to Blade's arms and hands. He realized his right Bowie was gone, but he had retained his grip on the left knife.

"All I need do," the Doktor was saying, "is move my hand a certain way and, presto! My target receives enough juice to kill a horse! Simplicity itself!"

Blade glared at the Doktor, his intense hatred welling up inside of him. The man had assassinated his father and claimed to have murdered Joshua; he had caused untold hardship and suffering to the Family; he had used countless infants as fodder for his rejuvenation technique. Who knew the extent of his atrocities?

It was time for the Doktor to die.

His bulging muscles rippling, Blade surged upward, his left arm driving the Bowie up and in, planting the blade in the Doktor's groin, imbedding the knife to the hilt.

The Doktor gasped and dropped the dart and wire. He uttered a feeble, rasping squeak and looked down at his ruined loins.

Blade gripped the Bowie in both hands and drove the keen blade upwards, slicing through the abdomen and reaching the ribs.

Whining, wimpering in abject fear at the prospect of his own demise, the Doktor managed to grab Blade's wrists. "Please!" he pleaded, his eyes silently begging for his life. "Spare me!" he entreated the grim-faced Warrior.

Blood was pouring from the Doktor's ruptured body, raining from his abdomen and spattering the floor with continual red drops. His intestines were seeping from their cavity, oozing slowly toward the concrete below.

"We can make a deal!" the Doktor cried in desperation. "We can make a deal!" A crimson rivulet suddenly spurted from the right corner of his mouth.

Blade allowed himself the luxury of having the last word. "A deal, Doktor? You want to bargain with me, a man who represents everything you loathe? Plato has told me a little about the contents of your journals. I know you don't believe in the

Spirit, Doktor. I know you think faith is for
simpletons. You see humans as nothing more than
animals. You consider love fit only for weaklings."
Blade paused.

The Doktor was breathing heavily and starting
to sag.

"Well, I don't, Doktor!" Blade stated, his voice
hardening. "I was raised to appreciate love as the
greatest of all strengths. I see all men and women as
spiritual children, all part of one vast cosmic family.
And I value my faith, Doktor. It's the foundation of
my life. And do you know what else?" Blade
growled. "I value wisdom, and my wisdom tells me
you will never see reality as I see reality. You will
always be as warped and perverted as you are now.
You will always be a menace, Doktor. People like
you think they have the right to reshape the world
in their own wicked image. And you don't!"

The Doktor's chin was drooping.

"And so," Blade said in conclusion, "there's
only one way to deal with people like you." He
tightened his hold on the Bowie. "And this is it!"

The Doktor's head snapped up, his eyes locking
on Blade's.

Blade rammed the Bowie upward, angling the
blade over the sternum and burying the knife in the
Doktor's neck below the chin. Warm blood flowed
over his hands and arms and sprayed on his face.

With a protracted, labored wheezing sound the
Doktor expired, his arms falling limply at his sides.
He started to fall forward.

Blade wrenched his Bowie free and stood aside.

The Doktor toppled over like a giant tree
plummeting to the ground in the forest, smacking
onto the floor and making an odd squishing noise.

"I admire your style, bub," someone said from
the doorway.

Blade looked up.

Lynx was leaning on the jamb, his arms folded across his hairy chest. His body was covered with red splotches. "I wanted the Doc for myself," he remarked. "But I didn't want to interrupt your work of art." He chuckled, gazing at the form on the floor. "I couldn't of done better, chuckles."

"What's happened?" Blade queried. "Where are the rest."

"Come take a look," Lynx responded.

Blade spotted his other Bowie on the floor near his feet. He scooped it up, wiped the knife he used to slay the Doktor on his pants, and slid both Bowies into their sheaths.

Lynx stood to one side as the Warrior strode past.

Blade stopped just outside the front door, surveying the scene before him.

The town square was packed. Bodies littered the ground, the majority of them G.R.D.'s or troopers. Cavalry riders were everywhere, tending to wounded comrades or mopping up, checking on the prone figures of their enemies to ascertain if any were still alive. A veritable stack of soldiers and genetic deviates was piled on the east side of the half-track.

Blade glanced up at the rear of the vehicle.

Bertha was slumped over the machine gun, her arms dangling in midair.

"Bertha!" Blade ran to the back of the half-track and vaulted over the tailgate. He took her in his arms and examined her.

Blood was trickling from her right thigh and the wound on the left side of her head. There was an additional injury, a bullet hole in her shirt on the left side of her chest.

Blade pressed his right ear to her bosom.

Thank the Spirit!

Bertha was breathing, but barely.

Blade scanned the crowd below and recognized Yama walking toward the half-track.

"Yama!" Blade shouted.

The man in blue immediately ran to the vehicle and climbed up to Blade's side.

"Take care of her," Blade ordered. "I'll locate Kilrane and have him send over one of his men skilled in medicine."

"I will tend her," Yama promised, then added, "Rikki needs to see you at the fountain."

Blade jumped from the half-track and headed for the fountain. The strain of the combat was beginning to be felt; his left side was a mass of torment, his right side along the ribs ached, and his body was feeling extremely fatigued.

The Cavalrymen readily parted for the crimson-coated apparition moving among them, many gaping at his barbarous appearance.

A cool breeze was blowing in from the northwest.

Somewhere nearby, a man was groaning in agony.

The fountain abruptly loomed directly ahead.

Blade stopped, shocked, forgetting his pain at the sight before him.

Rikki-Tikki-Tavi, Teucer, and Kilrane were standing near the fountain.

Lying on the ground at their feet were four bodies.

Blade ran the final yards.

Hickok, Geronimo, Rudabaugh, and Orson were each on their backs. Before Rikki could say anything, Blade knelt alongside Hickok and placed his left ear on his chest. He detected a strong heartbeat, and a flood of relief washed over him.

Rikki squatted next to Blade. "He'll live," he stated, and pointed at a huge bruise on the gunman's right temple. "I saw him get hit by a G.R.D. with a club. He should be coming around soon."

Blade turned to Geronimo. The third member of Alpha Triad was obviously alive, his chest rising and falling rhythmically. There was a bloody furrow parting the center of his hair.

"It's deep," Rikki said, "but he'll be fine." He looked at the remaining two forms. "I wish I could say the same about them."

Blade went down the line.

Rudabaugh's clothes were drenched. He had been shot three times, high in the back, between the shoulder blades. The bullets had exited on either side of his sternum, and two of them had made a sizeable hole above his heart. He was dead.

Orson was dripping wet. A slug had caught him on the left side of his chest and perforated his heart. He had probably died instantly.

Blade slowly stood, sighing.

"You look like you could use some tending, yourself," Kilrane interjected.

Blade looked up. "First things first. How did the battle go?"

"Much easier than expected," Rikki replied. "There weren't as many of them as we thought there would be. Kilrane led the Cavalry, charging right into the middle of Catlow. Resistance was minimal until we reached the town square, and even here we outnumbered them by about four to one." He paused and scanned the town square. "It was over almost before we knew it."

"What if some attempted to escape?" Blade asked.

"Some did," Rikki detailed. "I sent the Clan to

cover U.S. Highway 85 to the south, and the Moles
to the north. We heard some gunfire to the south,
but it didn't last long." He nodded at a dead G.R.D.
"What happened to the great army we were
expecting to encounter?"

Blade shrugged. "I don't know," he admitted.
"I estimated there were several hundred, tops." A
question suddenly occurred to him. "Rikki, don't
misunderstand me, because I'm glad you showed up
when you did, but what are you doing here so early?
Did Kilrane's man inform you we were in trouble?"

Rikki shook his head. "Thank Red Cloud."

"Red Cloud?"

"Red Cloud linked up with our column
yesterday," Rikki elaborated. "He was concerned,
afraid we were recklessly exposing you to danger by
relying on only one man to alert us. I decided he was
right, and acting on my own initiative I sent in
another rider last night as insurance. When he
couldn't locate our contact man, he rode back to us
and reported it. We departed for Catlow immediately."

Blade put his right hand on Rikki's narrow left
shoulder. "You performed well. I will commend you
to Plato after we return to the Home."

"A commendation isn't necessary," Rikki
declared. "I was only doing my duty as a Warrior."

Blade looked at Kilrane. "I almost forgot!" he
exclaimed, appalled at his neglect. The sight of
Hickok and Geronimo on the ground had rattled his
senses. "Find one of your menders and get over to
the command post. Bertha took a bad hit."

"On my way," Kilrane said, and left on the run.

Blade walked to the fountain and sat down on
the basin rim. How could he have forgotten Bertha?
Damn! What an idiot! Sure, he was on the verge of

exhaustion, but that was no excuse. He frowned,
displeased at himself. If anything happened to her,
he would never be able to forgive his part in her
death. She had been right all along. She usually was.
Bertha had given him sound advice before, in the
Twin Cities, and he'd disregarded it with disastrous
consequences. Now he'd done it again! He should
have heeded her and used the SEAL. All of them
might have survived in one piece. Rudabaugh and
Orson were dead because—

Someone moaned at his feet.

Hickok opened his eyes and gazed around. He
raised his right hand and gingerly touched the welt
on his temple. "Howdy," he mumbled.

Blade knelt next to the gunman. "Take it easy,"
he advised.

"I ain't gonna take it any other way, pard,"
Hickok muttered.

"You were struck on the head," Rikki
mentioned.

"Oh, really?" Hickok quipped. "You could of
fooled—" He suddenly sat up, anxiously looking
around. "Geronimo—"

"He's right here," Blade said, indicating their
companion. "He'll be all right."

Hickok stared at the wound on Geronimo's
crown. "Yeah. I see they shot him on the noggin.
I'm plumb surprised the bullet didn't ricochet off."
His gaze moved to Rudabaugh and Orson and he
instantly lost his levity.

"They died bravely," Blade said in tribute.

"That's how I'd like to pass on from this
world," Hickok remarked. "With my guns blazing."
He glanced at Blade. "Say! Where the blazes is
Black Beauty?"

Blade averted his eyes.

Hickok reached out and grabbed Blade's left arm. "Where is she?" he demanded.

"The half-track," Blade responded despondently, pointing. "She may not make it."

Hickok rose to his feet.

"You should rest," Rikki told him. "Don't push yourself."

"I gotta check on Black Beauty," Hickok declared, and stalked off.

"Why arc you so depressed?" Rikki asked Blade.

"Who says I'm depressed?" Blade retorted, standing.

"Your face," Rikki revealed. "If there is something troubling you, perhaps I can help?"

Blade shook his head. "Thanks. But I'll be okay."

Rikki elected to change the subject. "Do you know what happened to the Doktor?"

Blade glanced toward the command post, remembering. "We don't need to worry about him anymore."

"Then our mission was a success," Rikki said.

"Tell that to Rudabaugh and Orson," Blade suggested, "or Bertha."

Rikki's brow furrowed. "Casualties in an operation of this magnitude were inevitable. You knew that."

"Yeah," Blade sighed, "I suppose I did. But intellectually recognizing a fact and actually experiencing it are two different things."

"Do we proceed to Denver as planned?" Rikki inquired.

"After we finish here," Blade confirmed.

"I will pray we meet with equal success in Denver," Rikki said. "The sooner we conclude this affair, the sooner we can return to our Home. I miss it."

Blade thought of his wife, Jenny. "So do I." He wondered how Plato was faring, and then he remembered what the Doktor had said. "Joshua!" he stated in alarm.

"What about Joshua?" Rikki questioned him.

"The Doktor told me he killed Joshua," Blade disclosed.

"What?" Rikki responded incredulously. "That's impossible."

"The Doktor told me he killed Joshua," Blade insisted.

"But Joshua is back at the Home," Rikki noted. "There's no way he could have . . ." He paused, stunned, insight dawning.

"What is it?" Blade asked.

"One of our horses was stolen," Rikki divulged.

"Stolen? You're sure?"

"Yes. And there was a report of one extra man in one of the trucks. You don't think . . ." Rikki left the sentence unfinished.

Blade reached into his right front pants pocket and removed a set of keys.

"Where are you going?" Rikki queried.

"I'll be back," was all Blade would say as he started to walk away.

"Take somebody with you!" Rikki recommended.

Blade shouldered his way through the crowd, oblivious to his surroundings.

28

She jammed on the brakes and the speeding jeep drew to an abrupt stop.

He was still up there where they had left him.

She threw the gearshift into Park and hopped from the vehicle. Her remorse was overwhelming, her sorrow affecting her to the core of her being.

His eyes were open and watching her as she approached.

Tears crisscrossing her scaly cheeks, she gazed up at him, at the symbol of all she despised. "He's dead!" she wailed. "I know he's dead! I can feel it!" She fought to control her grief. "I wanted to go with him, but he wouldn't let me. He made me stay behind. He must have known what was going to happen!"

"I'm sorry," the figure croaked in a barely discernible voice.

"I don't want your sympathy!" she screamed at him. "I hate you!" she shrieked. "I hate you! I hate you! I hate you!"

His eyes were pools of sadness.

"I hate all of you!" she raved. "I won't rest until every one of you has paid for what you've done! I will avenge him!" She threw back her head and cackled. "He'll have the last laugh yet! He dispatched a surprise package for your precious Home. If there is someplace we go to after we die, then you can die knowing you will see your friends there very shortly!"

His chin slumped to his chest.

She whirled and returned to the jeep, her purpose set, her determination firm.

Denver was her destination.

Denver was the first step in her plan.

Exterminating Blade was the second!

29

The SEAL rolled to a stop and Blade threw the door open and leaped to the ground. He ran up to the stark figure and paused, his very soul in agonizing distress.

No!

Dear Spirit, no! He seemed to be dead!

"Hey! Wait for me, dimples!" Lynx emerged from the passenger side of the transport and joined Blade. He stared at the object before him, puzzled. "What is it?" he asked. "I ain't never seen one of these before."

"It's a cross," Blade replied softly.

"Is Josh alive?" Lynx inquired.

Joshua had been stripped naked. Two boards had been nailed together at right angles to one another in the traditional form of a cross, with the upright beam imbedded in the ground not ten feet to the east of U.S. Highway 85. Large nails had been used to tack Joshua's arms to the crossbeam, with one nail in each wrist serving to secure him to the wood. A third nail had been utilized to fasten his legs to the upright beam; they had crossed his legs and hammered the nail through both of them just above his ankles, effectively impaling his slim body to the cross.

"That must hurt like crazy," Lynx callously remarked.

Blade frowned. "Lynx, I want you to go look in the back of the SEAL. There are some tools in a metal box under the rear storage area. Dig through our pile of supplies and find the tool box.''

"No problem, chuckles,'' Lynx said.

"The tool box is in a recessed compartment under the floor,'' Blade clarified as Lynx hurried off. "Look for a small handle near the back seat and lift it up.''

Lynx nodded and kept going.

Blade walked up to the cross and gently laid his right hand on Joshua's knees. "Joshua? Can you hear me?''

Joshua's brown eyes slowly opened. "Blade?'' His voice was a ragged whisper.

"None other,'' Blade affirmed. "We'll have you down in a bit. Hang in there.''

Joshua, incredibly, mustered a feeble grin.

"Can you talk?'' Blade inquired.

"Yes,'' Joshua replied, the word scarcely audible. "Throat . . . so . . . dry.''

"I'll give you some water as soon as we have you down from there,'' Blade promised.

"Thank you.''

"How long have you been here?'' Blade queried.

Joshua licked his parched lips. "Lost track . . . of time. Two days . . . I think. Not . . . certain.''

Blade glanced at the SEAL, wishing Lynx would hurry.

"The . . . Doktor?'' Joshua asked.

Blade looked up. "Dead,'' he succinctly answered.

Joshua closed his eyes and sobbed.

"Joshua? What is it?'' Blade inquired apprehensively.

"Failed,'' Joshua mumbled. "Failed all . . . of . . . you.'' He spoke haltingly, as if the mere act of speaking entailed monumental effort.

"Joshua, this may not be the right time to bring

it up," Blade stated, "but if you can tell me, I'd really like to know what you were doing here."

Joshua tried to laugh, but it sounded more like a sorrowful wheeze.

"Why, Joshua?" Blade pressed him. "I know Plato didn't send you. So why?"

Joshua stared into the Warrior's eyes. "Wanted to . . . prove to all of . . . you. Wanted to do as . . . I . . . did in . . . Twin Cities."

"The Twin Cities? You succeeded there because everyone wanted to end the decades of bloodshed. The Doktor was just the opposite. He reveled in spilling innocent blood, in slaughtering others for the thrill of it." Blade paused. "Did you really believe you could change him?"

"Had to try," Joshua insisted. "But . . . forgot . . ."

"Forgot what?" Blade queried.

Joshua quoted from memory: "Give not that which is holy unto the dogs, neither cast ye your pearls before swine, lest they trample them under their feet, and turn again and rend you."

"You must realize by now that not every man and woman craves peace and brotherhood," Blade emphasized diplomatically. "Until everyone does, those who do must beware of those who don't."

"I think . . . I've . . . learned my lesson," Joshua said. His chin dropped and his eyes flickered.

Blade spun around and cupped his hands around his mouth. "Lynx! Where the hell is that tool box!"

The gusting wind blew his dark bangs over his eyes as he stood on the small rise five hundred yards south of Catlow and surveyed the column on the road below. Was the chill air a harbinger of a winter storm sweeping in from the northwest, or a portent of events to come as they continued their invasion of the Civilized Zone?

Loud shouts and laughter rose from the town. The residents of Catlow were celebrating their newfound freedom with a vengeance. They had returned the evening before and assisted in the cleanup. Afterwards, they had conducted a town meeting in the square, held a vote, and formally elected to align themselves with the alliance being forged by the Freedom Federation.

The SEAL was parked on the highway below the rise. Mounted and raring to depart were 484 Cavalrymen, lined up five abreast across the road between the transport and the town. Next came the troop transports bearing the contingent of Moles, then the trucks containing the force from the Clan.

He stared at the rising sun and saw a flock of birds silhouetted on the far horizon, winging their way south. Whimsically, he found himself envying those birds and their carefree existence, and he wished his own life could return to a simple level again. But would it? Could it? Oh, to enjoy a quiet day at the Home, secure within those four walls, frolicking hand in hand with Jenny!

The introspection troubled him.

He glanced to the north, wondering how many miles Hickok had logged since leaving Catlow. There had been no other recourse. Bertha and Joshua were both critical, and Catlow lacked the facilities to treat them properly. Transporting them to Denver was completely out of the question; a battlefront was hardly the ideal location for rest and recuperation. At Hickok's insistence, and because there was no other viable option, he had sent the gunman, a recovered Geronimo, Bertha, Joshua, and a Cavalryman somewhat skilled in medicine back to the Home in a troop transport. They could easily spare the vehicle, and the Family Healers were extremely proficient at their craft; if anyone could save Bertha and Joshua, it would be the Healers.

"Yo, chuckles! You plannin' to grow roots there or what?"

Lynx, Rikki, Yama, and Teucer were waiting by the SEAL.

Blade grinned and placed his hands on his Bowies.

One down, and one to go.

Lookout, Denver, here we come!